"MISS J–JESSIE STARBUCK?"

"What?" Jessie turned, startled, to face a man standing beside her table. He was lean, sandy-haired, wearing faded twill trousers and a worn plaid shirt. His big, sad eyes were veined with red, and the stink of sweat and whiskey was in his clothes.

"Yes," Jessie said cautiously. "I'm Jessie Starbuck. What do you want?"

"If you know a k–kinda slant-eyed lookin' feller," he said nervously, "you might better c–come and see him off. They're fixin' to hang him..."

Also in the LONE STAR series
from Jove

LONGARM AND THE LONE STAR LEGEND
LONE STAR ON THE TREACHERY TRAIL
LONE STAR AND THE OPIUM RUSTLERS
LONE STAR AND THE BORDER BANDITS
LONE STAR AND THE KANSAS WOLVES
LONE STAR AND THE UTAH KID
LONE STAR AND THE LAND GRABBERS
LONE STAR IN THE TALL TIMBER
LONE STAR AND THE SHOWDOWNERS
LONE STAR AND THE HARDROCK PAYOFF
LONE STAR AND THE RENEGADE COMANCHES
LONE STAR ON OUTLAW MOUNTAIN
LONGARM AND THE LONE STAR VENGEANCE
LONE STAR AND THE GOLD RAIDERS
LONE STAR AND THE DENVER MADAM
LONE STAR AND THE RAILROAD WAR
LONE STAR AND THE MEXICAN STANDOFF
LONE STAR AND THE BADLANDS WAR
LONE STAR AND THE SAN ANTONIO RAID
LONE STAR AND THE GHOST PIRATES
LONE STAR ON THE OWLHOOT TRAIL
LONGARM AND THE LONE STAR BOUNTY
LONE STAR ON THE DEVIL'S TRAIL
LONE STAR AND THE APACHE REVENGE
LONE STAR AND THE TEXAS GAMBLER
LONE STAR AND THE HANGROPE HERITAGE
LONE STAR AND THE MONTANA TROUBLES
LONE STAR AND THE MOUNTAIN MAN
LONE STAR AND THE STOCKYARD SHOWDOWN
LONE STAR AND THE RIVERBOAT GAMBLERS
LONE STAR AND THE MESCALERO OUTLAWS
LONE STAR AND THE AMARILLO RIFLES
LONE STAR AND THE SCHOOL FOR OUTLAWS
LONE STAR ON THE TREASURE RIVER
LONE STAR AND THE MOON TRAIL FEUD
LONE STAR AND THE GOLDEN MESA
LONGARM AND THE LONE STAR RESCUE
LONE STAR AND THE RIO GRANDE BANDITS

WESLEY ELLIS

LONE STAR
AND THE
BUFFALO HUNTERS

A JOVE BOOK

LONE STAR AND THE BUFFALO HUNTERS

A Jove Book/published by arrangement with
the author

PRINTING HISTORY
Jove edition/July 1985

ISBN: 0-515-08233-3

Jove books are published by The Berkley Publishing Group,
200 Madison Avenue, New York, N.Y. 10016. The words
"A JOVE BOOK" and the "J" with sunburst are trademarks
belonging to Jove Publications, Inc.

PRINTED IN THE UNITED STATES OF AMERICA

★
Chapter 1

The storm swept in from the west, a slate-black wall that spit lightning in its path. It caught them just short of Bear Mountain and dogged them through dark, narrow valleys and steep hills. Rain lashed the stage furiously, turning the dirt roads into mud. The driver whipped his team up the slope, one wary eye on the churning river below. The horses pawed frantically for a hold, digging at the slick muck. Suddenly the lead horse slipped, floundered, and went to its knees.

Jessie Starbuck gasped, gripped the edge of her seat, and held on. The stage swung sickeningly to the right. For a moment one rear wheel spun out over empty air. Then the team found its footing and lurched to the crest of the hill.

Jessie shot Ki a narrow look. "One more *inch,* friend, that's all." She made a tiny space with her fingers. "Lord, that driver is out of his mind!"

Ki answered with a grin. Lightning caught his features in quick relief—the sharp planes of his cheeks, eyes tilted slightly at the corners.

"Maybe. Maybe not," he said dryly. "Maybe he's just new. Maybe this is his first trip—"

"That's not funny and you know it."

The man across from Jessie laughed aloud. "That's ol' Charlie Breed, miss. I know'd him down at Fort Zarah in Kansas. Reckon you're right and your friend's wrong. Charlie ain't new at anything, but he's damn close to crazy."

"Thanks," Jessie said shortly. "That helps a lot, Mr. Cole."

"Glad to be of service." Cole gave Jessie a crooked grin and let his eyes roam boldly over her body. He hadn't stopped looking since they'd left the North Platte. Ki's warning glances

1

didn't bother him at all. He was a big, heavyset man with water-blue eyes, tangled hair, and a matted beard. His clothes were greasy leather, worn to fit him like skin. Cole claimed to be the best damn skinner in the west. "Better'n George Newton or Jim White," he'd boasted more than once. "I can do thirty-five buffalo a day without stopping for a breath!"

Jessie didn't doubt it. Cole stank to high heaven and his clothes were stained dark with the blood of his kills. There was nothing wrong with good, honest labor, or the smell of it on a man. Jessie, though, had no liking for the army of hide hunters who stalked the northern herd. To her way of thinking, there was plenty of other work a man could do.

"Looks like we're heading down again," said Ki. He drew back the slicker they'd tacked to the window. Rain lashed his face and he quickly shut it tight. "There are some buildings down there. Might be part of a town."

"Deadwood," Cole said flatly. "Ass-end of the world."

"Watch your tongue, mister," Ki said flatly.

"Watch your own," said Cole, "or I'll cut it out and roast it."

Ki's eyes went gunpowder-black. His muscles went taut about his shoulders.

"Ki, let it go," Jessie said calmly. She laid a hand on his arm. "It's all right."

Ki sat back but didn't take his eyes off Cole. Cole shot him a grin. His hand rested easily on his belly, an inch from the big Wilson skinning knife in his belt. Ki had studied the weapon before and wondered if Cole could use it on anything livelier than a hide. He half-wished the man would give him a chance to find out.

Jessie peered out of her own window as the stage slogged into town. Deadwood, a collection of dreary buildings spilling out of a narrow gulch, had grown some since Dakota gold breathed it into life, but it was still nothing to look at twice. Mud ran down the mountain and swelled the streets into a river. Rain drew a curtain over the somber Black Hills and turned midday into night.

Cole opened the door, slipped into the driving rain, and

2

didn't look back at Jessie and Ki. Jessie pulled a slicker over her head and ran for the cover of the station. Some kindly soul had laid planks to the porch, and she was grateful for the favor. Ki scraped mud off his boots and set their valises on a dry patch of wood.

"I've been in drier creeks," Jessie said soberly. "You think it's ever going to stop?"

"I wouldn't count on it," Ki told her. He squinted past the station to his left. "There's a hotel down the street, and cover most of the way. We can wait it out here or give it a try."

"Let's go," Jessie sighed, "we can't get any wetter than we are."

The rain had let up by the time she walked downstairs to the lobby. The Dakota Hotel was nothing special, but the rooms were clean and warm. Jessie longed for a hot bath, but settled for dry clothes. She wore a light blue dress that did little to hide the lush lines of her figure. Strawberry-blonde hair tumbled freely past her shoulders. The hair framed startling green eyes, a classically straight nose, and a full and generous mouth. Even in dreary half-light, the creamy texture of her skin worked its magic, turning the soft color of honey-gold.

There were half a dozen men in the lobby, talking and keeping out of the rain. To a man they followed Jessie's path down the stairs. With few exceptions the females in Deadwood were overpaid whores or honest wives who'd lost their beauty to the rigors of frontier life. A woman like Jessie was something to see, a sight to talk about later over a drink.

From the small dining room off the lobby Ki spotted her, left his place, and went to meet her. He'd changed from traveling clothes to a worn blue shirt, black trousers, and rope-soled sandals.

"Well, you look dry," he said. "Hungry yet?"

Jessie wet her lips. "Do you really have to ask?"

"The menu says antelope steak. Around here, I imagine that means elk or deer or whatever got brought in last. Oh—Colonel Henry's here. He was waiting when I came down."

"Good!" Jessie's face brightened. "I can't wait to see him."

3

Ki touched her arm. "Jessie, don't be real surprised. He isn't the man he was five, six years ago."

"Ki, the man has to be close to eighty."

"He says eighty-one," Ki stated. "Come on, I just wanted to let you know."

Ki was right. The years were dragging the old man down, thinning out his flesh and turning the thick mane of hair pale as ivory. Still he was Colonel Henry Dodd and, to Jessie Starbuck's eyes, one of the most imposing men she'd ever seen. He wore a plain black suit, white shirt, and string tie. Jessie was almost certain the old, polished boots were the same ones he'd worn as a Confederate cavalry officer. He smiled at Jessie's approach and brought himself slowly erect.

"By God, you are prettier than ever, girl!" He held Jessie close and kissed her soundly on the mouth.

Jessie colored and burst out laughing. "You haven't changed a bit, Colonel—might be you're a bigger rogue than ever."

"It is my fervent hope that you are correct," he said solemnly. His blue eyes sparked with mischief and he eased himself back in his chair. "You folks go ahead and order. I'll take myself a nip of good whiskey. Goddamn teeth won't take a thing but mush these days."

"You have to eat something," Jessie protested.

"Don't start woman-talkin' me, Jessie Starbuck. You haven't got the stomach for it."

Jessie grinned. "Don't you count on it, Colonel."

Colonel Henry made a face, glanced over his shoulder, and leaned toward Jessie across the table. "Sorry I didn't meet you, rain isn't good for my joints. Too many arryheads and minnieballs stuck to my parts." He paused to gather his thoughts. "I got your message roundabouts. I been doing a little hunting down on the Wounded Knee and I come back up to Lead to get warm. I've known old Jeff Hawkins runs your Starbuck office for thirty years. He told me you were sending out the word about a girl. I got a message back soon as I could."

"Do you think you've seen her, Colonel? Are you sure she's the one?" Jessie asked.

"*Course* I'm sure!" Colonel Henry stuck out his jaw.

"Hawkins had a photograph picture you sent out. It's her, all right."

"Your message said she was here. In Deadwood," Jessie said.

"She was. I saw her plain as day, right in the lobby of this hotel. She isn't calling herself Angela Halley. It was Louisa somethin' or other. But it's the same gal, all right."

"You said she *was* here, Colonel," Ki put in. "You don't think she is now?"

"Doubt it real strong," Colonel Henry's brows came together in a frown. "If she's got good sense she's long gone. The thing is, you two aren't the only folks looking for her."

Jessie exchanged a quick glance with Ki. Colonel Henry caught it and nodded. "Uh-huh. Figured it was something like that."

The old man told them what he knew. Angela Halley had come to town some three weeks before, no one knew from where, and no one bothered to ask. She was a breathtaking beauty, and every man in town sought her favor. According to the Colonel, more than one succeeded.

"Christ a'mighty," he said flatly, "that little gal took to men like a kid takes to candy. Had 'em fightin' like dogs in the street. Finally wound up with the meanest son of a bitch in Deadwood. Buffalo skinner named Pig-Eye Foley. That's the last I heard. I got an idea, though, they both skedaddled out of town." He raised a brow at Jessie. "I don't know where they are now, but I know who wants to find out. Half-breed Shoshoni they call Copperhead. Him and six or seven other no-goods rode in a couple of days back."

"And they're still here?" asked Ki.

"Oh, yeah, they're still here. Askin' the same questions you are, too."

Jessie sipped her coffee and set it down. "This man called Copperhead . . . do you know where he's from, Colonel? Where he was before?"

Colonel Henry shrugged. "Man like that doesn't come from much of anywhere, Jessie. And he sure doesn't talk about his business. I heard about him, though, couple of years back. Did some pretty nasty work for a big cattle outfit down in New Mexico Territory."

"He's for hire, then," Ki said bluntly. He glanced narrowly at Jessie. "Hell, he's got to be the one."

"We've been looking for this girl for six months," Jessie explained. "Someone wants her dead, Colonel. She's been hopping across the country like a frog, and she doesn't have the sense to lay low. Her pattern's about the same wherever she lights. Raises hell all over town, gets men heated up, then takes off with the one she likes best. The people who are after her nearly got her in Kansas City. We just missed her in Denver. And from the way you describe this Copperhead, I think maybe he was there too."

"She was living with a high-rolling gambler," Ki added. "They had about half of one floor of the Windsor Hotel. A half-breed shot the gambler dead, right in the middle of Chase's Palace. Angela got away. We stuck around awhile, then got word from you she might have showed up in the Dakotas."

"Busy little lady," Colonel Henry said wryly. "Don't much mind pushing her luck."

"Angela's too pretty for her own good," Jessie sighed, "but she's *not* as dumb as she acts. Foolhearty, maybe, but not dumb. She just can't stay out of trouble, especially where men are concerned."

The waiter came with food, thick steaks running with juice and bowls of mashed potatoes and greens.

"You all get on with your eating," Colonel Henry said dourly. He finished off his whiskey, made a face, and pushed back his chair. "I'll ask around some and get back—but I can tell you right now the girl's gone."

"Be careful," Jessie warned. "This Copperhead fellow isn't real friendly."

"Huh!" The old man shot Jessie a withering look. "Better tell *him* to watch his step. I didn't fall off the wagon yesterday morning, girl."

Jessie laughed. "Colonel Henry, according to my father's stories the only thing you ever fell off was some young widow gal's bed."

6

Colonel Henry colored and cleared his throat. "Alex Starbuck was a fine man, rest his soul. But you don't want to believe everything your daddy said, especially 'bout me." He frowned and looked at the floor. "None of my business, Jessie, and you haven't said it, but I hear things now and then. This gal you're after, and the men that want to kill her. They wouldn't have something to do with the bastards that gunned down your father, now would they?"

Jessie met his piercing blue eyes. "Yes, Colonel. They would."

"Figured as much." He nodded and squeezed Jessie's shoulder. "Be talking to you. He turned then and walked through the tables to the lobby. He was slow on his feet, but he still stood straight and tall as a pine.

"Lord," Jessie sighed, "there isn't another like him in the world. You know that, Ki? He grew up with this country! My father said when the Colonel was a boy, he knew Daniel Boone himself. Went hunting with him in Missouri. I know for a fact he fought in the Seminole War with Andy Jackson, and with Sam Houston at San Jacinto. He trapped all over the west with Jim Bridger and Joseph Walker. And he comes by that 'Colonel' business honestly—Gettysburg and Antietam and the whole thing, right to the end." Her smile faded then, and she shook her head in concern. "I don't really like him out asking questions, but there's no way to stop Colonel Henry. I could've lied about Angela, but I'm sure he would have seen right through me." ,

Ki finished his steak and wiped bread around his plate. "I've got to start asking questions myself sooner or later. Might as well be now. I'll try and track down the Colonel while I'm at it." He set his napkin aside. "If this Copperhead's working for Heydrich, it isn't going to take too long for him to put two and two together. He's bound to know who you are, Jessie. Or he will soon enough. Everyone in Deadwood knows a good-looking woman checked into the hotel. By now, they know who's name is on the register. If Copperhead works for the cartel—"

"I know," Jessie finished, "we don't have much time to

waste. I'm going with you. There's nothing I can accomplish here at the hotel."

"No," Ki said flatly. "That's not a good idea and you know it."

"Ki—"

"Look, Jessie, I can't make you stay, but it isn't going to be much help, you marching all over town. All you'll do is attract attention and make it hard for me to ask questions. You're, ah, not exactly the easiest woman to ignore."

"I'm not, huh?" Jessie grinned, enjoying Ki's discomfort. "All right," she said finally, "you win. And thanks for the compliment—I think. Be careful, friend."

"I'll do that," he told her.

Jessie watched him disappear through the lobby, then signaled the waiter for more coffee. She didn't like waiting, but had to admit he was right. He could do a lot better in the backstreets and saloons without her. A woman any prettier than a duck drew a crowd real quick in the Dakotas. Angela Halley was proof enough of that. *Lord,* thought Jessie, *that girl doesn't have the sense God gave a mule!*

Still, what could you expect from a girl like Angela Winston Halley? She'd crowded more living into nineteen years than any two hundred women put together. Her father, Andrew Halley, owned half of St. Louis. But money didn't impress Angela at all. Born with a silver spoon in her mouth, she had a liking for raw whiskey in tin cups. At eleven, she was stealing her mother's jewels and running with river thieves on the Missouri. At fifteen, she'd been kicked out of three eastern schools. A year later, she ran off to Europe with a phony Italian count. A year after that, at seventeen, she was back in this country, the mistress of Ernst Heydrich.

Then Angela came to Jessie's attention. Heydrich was a name she knew only too well. If her information was right, he was one of the cartel's key men in the United States, a guiding force behind those who had taken her father's life.

For some time Jessie had heard only rumors of Ernst Heydrich and the rebellious young girl who'd become his lover. Then, six months ago, startling news reached her at the Circle Star ranch in Texas. Angela Halley was gone. She'd left Ernst Heydrich, jumped naked off his private railcar outside of Chicago. According to Jessie's informants, Heydrich had alerted every cartel assassin in the country to find her and kill her. As an incentive, he was offering an unbelievable sum—fifty thousand dollars to whoever completed the task.

Heydrich, Jessie knew, had every reason to be concerned. When Angela Halley left, she deprived her former lover of more than her supple young body. She also took a list containing the names of the cartel's top agents in the country. The men and women on the list, Jessie was sure, were in key positions in government, business, and high society. The cartel had taken great pains to place them there. If Heydrich couldn't get the list back, he was dead. His associates wouldn't tolerate such a costly, foolish mistake. If they *guessed* he'd let such a prize slip out of his hands . . .

Jessie sat back and gave a deep, weary sigh. If she could find Angela Halley, get to her before Ernst Heydrich's men, get her hands on that list . . . ! She was almost afraid to hope. A find like that would set the cartel back on its heels. By God, she'd *make* people believe they were a danger with a weapon like that in her hands.

"Uh, Miss Starbuck? Miss J—Jessie Starbuck?"

"What?" Jessie turned, startled, to face a man standing beside her table. He was lean, sandy-haired, wearing faded twill trousers and a worn plaid shirt. His big, sad eyes were veined with red, and the stink of sweat and whiskey was in his clothes.

"Yes," Jessie said cautiously. "I'm Jessie Starbuck. What do you want?"

"If you know a k—kinda slant-eyed lookin' feller," he said nervously, "you might better c—come and see him off. They're fixin' to hang him down back of the livery."

★

Chapter 2

Ki walked through the lobby and out the glass front door of the Dakota Hotel. The hard, driving rain had eased to a slow and steady drizzle, and clouds hung low over the valley, washing all colors into gray. It was the kind of weather that intended to settle in and stay.

· He headed left, toward the busy center of town, keeping to the walkway that bordered the street. The street itself had disappeared. He passed a heavy wagon mired halfway up its wheels in mud. The hapless driver had given up, hauled his team to safety, and left the wagon.

Past the general store was the assay office, the livery, and two saloons. Ki paused before the bat-wing doors of the Golden Eagle, peered inside, and walked on. A saloon was the best place in town to sit and listen, the worst place to ask questions. He'd likely have to try sooner or later, but there were better things to do before that.

"Mister, you f–figure you could stake a poor fellow to a meal? I'm lookin' for honest work but there isn't any around t–to be had."

Ki took the man in quickly. It was easy to spot the truth; the man wasn't trying hard to hide it. He didn't want food or hard work and likely couldn't handle either one. What he needed was a drink to stop the shakes. "You want a hot meal I'll buy it," said Ki. "I've got a couple of things to do first."

"Huh?" The man blinked in dismay. "You d–don't have to go with me or nothing, friend. I can f–feed myself, you know."

"I'll be back, all right?" He nodded and started off. The man reached out, touched his sleeves, and blocked the way.

10

"I can show you where J–Jack McCall shot Hickock. Know right where it is. You sure ought to see that."

"No thanks, not now."

"That's a real f–famous shootin'," the man insisted. "Why d–don't you want to see it?"

"Look," Ki said, "I don't have the time."

"I can show you ol' Wild Bill's grave. Take you right to it."

"Hey, friend—"

"Shit," the man blurted, "why don't you just give me the goddamn money so I c–can get myself a drink!"

Ki was startled by the sudden outburst. There was anger in the young man's eyes, a spark of pride still very alive.

"You ought to get yourself together," he said evenly. "You're too young to be a drunk."

"Yeah? How old do you h–have to be?"

Ki had to grin. "Sorry. You can kill yourself if you want. I'm not going to help."

"Jesus—" The man shook his head in disgust. "You a preacher or what?"

"Not even close."

The man licked his lips. "All right. You don't care nothin' about Hickock. W–what is it you want? You're lookin' for something, mister. Might be I could help you f—find it."

Ki studied the man a long moment. "Friend, you're wrong. I'm not looking for anything at all."

There was a hint of warning in his voice. The man caught it but let it pass. "Might as well t–talk to me as the next man," he said calmly. He nodded, a gesture that took in the whole street. "Everybody knows you're here and where you're staying. We don't get a lot of pretty ladies like M–Miss Starbuck in Deadwood. Everybody'd l–like to know why we got one now. You understan' what I'm saying?"

Ki understood very well. He wasn't surprised the drunk knew Jessie's name. She'd made no secret about that. He wondered, now, if that had been a mistake. He made a quick decision, pulled a half-dollar from his trousers, and dropped it in the man's shirt pocket. "Maybe I'll talk to you again," he

11

smiled, "if I can think of something to ask."

"Yeah, well—thanks!" The man blinked in surprise. He'd given up completely on Ki.

Ki nodded and walked away. The drunk could likely answer questions, but Ki knew he couldn't trust him. A fellow addicted to the bottle was always for sale. The next half-dollar or a dime was as good as his own.

He crossed the street quickly, staying to the narrow plank boards laid over the mud. Men were getting restless indoors; cattlemen, prospectors, and drifters began to wander out and stare at the leaden skies. Ki noted a number of men clearly in the hunting and skinning trade. They were lean, hard-eyed fellows, years of dusty summers and long winters etched in their faces. Their hats were broad-brimmed against the sun, their clothes of faded leather. They'd hunted the herds south, wandering from Dodge City to Fort Griffin and back again. Now with the buffalo nearly gone south of the Powder, they'd come to try their hand with the northern herd. Some, Ki knew, were on their way to Miles City in Montana Territory. Many were gathering parties for the Cave Hill region of the Dakotas to the north. Rumor had it a large herd had moved into that area for the first time in years.

Ki shared Jessie's dislike of men who made a living killing and skinning the big shaggies—and the large organizations that paid top dollar for the hides. They were driving the beasts to extinction and starving the Indians in the bargain. Seventy-five million buffalo had once roamed the Great Plains, the herds stretching all the way from Texas past the Milk River in Canada. Now, there were a million or maybe less, easy to get to and ripe for the slaughter. Another year, some said, maybe two or three—after that they'd all be gone.

"They won't stop shooting till it's done," Ki muttered under his breath. "Then, they'll wonder where the hell they all went."

He passed another saloon. Ki came instantly alert as a man sauntered lazily out of an open doorway ahead. He knew the fellow at once: Cole, the skinner who'd shared their coach a few hours before.

Cole looked up, saw Ki, and pretended surprise. "Well now,

12

small town, ain't it? How you takin' to Deadwood, friend?"

"Finest place I've ever seen," Ki said without expression.

Cole threw back his head and laughed. His fingers hooked his belt and he made no effort to move aside. Ki could either wait, or step into the muddy street and go around.

"You want something," he said flatly, "or just passing the time?"

"Matter of fact," said Cole, "I was kinda hopin' to run into *you*."

"What for?"

"Well, you know . . ." Cole shrugged and squinted at the sky. "Business is what I was thinking. Maybe a little business transaction."

"I'm not in the market for hides," Ki said irritably. "If you don't mind stepping aside . . ."

"Hey, now, take it easy, friend." Cole held up a hand, leaned in close and gave Ki a whiff of beery breath. "I ain't selling. I'm buying."

Ki had no idea where in hell the man was going, but he didn't like the broad, crooked grin that went with his words. "Buying what? I've got nothing to sell, mister."

"Now I kinda figure you do." Cole scratched his jaw and nodded over his shoulder. "See, those ol' boys and me are headed up to buffalo country. Figure on ridin' out in the morning." Ki looked past Cole. Three men were lazing before the saloon maybe thirty feet away. They looked enough alike to be related.

"Yeah, so?" Ki gave Cole a puzzled look. "What's that got to do with me?"

"Well now we're goin' to be gone all fall and through the winter," Cole explained. "That's a powerful long time. Shit, you run out of tobacco and whiskey right off and there isn't nothin' to do but freeze your ass and look at some bastard's hairy face. What me and the boys was thinking, now, was it'd be worth a hell of a lot to have us a little comfort. You know what I'm saying? 'Course pleasure's got a price and that's a fact. We figure if huntin's good we could take five, six thousand hides or maybe more. They're supposed to be paying two-dollar seventy cash at Miles City. We'd be willing, now, to cut a man in for, oh, five percent of the take, and that'd be right off the top you understand." He gave Ki a broad wink. "Shit, mister, that's close to seven hundred dollars."

Ki shook his head. "Damn it, what are you talking about, Cole!"

"Ain't you been listening at all?" Cole looked pained. "I'm talking about *business*. You get good cash money come spring, and me and the boys get us that pretty little gal to take north. Hell, you could even have her back if you want. 'Course we'd have to take somethin' off your share if you did that. Be the fair thing to—"

Ki's right hand shot out in a blur, fingers stiffened into a wedge. Cole turned white, gasped for air, and bent double. Ki brought his knee up hard and felt the man's nose turn to mush. Cole bellowed in pain, flailed out blindly, and went sprawling into the street.

Ki stared at the man through a red curtain of rage, hard fists trembling at his sides, not believing what he'd heard. He was trying to buy Jessie for the winter! It was no different to him than bargaining for a team of good mules!

Ki saw a white flash and felt splinters sting his cheek. The roll of thunder took forever crossing the street. He threw himself aside as the pistol roared again. Lead chewed wood and he rolled to the right, hit the muddy street, and tumbled on his side through the muck. Jerking to his knees he saw them coming, three bearded men as big as bears. One fired his pistol until it was empty. Another shook a blade in his fist, shouting and slashing the air with a vengeance.

"Oh, hell—" Ki stared at the big skinning knife. It looked a foot long and he knew he wasn't off more than an inch. The first man reached him, a skinner with pit-black eyes and a thick neck. Ki thought about the slim *tanto* blade in his belt, wiped mud from his eyes, and left the weapon where it was. He leaped aside as the skinner's knife carved a long, wicked arc. The man slashed out again and Ki struck, caught the man's wrist, and jerked it sharply to the left. The skinner howled and

14

staggered back, his arm hanging loosely from his shoulder. Ki kicked out with the side of his foot and slammed the man solidly in the throat.

He didn't stay to watch the man fall. He sensed rather than saw the cold blade coming at him to his right, whirled about in a half circle, and jumped. The mud slowed his actions and his foot slid past the man's belly. The blade thrust out, painting a red line across his thigh. Ki fell back, slipped, and lost his balance. The knife whipped straight for his gut and he threw himself desperately out of its path. The skinner roared, a bright gleam of triumph in his eyes. He kicked out at Ki with his boot and plunged the knife at his groin in a killing blow. Ki crabbed aside, scooped mud with his hands, and threw it into the skinner's eyes. The man bellowed in rage, backed off, and clawed at his face. Ki came out of the mud in a blur. His fingers bent slightly, the joints a wedge of hard bone and cartilage. The blow snapped in and out, catching the man directly beneath his chin, and he went stiff, then dropped to the mud like a tree.

Too late, Ki turned to meet the quick whisper of sound. He'd known it was there a breath before, heard it coming at him, and tried to guess its path. Pain seared his chest as the leather caught him turning, whirled him harshly, and jerked him off his feet. Ki rolled away, clawed for the whip, and felt it razor through his fingers. He saw the hunter then as he circled the weapon sharply around his head. The tip exploded an inch from Ki's cheek. The man laughed, struck out again. Ki lunged straight for the darting leather, ducked his head between his shoulders, and let the coil punish his back. The hunter cursed and drew the whip back fast. Ki spun on his heels, caught the coils in his arms, and yanked as hard as he could. The hunter stared at his bare hands and darted through the mud, his big fists moving before his face. Ki shifted his feet and let him come. The man swung wide, his right glancing off Ki's shoulder. Ki lashed out, landing short, punishing blows to the face that rocked the man. The hunter gasped in surprise, staggered back, and stared. Ki's open hand snaked in repeatedly. Blood flowed from the hunter's ruined nose and filled his mouth. Ki

15

delivered a quick, punishing blow with stiffened fingers. The hunter's eyes glazed, his features went slack, and he dropped to the mud like a sack.

Ki shook his head, drew a deep breath, and wiped a hand across his eyes. Shouts of anger brought him around. The plank sidewalk to his right was crowded with men—most of them hunters and skinners and all of them madder than hell. Ki jerked around and saw them coming, spilling into the street straight for him. He turned and ran through the mud. The rope dropped over his shoulders and lifted him off his feet. He sprawled on his back and the crowd roared in delight. They were on him in an instant, pounding him with their fists and kicking with their feet. Ki fought back but they smothered him under their weight. They were a pack of wild dogs and he was the fox. They meant to tear him apart before they were through.

He felt himself lifted off the ground, passed roughly over the crowd. Another rope snaked around his neck. They carried him down the street and through an alley, out behind the livery to a dead yellow pine on the hill.

"Billy Karl's dead," someone yelled hoarsely, "Christ, the son of a bitch broke his neck!"

"Hang him," another shouted, "hang the goddamn chink!"

The crowd roared in anger. Someone punched Ki in the belly. He gasped for breath; the man hit him again. The rope tightened around his neck and he saw the loose end snake over a branch high above. *Where the hell's the law in this town?* he wondered angrily. The answer came quickly enough: If they were smart, they were minding their own business. A crowd of hunters and skinners out for blood was a lot for any lawman. Why take them on for a stranger—one who clearly wasn't pure-blood white in the bargain?

The noose began to tighten around his neck. He stood on his toes and gasped for air. A hunter stepped up to tie a dirty bandanna around his eyes. Another grabbed it out of his hands and tossed it away.

"Let the bastard see hell coming," he said tightly. "He's got no favors due from us!"

The men muttered approval. "What'll it be," the hunter with

16

the rope said to the others, "you want it slow or fast?"

"Slow!" the men yelled, shaking their fists in the air.

"By God, yes!"

"Squeeze him dry, Pete!"

Out of the corner of his eye, Ki saw Cole and one of the others he'd fought in the street edge their way roughly through the crowd. The men stepped back to let them through. Cole glared wildly at Ki, glanced to his right, and drew a blade from a man's belt.

"You boys can hang him," he growled between his teeth, "but I'm going to cut him good first."

The hunters went silent as Cole stepped up to Ki. His nose was a swollen mass across his face.

"You going to remember me, friend," he said tightly. "I'm the last man you're ever going to see." The knife lashed out and ripped Ki's trousers to the crotch. A terrible grin stretched Cole's features. "Reckon this is going to *smart* just a might. I'll make sure they hang your pecker right with you, by God. Least I can do for a friend."

The cold blade lifted Ki's member. Cole looked at it and grinned. Ki's stomach tightened into a knot and bile rose up in his throat. Cole grasped his member, pulled it out straight and chopped down savagely with the knife.

★

Chapter 3

The bullet ripped Cole's fingers away and sent the blade arching through the crowd. Cole howled and grabbed his ruined hand. The rifle roared again. A side of Cole's skull disappeared. The skinner twisted around and fell on his face.

"All right, who wants to be second?"

The men didn't move. Ki turned his head as well as he could and saw Colonel Henry, his Winchester steady at his waist.

"Mister, this ain't your affair," a bald man told him.

"You want to ask that dead feller 'bout it?" the Colonel drawled. "Drop that noose, boy; the fun's over."

The man laughed. "Put the piece away, old man, 'fore you get hurt."

"Pete," one of the men said calmly, "he ain't just any old man, I don't reckon. That's Henry Dodd you're talking to."

Pete's eyes widened in surprise, then his jaw shot out in defiance. "Shit, I heard tell ol' Dodd was dead. Looks to me like you aren't far from it—"

The rifle thundered twice, two shots close enough together to be one. Pete dropped the rope and howled, staggered back and slapped his head. The first shot had taken half his ear. The second had carved a long red furrow across his neck. The buffalo hunters watched the Colonel, who didn't move. A man on the edge of the crowd turned and started down the hill. Another followed after, and in a moment there was no one left but Ki the dead man on the ground, and the Colonel.

"How many'd you take on?" asked the Colonel.

"Four, counting him."

"How many'd you beat?"

"All four I guess."

Colonel Henry nodded. "Sounds like a fair fight to me."

18

• • •

"You don't look *real* bad," said Jessie, "I guess I've seen worse."

"Thanks," Ki said dryly, "that's a comfort." He brought a fork to his face and winced, then forced himself to chew. An hour in a steaming hot tub had helped some, but every inch of his body was sore and bruised. "I'd be just fine," he complained, "if Colonel Henry hadn't rubbed my skin raw with that Cheyenne snake oil, or whatever the hell it was. Damn, Jessie, I burn all over from that stuff!"

"Uh-huh . . ." She made a tent with her fingers and studied him over the table. "Smell real nice, too. Like old grease and dead cows. You don't mind having supper up here, do you? I mean, you've made so many friends around town I thought you'd like to get off to yourself."

Ki looked up, caught the mischievous sparkle in her eyes and laughed with her. "It's an Oriental custom. We like to meet new people."

"In muddy streets in the rain."

"I'm only half Japanese," Ki reminded her. "It's the American half that can't resist a fight."

"Oh, sure." Jessie's smile suddenly faded. She reached across the table and squeezed Ki's hand in her own. "God, I was scared," she said shakily. "When that man came in and told me they were getting ready to hang you . . . that if I wanted to see you again . . ."

Ki read the deep concern in her eyes. "Hey, I'm all right. It's over." A broad grin suddenly creased his features. "That old man, I never saw anything like it. He faced that crowd and they backed off. I can't say as I blame 'em."

Jessie poured them both coffee, stood, and crossed the room. Lightning lit the sky and rain rattled the dark panes. She touched the glass and brought her fingers away cold.

"Colonel Henry was coming back here when he heard the commotion behind the livery," she told Ki without turning. "He found a couple of things that might help. This Copperhead isn't in Deadwood, but he's not far off. A man the Colonel trusts says he's camped somewhere out of town, this side of Elk Creek. He's got about eight or ten hired guns with him. He, or one of the others, rides into Deadwood now and then."

Ki gave her a thoughtful look. "If he's still around here, that means he doesn't know where Angela is."

"Exactly," said Jessie. "It also means we were right in thinking he'll know who *we* are soon enough, if he doesn't know already."

Ki's dark eyes didn't waver. "There's more. What is it?"

Jessie made a face. "I don't like you knowing everything I think."

"It works two ways. What else did Colonel Henry say— the part you aren't sure you ought to tell me?"

"I was going to," she said irritably. "It's just *when* is all. I don't want you runnin' off all crippled up."

"I'm not all crippled up."

"Oh well, 'course you're not," she said dryly. Jessie swept amber hair off her shoulders. "All right. It seems this Pig-Eye Foley Angela took up with is a real ladies' man. One of his favorite girls works at the Golden Eagle. A lady named Canary. Only this friend of Colonel Henry's says nobody knows about that. He had a couple of other girls going and didn't want either of 'em to know about her."

"Real slick fellow."

"Uh-huh. At least it's a break for us. Copperhead hasn't found out about her. Not yet, anyway."

Ki gave Jessie a thoughtful look. "All right. I think I see what's happening here."

"What? What are you talking about?"

"What you were going to do. Go see this Canary yourself, so I wouldn't get in any trouble."

"It doesn't seem like a bad idea, now does it? Considering those buffalo hunters are still in town—and they *might* just decide to have a drink now and then."

"You're probably right. The safest place for me is under the bed."

"Ki..."

"Don't worry, I'm not going anywhere tonight." He stood painfully and stretched his limbs. "All I want right now is a good night's sleep. We can talk about this Canary in the morning. You want to see her, fine. But daylight's the time to do it. What kind of a name is that anyway? She sing like a bird or something?"

"I wouldn't be surprised," Jessie said flatly. "According to Colonel Henry, she's pretty good at everything else."

"Well, that's real interesting."

"Ki..." Jessie's eyes turned a menacing shade of green. "You're going straight up to bed. Remember?"

"Isn't that what I said?"

"I know what you said. It's the look on your face I don't like."

"What look? You can't tell what us Orientals are thinking."

"Get out of here," she grinned. "Like you say, we'll worry about Canary in the morning."

Ki moved to the door, stopped, and turned to face her again. "I'm not ever going to forget that business with Cole, you know? Damn it, Jessie, I couldn't believe it, him standing there dead serious offering me seven-hundred dollars for you."

"Ki, nothing surprises me anymore."

"I know, but—seven hundred dollars? Eight, maybe. Eight and a half..."

Jessie's face fell. She reached for a plate of hard dinner rolls. Ki grinned and slipped through the door as the missiles began to pelt the wood panel at his back.

He crouched on the saloon's flat roof, shielding his head against the rain. When he'd left his room and slipped down the backstairs the rain had slacked off to a light and easy mist. The storm hadn't dampened the town's spirits. The streets and saloons were crowded, and horses lined the hitching rails.

Now the rain had come again, lashing through the Black Hills with a vengeance. Ki welcomed its appearance. It would drive everyone inside, help him do what he had to do next.

Bringing his legs over the edge of the roof, he lowered himself down the side of the building, then dropped to the porch below. A narrow balcony ran along the upper floor of the Golden Eagle. He'd visited more than one such establishment and knew what the second floor was for. He ignored the lighted windows, though several offered interesting sights. On the far side of the saloon he found the entry he wanted. Pressing his face to the rain-spotted glass, he saw a dark and narrow hall. Luck was running with him: for the moment, the hall was empty. After raising the window he slipped quickly inside. His

21

heart pounded and he drew a calming breath. He was wet, crouching in a corner where he clearly didn't belong. The doors all looked alike. Except one. It was half the width of the others. He moved quickly, jerked the door open, and slipped inside.

He could feel the shape of the brooms and smell soap and fresh linens. The closet was stuffy and he opened the door a crack. He'd brought no weapons, deliberately leaving behind the *tanto* knife and the *shuriken* throwing blades he usually carried. This wasn't the place for weapons; his hands and feet would serve him well enough. If there were trouble, he didn't intend to stay and face it.

A man laughed; a girl shrieked with delight. She stood in yellow light before her room. She was short, dark-haired, and naked to the waist. The man swayed drunkenly and pawed at her breasts. The girl playfully shoved him away. The man laughed and reeled down the hall. The girl made a face at his back and shut the door.

Ki waited. A girl came up the stairs, a customer in tow. Ki already had the envelope in his hand. He'd kept it dry inside a small oilskin packet. Before the man and girl reached the hall, he flipped it along the floor, directly in their path. The pair walked past without stopping and entered a room. Ki cursed under his breath.

A moment later the dark-haired girl opened her door, tucking a low-cut blouse into her skirt. She started down the hall, hesitated, picked up the envelope, and turned it right side up. He could see her lips move as she read the name Canary. With a shrug she poked it between her breasts and pranced down the stairs.

Ki ran a hand over his face. It was hot in the closet and the water on his body was mixing with sweat. He wondered if the girl would even remember she had the note. If she found another customer, if someone bought her a drink . . . *Too many ifs,* Ki thought grimly. Still it was the only way he knew to get the girl named Canary alone, to pick her out from the others.

Footsteps and the silken rustle of clothing alerted him. The girl was tall, slender as a snake. She wore a bright yellow dress, and wheat-colored hair tumbled over bare shoulders. Ki allowed himself a smile. Canary, of course. Yellow dress and yellow hair. He knew he was right when he saw the note crumpled tightly in her fist. She stopped at a door nearby, opened it, and started inside. Ki came out of his closet, slipped in behind her, and shut the door.

The girl whirled around to face him, blue eyes flashing in anger. "Who the hell are you," she snapped. "Get out of here, mister!"

"I just want to talk," Ki said calmly. "Take it easy, all right?"

"*Talk,* huh?" She gave him a scornful little laugh and set her hands against her hips, thrusting her pelvis forward and giving her breasts a saucy tilt. She looked Ki over from head to toe, anger turning to a bold and mischievous grin. "You aren't bad-looking, you know? You want to get out of those wet clothes, so we can *talk* some better?"

"I don't see how that'd hurt," Ki told her.

"Won't hurt at all," she said softly. "Might even feel good."

It wasn't what he'd come for, but he couldn't tell her that. Not until he'd eased her fears. The sullen, lazy smile hadn't impressed him at all. He could see the lines of tension around her mouth, the quick, wary movement of her eyes.

"You just get undressed and dry off," Canary told him. "I'll slip out of this dress. Wouldn't mind watching me do that, now would you?"

"I've got an idea it'd be a pleasure," Ki said. The girl bit her lip and raised a hand to the swell of her breasts. Ki had no trouble at all showing his interest. The girl had a slender, almost fragile figure. The wheat-colored hair framed enormous, smouldering blue eyes. Her full, sensuous mouth hinted at pleasures that stirred his loins with growing excitement.

"You're not gettin' ready," she pouted, opening another button on her dress. "You going to keep me waiting?"

"I kinda got caught up watching you," Ki told her.

"Did you, now? Isn't that sweet!" She laughed and twirled in a quick half-circle, sweeping past him toward a table and pitcher in a corner of the room. When she faced him again the smile was gone, and the silver Smith & Wesson .38 was aimed at his belly.

"Glad I didn't try to pour a drink of water," said Ki.

"Keep laughing, mister," she said coldly. "Now who the hell are you and what do you want with me?"

"Like I said, I want to talk, Canary."

Canary showed her teeth. "You write this trash, I reckon?" She thrust the crumpled note at his face. "'Canary, I left a little something extra under your pillow. A grateful friend.'" She spat a curse in Ki's direction. "Real cute. Figured that'd get me up here fast, did you?" Her arm came up and she thumbed back the hammer of the revolver. "You want to talk? Well *talk*, mister, and by God it better be good!" She paused and a frown creased the center of her brow. "Say, how'd you get up here, anyway? Know it wasn't the stairs; a man isn't allowed up here alone."

"I came through the window in the hall."

"Christ, what for? You ever hear about doors?"

"I wanted to see you. I didn't know what you looked like. And, I didn't figure it'd be a good idea to show my face down there. There's some fellows around town I'd just as soon not tangle with again."

"What? Look, I don't get this friend. If you're a—" Canary's eyes went wide. "My God, you're him—the one those hunters tried to hang!"

Ki forced a smile.

"Shit, you got a nerve," the girl said darkly, "I'll have to hand you that. We got hide hunters and skinners wall-to-wall down there tonight." She cocked her head curiously at Ki. "That doesn't say what you wanted with me, now does it?"

"Do we have to talk with you pointing that?"

"Yeah, we sure do," she said flatly.

Ki drew in a breath. "A girl was here in Deadwood. She went by the name of Louisa. The word is she went off with a fellow named Pig-Eye Foley—"

"Damn you, mister!" Canary blurted.

"Hey, now hold it." Ki pushed air with his hands. "I don't know what you feel about this Foley. Maybe you're madder'n hell and maybe you're not. I'm not interested in him. Not any. I'm trying to find the girl."

Canary's mouth went tight. "How—how do you know about him and me?"

"I just heard is all."

"Well I don't know a damn thing. About Foley or no girl or anything else. All right?"

"Canary," Ki said carefully, "I know I'm not the only one

24

asking questions around town. There are other people interested in the girl, people you don't want to meet." Canary's eyes told him she knew exactly what he was saying. Copperhead's men had been busy. "I'm not one of them. Believe me."

"Oh, well sure," she said dryly. "'Cause you'd *tell* me if you were, right?"

"No. I wouldn't tell you a thing." Ki's dark eyes bored into hers. "What I'd do is take a knife to your throat the second I came through the door. I wouldn't waste time talking. If you didn't come up with what I wanted I'd kill you on the spot."

Canary flinched at his words. Her hand started shaking and the pistol began to waver. Tears filled her eyes, and her face suddenly twisted in pain. The gun fell to the carpet and she covered her face and wept.

Ki moved to her and took her in his arms. "Look, I'm sorry," he said softly. "I didn't mean to scare you."

"Christ, mister," she blurted, "I was scared 'fore you even got here. Hell, I don't care about her. You think I don't know Foley's got other women? I'm a whore in a goddamn saloon. I don't figure a man's going to worry 'bout being faithful and true to Suzanne Platt." She grinned at Ki through her tears. "Yeah, that's me. Canary sounds some better, don't you think?"

"It sounds just fine," Ki told her. "It's a real pretty name."

"Really? You think so?" The bold, wanton look in her eyes suddenly faded. Now, for a moment, she was the girl she'd likely been before Deadwood claimed her. Ki held her, bent to kiss her. She gave a little sigh and closed her eyes, then reached up and took his cheeks gently between her hands. Her mouth opened slightly and she guided his lips eagerly to her own. Ki explored the warmth of her mouth, savoring the sweetness of each small, secret hollow. Canary answered his need, drinking in his kisses. Ki let his lips trail past her cheeks to the column of her throat. His hands found the curve of her shoulder and slipped the loose dress down her arms. Canary reached up to help. When she finished the last button, she slipped the hooks at her waist and let the dress whisper to the floor. For a moment she stood before him without moving. She wore nothing at all under the dress. The light from the flickering lamp turned her flesh the color of gold. Watching Ki from under a veil of tousled hair, she caught the folds of her gown on her toe and flicked it mischievously at his feet. Bending one leg slightly behind the other, she rested her palms gently on the silken yellow patch between her legs.

Ki's throat went suddenly dry. He was struck by the startling contrasts in this woman. She was bold, wanton, begging for pleasure. Yet at the same time she was a shy, hesitant little girl, caught for the first time without her clothes.

Canary caught his expression and grinned. "Everything look all right?"

"Everything is just fine." Ki swallowed hard, pulled off his shirt, and quickly slipped out of his trousers. Canary opened her mouth slightly, lips full and lazy. Twisting on her heels, she clasped her hands behind her back. The motion deepened the hollow beneath her ribs and thrust her breasts forward in a sharp and saucy tilt. In spite of her willow-slim frame, the lovely little mounds were firm and well formed.

Ki took a step toward her and cupped her small breasts in his hands. The sky-blue eyes followed his every move. He bent to kiss each rosy nipple, caressing each into a hard little point. She drew in a breath at his touch, rested her hands at his waist, and let them slide down the hardness of his belly.

"Oh my, *yes!*" A cry escaped her lips as she touched his swollen member. She looked right at him and showed him a wicked grin. "By God I'm goin' to have to keep my eye on that window. Never can tell what'll crawl in out of the rain!"

★

Chapter 4

"Lady, I'd by jumping through windows all night," Ki said, "if I figured my luck would hold up as good as this."

Canary laughed, twisted on the trim curve of her legs, and danced out of his arms. Her body was long and sleek, a sensuous mix of velvet curves and soft hollows. With an impish grin, she moved in close to him again, grasped his waist, and went slowly to her knees. Shaking long hair out of her eyes, she cradled his erection in her hands and softly touched the swollen tip with a whisper of a kiss. Ki sucked in a breath. Canary looked up with a smile, blew a soft breath across his belly, and slid his shaft gently into her mouth. At once the heat of her touch raced like a fire through his loins. Her fingers raked his hips as her tongue explored his length. She teased the hard flesh, nipped him softly with her teeth. The tip of her tongue moved lazily along the underside of his member. Again and again she stroked him with her warm mouth. Her pale blue eyes held him intently through a wisp of yellow hair.

Ki sighed a whisper of pleasure. Her tongue flicked out to tease him, stroke him quickly with moisture. Her lips opened around him, scarcely touching him at all. The hot breath of her mouth was a charge of pain and delight.

Ki, suspended on the fragile crest of pleasure, longed for the stroke that would hurl him over the top, shake his whole body like a storm. Canary, though, refused to let him go. She was a master at her game and plainly knew every trick in the book. She gave him all she had, every subtle kiss, every artful flick of her agile tongue, everything but the one, final touch that would bring him exquisite release.

"My God," Ki groaned, "you're trying to kill me, girl, or just plain drive my crazy!"

Canary didn't answer. Instead, she caressed his rigid member once again, a long and sensuous stroke from the base of his shaft to the tip.

Now—now—*now!* Ki shut his eyes. Canary took him nearly to the top—then let him down again. Ki gritted his teeth and stared at the ceiling. The feeling was almost unbearable, an agony that tightened every cord and tendon in his body, filled his shaft until he thought it would surely explode.

"Damn it, girl, I mean it. I can't take any more of this, you hear?"

Canary gave him a long and sober look. "Might be best if I quit right now. Save you any more worry."

"Huh?" Ki looked appalled. "Hey, now look—you wouldn't do a thing like that."

"I might," she said absently. "Then again, I might *not.*" Her tongue flicked out once more. The little pink tip darted at him like a snake. Suddenly the strokes grew harder and faster until her tongue disappeared in a blur.

Ki felt the storm surging within him, thundering up through his loins. Her brow slammed hard against his belly. Canary moaned with delight as he exploded into her mouth. He was sated, empty, drained of every desire. Then, her lips came together and kneaded him once again.

Ki clutched her tousled hair and pressed her hard against his belly. The orgasm shot like a bolt from his groin, bringing a new release even greater than the first. Ki staggered back, staring at the girl in open wonder. Canary looked smug and happy. "Damn, lady, I hope those buffalo hunters don't come bursting through that door," he said shakily. "You'll have to hold 'em off yourself if they do."

"Huh?" Canary sprang lightly to her feet and brushed yellow hair off her cheeks. "Don't give me that stuff, mister. I'm not finished with you yet!"

"You're not?" Ki blinked in alarm. "Well, uh—after a while, maybe, we could sort of—"

"After a while's right now," Canary announced firmly. She grabbed his hand in hers and guided him to her bed, caught the look in his eyes, and burst into laughter. Ki gave up and sprawled down beside her.

"You're some kind of lady, you know?" Ki told her.

Canary twined her arms around his neck. "I've been called a lot of things, friend. I reckon that's a new one." She cocked her head and ran a curious finger over his brow. "I can't get over those eyes," she purred. "They're all tilty at the corners. What kinda fella are you, anyway?"

"I'm half Japanese," he told her. "And half American."

"Uh-huh. And that pretty gal travelin' with you?"

"Jessie. Jessie Starbuck. I work for her, Canary."

Canary rolled her eyes. "Lord, if you *work* for her good as you do for me, I bet you get paid a heap of money!"

Ki felt himself color. "Jessie is my employer. My employer, and a good friend besides. That's all."

"Oh, well whatever you say." The girl's impish grin told him she didn't believe that for a minute. Ki didn't bother to take it further. At the moment her hand was snaking slowly down his chest past his belly, and he couldn't think of anything else. He was as stiff as a rod already from just being close to her honeyed flesh. Her touch made him swell even more.

"Well, now," she whispered, "for a man that was fixin' to rest up, you're sure coming along fine."

"You don't hardly give a man a choice."

"You want me to go away, I will. I wouldn't want you to—oh, Lord!"

Ki trailed his hands past her shoulders to cup the swell of her breasts. Canary groaned and arched her neck as he kissed the pliant skin, moving his tongue in small circles toward the dimpled rosettes. Canary sighed and kissed his shoulder. Her hand pumped his member as he drew the hard little nipples into his mouth. Her breath came in quick bursts of heat against his throat. She cried out and spread her legs wide, stretching her slender form up to meet him. The heady, woman-smell of her body assailed his senses.

"Please," she pleaded, "get in—inside me, do it *now!*"

Her nails raked his back. He could feel the heat of her body, almost taste the sweet honey between her legs. Canary moved her pelvis in a slow circle, begging him to thrust himself into her warmth. The supple tendons in her legs went taut, forcing tender hollows along her thighs. Ki teased her downy nest with the tip of his member, knowing the waiting heightened her pleasure as well as his own. Canary fought to bring him closer. She found his rigid shaft and ground her moist petals firmly against him. With a quick little cry she grasped his manhood in her fist, then thrust it into her body.

Ki gasped and drove himself deeply inside her. Canary gasped with delight. Her long legs scissored about him, pounding against his back. Once more Ki felt himself climbing toward a throbbing peak of pleasure. Heat surged through his belly, begging for release. Canary clung to him, matching his hunger with her own. The furnace between her legs spasmed against him, drawing him closer and closer to the edge. Ki found her breasts again and drew them deeply into his mouth. The musky taste of her flesh sent a sharp surge of excitement through his veins. Canary moaned loudly and thrashed her head wildly from side to side.

The fierce, churning heat in his loins threatened to rise up and pull him under. Canary knew exactly where he was and squeezed him deeper inside her with her legs. Ki threw back his head and roared. His orgasm triggered hers, stoking the fires within her: Her back came off the bed in a sensuous curve of pleasure. For a moment her whole body trembled like a sapling in wind. Finally she went limp beneath him, a ragged sigh of joy on her lips.

In the sudden silence, Ki heard laughter below and wind-driven rain against the window.

Canary snuggled into the hollow of his arm. "Damn, I don't want to leave you," she groaned. "I'd prefer to stay right here the rest of the night." She gave him a harsh little laugh and pulled away. "I'm a workin' girl, you know. Those bastards downstairs will be wondering where ol' Canary's been hiding."

"I'm sorry," he told her.

"Yeah, so am I. Isn't a hell of a lot I can do about that now, is there?"

Ki watched as she rose and walked naked across the room to retrieve her clothes. The sight of her pouty little breasts, the golden skin, and slender legs stirred him again. He stood and pulled on his trousers and found his shirt. Reaching into the folds of his belt, he cupped the leather and shook four double-eagles into his palm, then laid them on the table. Canary heard the noise and turned. Her body went rigid and her blue eyes blazed with anger.

"Damn you," she flared, "who said a thing about paying? That—that wasn't what it was!" Her eyes filled with tears. "You so dumb you don't know the difference 'tween business and pleasure?"

"No, Canary, I'm not." He reached out and drew her into his arms. She beat against his chest in a fury but he refused to let her go. "Listen to me, will you?" he said gently. "The money's not for that. It's for just the opposite of what you think."

"And what's that supposed to mean?"

"There's eighty dollars there. It's all I have on me. I thought maybe it'd help you get out of this place . . . go somewhere else."

Canary's eyes softened. She gave him a long, tender kiss and slipped out of his arms. "And give up my sinful ways, right?" She tossed him a weary smile, then picked up the coins and squeezed them tightly in his hand. "I love you for the thought, but I'd be lyin' if I said it'd do any good." She bit her lip and looked away. "I've tried it before. A dozen times, I guess. I ain't a schoolteacher, friend, and I don't sing good enough for the choir. I'm a whore pure and simple and that's that. Hell, it's a living." She forced a bright smile, glanced in the mirror, and patted her golden hair. She turned then, the smile suddenly gone, and looked him in the eye. "Foley lit out of here fast with that gal. Whoever's after her wants her bad. You won't know them when you see them but they're here, ridin' in and out of town asking questions. A girl I know says they been over to Lead and everywhere else. Every little hole in the wall on the Belle Fourche River and down on the Rapid." She paused and touched the corner of her mouth. "Only place Pig-Eye Foley could've run is to the north. Miles City. He's got a place he can hole up there. Some kinda cabin ten miles or so south on the Yellowstone River. I don't think anyone knows about it 'cept me."

"Thanks, Canary," Ki said. "I'm grateful."

Canary's laugh was cold. "If you find him, try and get that bitch out of heat long enough to shake him loose. He isn't a bad fella, you understand. He's just got to sniff every stray that comes along." Her glance dropped to the floor. "If they catch him with her, he's as good as dead, too. I wouldn't want to see that, mister."

"Take care of yourself," said Ki.

Canary shot him a rakish grin. "Hell, I can do that. Reckon I've had enough practice." She walked to the door, opened it slightly, peered out, and then disappeared down the hall.

Ki found the Smith & Wesson where she'd dropped it. He put it back in the pitcher, then poured the double eagles on top. The girl had given her loving freely; he had no question about that. Still he was determined to leave her the money—for herself and for a reason she'd never know. If Foley had taken Angela Halley to the north, if they could find her and get her away, Canary had earned a hell of a lot more than eighty dollars.

It was close to one in the morning when he made his way back through the rain and up the backstairs of the Dakota. He paused at Jessie's door to make sure it was locked securely, then went to his room next door and stripped off his soaking clothes. He was tired and sore all over from his encounter with Cole's men and the hunters and skinners. Still sleep wouldn't come. Too much was working in his head. They'd have to leave Deadwood fast, get to Miles City as soon as they could. Maybe Canary was right—maybe no one else knew about Foley's retreat. But they sure as hell couldn't count on that. With the kind of money the cartel was offering for Angela's head...

A thought suddenly struck him and he sat up and listened to the thunder. What difference did it make if they were the only ones who knew about Foley? The half-breed wasn't a fool. He'd learn soon enough Jessie Starbuck was heading out of town. He'd follow, of course, knowing exactly what she was after.

And would they risk just trailing along, maybe losing Jessie somewhere along the way? It was two hundred long and lonely miles to the Yellowstone. Why would Copperhead bother to wait when he could take Jessie and make her tell him everything she knew?

She opened the door with sleep in her eyes, a veil of strawberry hair across her cheek.

"You're real early," she said dryly, "considering you were late getting in. Goin' straight to bed, huh?"

Ki felt his face color. Jessie gave him a knowing grin. "Don't tell me," she said, "it's too early in the morning. Sit down. Look at the wall or something while I get dressed."

Ki sat. She walked hurriedly past him, showing a patch of bare thigh through the side of her dressing gown. Ki looked away and stared dutifully at the window. The rain had let up again, but clouds still hugged the valley floor.

"Go on," Jessie said behind him, "I'm listening. What did you find out?"

"I talked to the girl called Canary, as you, uh—guessed. She thinks Pig-Eye Foley took Angela up to Miles City. Somewhere on the Yellowstone."

"Hey, that *is* news," Jessie said eagerly. "Is she sure?"

"I believe her. I think she knows Foley pretty well."

"Then let's get the hell out of Deadwood," Jessie said firmly. "The sooner the better."

"Jessie, I want to talk about that." He almost turned around, caught himself, and stared at the wall. He told her his thoughts about Copperhead, the dangers of heading north across the plains.

"I can't argue that," she said when he was finished. She pressed a hand solidly on his shoulder, then moved around to face him. She'd traded her dress of the day before for faded sky-blue denims, a matching jacket, and cordovan boots. A wide leather belt emphasized the natural slimness of her waist. The plain white blouse beneath her jacket flared provocatively at the *V* of her breasts.

"You can't argue," Ki said ruefully, "but that isn't going to stop you, right?"

"There's too much at stake here and you know it. We've *got* to follow through. That list, Ki. The *names*. You know what that could mean."

"I know what it'll mean if this Copperhead get on our tail—" Ki stopped and sat up straight as someone hammered loudly on the door.

"Yes, who is it?" Jessie said cautiously.

"It's me," Colonel Henry said. "Are you decent? If you aren't, all the better."

Jessie grinned and Ki moved to open the door. Colonel Henry gave him a nod and stepped inside. Behind him, a small boy carried a tray covered in a clean, white cloth.

"Put it down over there, son," the colonel told him. "Here's a nickel for your trouble, and don't go spending it wisely. You'll regret it all your life." He shot the boy a grin. The young man caught the coin in the air and disappeared.

"Figured you folks'd be up. Brought you some breakfast from downstairs. Coffee, sausage and eggs, some bread, and fried potatoes." He pulled the cloth aside and made a face. "I'll have me some dry toast and a little touch of rye whiskey, you don't mind."

"You're going to die if you don't eat," said Jessie.

"Christ, I'm going to die if I do—what the hell difference does it make?"

"We've got a little news," Jessie told him, pouring coffee for Ki and herself. "Your information on the girl at the Golden Eagle paid off." She told him quickly about Canary and what Ki had learned. Ki added his feelings about risking a trip to Miles City.

"There's a risk, all right," Colonel Henry agreed. He ran long fingers through a shock of white hair. "We can cut that some if you're determined to go. And being your father's daughter, I reckon you are. There's wagons going up carryin' freight all the time. And plenty of hunters traveling to Miles City."

"That's all we need," Ki said dryly. "A couple of days on the trail with more hunters."

"There's hunters and there's hunters," Colonel Henry said sharply. "Don't go judging one man by the next. They aren't all like the bunch you tangled with. If you're fixing to go, leave the travelin' companions to me. I'll put you in good company. This Copperhead bastard'll think twice 'fore he takes on the fellers I got in mind."

"We're going," Jessie said firmly. She shot Ki a determined look. "We *have* to, Colonel Henry."

"Uh-huh. I'm sure real surprised," the Colonel teased.

"Colonel—" Jessie paused and narrowed her eyes. "That man Ki killed in the fight. And Cole, the man you shot . . ."

"Will there be any trouble, you want to know?" Colonel

Henry gave her a crooked grin. "Told you not to concern your-self with that. Self-defense pure and simple. The law isn't real particular here in Deadwood, can't afford to be. Besides, I trapped with the old bastard who wears the badge. Him and me and Jim Bridger." Colonel Henry pulled himself painfully erect. "I know the man at the livery. I'll talk horses with him, work you up some supplies."

"I appreciate your help," Jessie said gently. She rose and kissed him soundly on the cheek.

"By God," the old man said, "between you and the rye whiskey, I think I'm goin' to live through the day." He paused then and squinted thoughtfully out the window. "There's some-thing I want you to think on, Jessie—you and Ki both. Don't figure it'll change your mind any, but you got to know where you stand." He drew in a breath, his blue eyes turning hard as stone. "You have good reason to worry 'bout this half-breed, Ki. He knows you're here, all right. And might be he knows more'n that."

"What is it, Colonel?" Ki felt something cold in the pit of his stomach. "Something's wrong. You—"

"Yeah, something is, all right." He looked straight at Ki. "What time did you see that gal at the saloon?"

"I was there a few hours. From right after ten, maybe. I was back here by one. Why?"

"Anybody see you with her?"

"No, no one," he said flatly. "Look, Colonel Henry—"

"They were bringing her out when I passed the Golden Eagle," Colonel Henry said darkly. "Couple of minutes ago. She's dead, Ki. Someone took a shotgun to her—up close, right in the face."

Chapter 5

They rode northwest through the Black Hills, the limitless stretch of the Great Plains opening before them. The Belle Fourche River was ahead, and past it, Montana Territory and the Little Missouri. Beyond the Chalk Buttes they'd find the Powder, and the high, rolling prairie that led to the Yellowstone. They'd left the bad weather behind around noon. The sun was hanging low under a heavy bank of clouds to the west. Silas Easter told Ki they'd left the Dakotas a few miles back. They were crossing a little corner of Wyoming and they'd camp on the banks of the Belle Fourche.

"Fine," Ki said absently, not sure at all what the old man had said. He glanced over his shoulder and saw Easter's four wagons just behind, the mule team easing down a grade. Ahead, a dozen riders stretched along the trail. Some carried heavy rifles on their saddles; every other man led a string of pack animals in his wake. The buffalo men carried most of what they needed for the hunt. Word was everything cost an arm and a leg in Miles City, and they'd bought what they could farther south.

Ki felt Jessie pull up beside him. He nodded, but stared ahead into the hills.

"I'm getting kind of tired of talking to myself," Jessie said. "You going to keep this up, I'd like to get some idea how long it's going to last."

"I'm sorry," Ki muttered. "I haven't felt a lot like talking."

"That's one way of putting it, I guess. Not saying two words all day, riding off by yourself every time I try to—"

"Jessie, look—"

"No," she said firmly, "*you* look, friend." She leaned out in the saddle and laid a hand on his arm. "I'm sorry about the girl. There wasn't anything you could do. Taking on all of

Deadwood wouldn't have brought her back."

"I got her killed," he said tightly. "She's dead because of me."

"No, that simply isn't true." She trailed her hand along his shoulder, gentling him with her voice. "No one saw you. I know better than that and so do you. If you were thinking straight, damn it, you'd see it. The half-breed found her, but it had nothing to do with you. She was one of Foley's girls. Copperhead asked someone the right question. We found her. Why couldn't someone else?"

Ki looked at her without really seeing her. "Lets me off easy, doesn't it?"

"No, there's nothing easy about it. But that's the way it happened and you know it."

"Maybe. That isn't real important, is it? The girl's dead."

"Yes, Ki, she's dead."

He'd played it over a dozen times in his head. If there were anything good about her dying, he had to tell himself Canary had gone fast. Colonel Henry said they'd found the .38 in her hand, three shots missing and a slug in the wall beside the door. They'd come to kill her slowly, to find out where Foley had taken the girl. Only Canary had heard them coming, gotten to the pitcher, and grabbed the Smith & Wesson. She'd fired at her intruder and the man had pulled the trigger without thinking. Maybe she'd hit him and maybe not. Ki was certain, though, she hadn't told him a thing. And one of Copperhead's men was in a hell of a lot of trouble.

Now all they can do is follow. They don't know I saw her but they know Jessie's heading for Miles City and that's enough.

Not for the first time, something cold stirred at the edge of Ki's thoughts. He could feel them, see them in his mind. Especially the half-breed, the one called Copperhead. He'd never seen the man but he knew him. He was a shadow, a patch of the night drawing close. Ki knew he was right. It had happened to him before. *Kime,* the sense without a name, told him it was so. The man would come. He would make a try for Jessie and Ki would have to stop him. The thing that troubled his mind was though he knew it had to happen, he could only see the beginning and nothing more. *Kime* never told him how it would end.

● ● ●

Silas Easter wasn't as old as Colonel Henry, but he'd been everywhere and back twice. He talked of men like Red Cloud and Liver-Eating Johnston. Places like the Snake and the Green River and the Beaverhead Range. And, long years after those times had come and gone, he told how he'd followed the shaggy herds from Texas up to Kansas and into the Dakotas.

"Got plain sick of it's what I did," he told Jessie, spitting a piece of gristle on the ground. He glanced at the hunters by their fire a few yards off down the draw. "Nothin' against them others, you understand. Can't fault a man for seein' things different. I just couldn't take all the killin' anymore, 'cept for what I needed to eat." He wiped his mouth and gave Jessie a near toothless grin. "Likely lived too long with the Flatheads, I reckon. Got to thinking Injun 'stead of white."

"There's nothing wrong with that," Jessie said fiercely. "My God, Silas, the whole thing is—it's crazy, insane!" She shook her head in anger. "I'm sorry—you say you don't fault those men but I do. It's slaughter and worse than that. The Indians are starving already and the buffalo's all they had. When they're gone . . ."

"That's the idea, ain't it?" Easter finished. "Kill the buffalo *and* the Injuns—make room for the damn cows and farmers. I oughta died back in the fifties 'fore it all started to happen," he grumbled. "Lord God, this country sure shined back then. Damned if it didn't."

After the good trapping days came to an end, Silas Easter guided and hunted for the wagons moving west. He made money and lost it digging for gold, drifted down to Mexico and back across the river into Texas. He spent ten years chasing the herds, and when he'd finally had his fill, bought into freighting in Dodge City. Dodge was still a good outfitting town at the time, a prime hide market for the Kansas hunters. For a while he and Colonel Henry ran the business together. Easter was content to settle down, but Henry Dodd got restless and sold out to his partner. Business wasn't for him, he explained, it fair gave a man the itch to get moving.

"It's done." said Easter, "Isn't nothing that can stop it. The Injuns are finished for good and they damn well know it. Hell, when the big kill started in seventy-one, there was still maybe forty or fifty million buffalo left. No one figured they'd *ever* run out. I drove through a big herd once on the way to Fort Larned in Kansas. They was fifty miles long and five days in the passing. And that's nothin' to what they was before that. In the thirties and forties, you'd see 'em covering fifty square miles, four million shaggies moving by at once."

"And now it's done," said Ki.

"Close enough to it," Easter said glumly. "Last year and the beginning of this they shipped out maybe ten thousand hides up north where we're headed. Time this year gets into winter an' then spring, they'll haul out a quarter of a million or close to it. Shit, it's all over, all right."

Jessie lay rolled up in her blanket away from the fire. A few of the hunters were still awake, talking and sharing a bottle down by the creek. They seemed decent enough, men trying to make a living as best they could. None were like Cole and his friends, and everyone she'd met made it clear they weren't sorry the man was dead. They all seemed in awe of Colonel Henry and Silas Easter. Henry and Silas were their gods—the trappers, and trekkers, the mountain men, the seekers they'd surely have been themselves a generation or so before. Jessie tried not to let her feeling show. She didn't like what they did, but telling them how she felt wouldn't keep a single buffalo alive.

The broad Wyoming sky was brilliant with stars. It was a sight that seldom failed to fill her with joy, then send her slipping quickly into sleep. Tonight, though, she scarcely noticed the stars were there. Ki had grown silent after supper, his eyes shifting restlessly in the dark. He said nothing at all, but Jessie knew exactly what he was thinking, what he was trying to do. He knew trouble was coming and didn't want to tell her. God, she could feel it, too!

Before she pulled the blanket around her, she checked the little ivory-handled derringer she kept snugged securely behind the buckle of her belt. By her side, within quick and easy reach, was the pistol her father had given her and taught her how to use. It was a .38 double-action revolver, mounted on a .44 frame. Its finish was slate-gray with a hint of blue, the grips polished peachwood carved to fit her hands.

39

Jessie needed no reminder of the past. Still, the familiar touch of the weapon never failed to bring her father's stricken features to mind again. Little more than a year after he gave her the gun, Alex Starbuck was dead—shot down before Jessie's eyes on the Circle Star ranch. Jessie knew a part of her father's story and learned the rest at his bedside, waiting for him to die. As a young man Alex Starbuck had begun his successful career with a fleet of trading ships to the Orient. Before long his interests had collided with a group of ruthless men, a Prussian business cartel that wanted the Eastern trade for themselves alone. They struck out at Alex, hijacking his ships and burning his goods. The young Starbuck gave as good as he got. Soon the stakes got higher, until murder was part of the game. Jessie's mother, Sarah, was killed on a European trip. Then the cartel assassins murdered Alex Starbuck himself.

In the space of one long and terrible day, Jessie found herself heiress to the far-flung Starbuck fortune—and the awesome legacy that went with it. She learned soon that the cartel wanted a great deal more than the Starbuck holdings. They wanted the country itself, control of the untold wealth and natural resources of a young and growing nation.

Jessie and Ki had fought them before and learned each time the faceless men behind the cartel would stop at nothing: Bribery, coercion, murder and extortion were only tools to achieve the goal of power. And now, finally, there was a chance she could deal the cartel a crippling blow, a blow that would tear away the masks of men and women in high places, cartel agents who could some day bring the country to its knees.

Jessie sighed and shook her head in wonder. The list she was after could change the course of history, maybe make or break a nation. And where the hell was it? With a good-looking girl who couldn't keep her legs together more than a minute—a girl likely rutting in the hay right now with a skinner named Pig-Eye Foley. God, it didn't make sense. Not any sense at all.

"You didn't sleep, did you?" she said. "You didn't go to bed at all."

"I was up some. I roamed around a little."

"A little."

"That's what I said."

Jessie made a face and threw the dregs of her coffee in the fire. "You were up all night, Ki. Watching out for me."

His dark eyes raised to meet her own. "You think that's a bad idea? I don't, Jessie. They'll come. They've got to try."

"Maybe. There are a lot of men here, Ki. It's a hell of a bunch to take on."

"They won't care about that."

"Damn it," Jessie said angrily, "I don't like this, Ki. We should've found another way. We're dragging this bunch into something that doesn't concern them. If Copperhead comes after us, we're going to get some people killed."

"Colonel Henry told 'em we had troubles," Ki said. "They were willing to have us. I wasn't the only one up last night. Silas Easter and some of the others were looking around."

"I still don't like it," Jessie muttered. She swept long hair off her shoulders and squinted into the morning. "I don't like it at all."

Ki looked up from his thoughts, guided his mount toward Jessie, and glanced across the broad vista ahead. The land was easy on the eye, gently rolling hills above wide river valleys. Bluestem and needle grass grew stirrup high on every side. The sun was midway in the sky, and he knew they'd made good time since breaking camp. The Little Missouri was at their backs and they were well into Montana Territory. Not a good place for an ambush at all, Ki decided. The land was wide open, no place to hide. You could see a man coming clear to Sunday.

And if all that was so, he wondered, why could he smell the sour odor of his sweat, feel his gut bunching up hard as a rock?

The team horses strained up the steep grassy slope, the drivers cursing and urging the animals on. The hunters were strung out ahead, waiting for the wagons to catch up. Silas rode between Jessie and Ki, bending Ki's ear with a fanciful yarn about Dodge City. Ki listened patiently without expression. He'd heard Easter's story a dozen times before. The old man had forgotten or likely didn't care. When he got to the part about Dog Kelly's saloon, Jessie shot Ki a grin and urged her mount ahead. Ki gave her a long and suffering look. Jessie knew she'd pay later—Ki would accuse her of desertion, cowardice under fire.

The big black gelding lunged eagerly ahead, cutting a swath through the high grass. A tall hunter rode nearby and Jessie slowed to greet him.

"'Bout as fine a day as you could ask," she called out. "Couldn't want for much better!"

"Why, I'd sure say it is," the hunter replied. "A *fine* day, ma'am." His face beamed with pleasure, delighted and surprised at Jessie's attention. He was young, likely short of twenty, with gray eyes the color of morning clouds. His beard was thin and scraggly, and Jessie guessed it was the first he'd tried to grow.

"Where are you from?" she asked. She bit her lip in a grin. "Wait—it's Missouri. I'll bet anything it's Missouri!"

"Well I'll be kicked." The boy's eyes went wide. "Now how'd you figure that?"

"I've got an ear for voices," Jessie told him. "And mister, you sure do *sound* Missouri."

"You hit it, ma'am. My folks got a farm outside of Liberty in Clay County. The James boys' place is just north. I been there and even saw Frank hisself once. I—" His face colored and the grin suddenly faded. "We're honest folks, you understand. My pa never took nothing he didn't earn."

"I understand." Jessie's warm smile eased his pain. "You been hunting long? Down south, maybe?"

"Well, it's kinda my first time," the boy admitted. "My brother, though—" he nodded up ahead—"he's been out lots. He's the best there is, I reckon."

"Oh. I see."

"Down in Kansas and Texas and everywhere. He says the buffalo was—" The boy paused as his horse jerked up tight and pranced aside. "Snake or something," he said irritably, struggling with the reins. "Dang animal ain't worth a—*what the hell!*"

Jessie shouted a warning as a man stood straight up out of the grass. Her horse pawed air; she jerked the reins frantically to one side to bring him down and saw the pistol explode out of the corner of her eye. The boy's face disappeared. His saddle

42

was suddenly empty and the man on the ground had the reins. Jessie kicked out hard with her boot. The man caught her leg and pulled her roughly to him. Something struck the side of her head. Her legs gave way and she went limp, feeling the sickness pull her down. She tried to move but nothing worked. Everything was happening too fast or too slow. The sky tilted up and met the ground. Her belly slammed hard against the saddle, the horn catching her sharply in the ribs. She felt the man's legs, one against her breasts, the other against her thighs. He kicked the horse hard and bent to the saddle. Angry shouts met her ears, then the sound of gunfire rolling over the prairie. The nausea took her again and she retched down the side of his leg.

★

Chapter 6

Ki heard the shot, jerked his mount to a halt, and saw the young hunter topple crazily out of the saddle. Jessie's copper-bright hair caught the sun and then she was gone. The rider hugged his horse like a Comanche, smothering Jessie's cries as the mount cut a path through the grass. Ki kicked his horse and sent it flying. A terrible cry of rage escaped his throat. Men shouted at one another and scattered shots rang over the prairie.

"Hold your fire," Silas Easter bawled, "you'll hit the girl, damn you!"

Ki whipped his horse into a fury, cutting the green wake of the rider ahead. He was vaguely aware of men behind him, Easter and the others taking up pursuit. The rider turned once, saw Ki, and cut sharply to the left. Two grassy hills sloped gently to the valley just ahead. The rider was heading for that, keeping to flat ground and high grass. Fine, thought Ki, only there's no place to go. Five hundred miles of flat prairie—did the man think his horse could make that?

Logic cut through cold anger. Ki cursed himself for setting reason aside. He raised one arm, frantically waving the men back, shouting out a warning lost in the wind. He'd ridden right into the damn thing and sucked Easter and the others in behind.

The men came over the rise straight ahead, flanking the sides of the two hills, letting the man with Jessie slip between them and disappear. Ki bent to the saddle and didn't stop. Smoke puffed on the grassy hills and the sound rolled in behind. Bullets sang past his shoulder and clipped grass, burned a raw furrow across the horse's rump. The horse shrieked, kicked out wildly, nearly tossing Ki from the saddle. He hugged the mount with his knees and struggled to bring it about. The animal

44

bolted, ears flat against its skull. Ki cursed and turned up the draw, knowing he'd lost precious seconds, that the rider with Jessie was gone.

He saw the men on either side, forty or fifty yards to the left and right, standing by their mounts or kneeling in the grass. The rifles sounded strangely flat in the open land, like a man slapping the skirt of his saddle. He didn't dare look back to find Easter and the others.

A man yelled suddenly to his left; a rifle opened up and then another. Riders joined in from the right, catching him in a crossfire from both flanks of the hill. Ki veered to the left, cut sharply back again, ripping drunken furrows through the grass. Suddenly he was through the narrows and out on the flats again. Scattered fire followed his path, then abruptly died away. Ki glanced back and pulled his horse up short, frantically searching the sea of grass. Nothing. Ki's heart sank. Where the hell were they? The man with Jessie had disappeared. There was nothing in sight except half of Montana, spread out flat before his eyes.

Ki felt a sudden chill in the air, an itch at the center of his back. His heels dug into the mount's flanks, sending the animal surging ahead. The bullet caught the horse below the eye. Ki heard the lead find bone and felt the fine spray of blood on his face. He jerked his feet free as the animal's legs folded and sent him flying. The rifle cracked again and he hit the ground, rolled and came to his knees in the grass. He heard them coming at him, felt the horses' hooves beating the ground. He could still see the image in his head, the quick second of sight as he heard the shot and turned and saw the riders bunched at the base of the hill. He could see it clear as glass, playing itself out before it happened. The men on the hill would keep the hunters busy, fall back and cover the riders below, the men who had Jessie. They'd ride and stop, form a line and fire, an orderly retreat across the prairie. And every time they took a stand, one of the hunters would take a bullet. Maybe some would die. How long would they risk their lives for a woman they didn't know?

Ki crawled through the chest-high grass, putting distance between himself and the dead horse. He kicked off his rope-soled sandals, feeling the raw earth with his feet. He could

45

hear the men calling to one another, hear horses and the squeak of saddles as they spread out to find him. He rolled on his back, slipped the razor-edged *shuriken* from his pocket. He palmed two of the deadly stars in one hand, holding another loosely in the other. He saw a rider coming close: ten, maybe twelve yards away; dark hat and thick neck bobbing above the grass. Bracing his knees on the ground, he shot his arm forward in a blur, the motion jerking his shoulders to the left. The circle of metal struck the rider above his eye, brushing the brim of his hat and driving steel sharply through his skull. The man slipped to the ground without a sound. The horses trotted off through the grass.

Riders shouted in alarm; someone emptied his pistol in the grass, nowhere close to Ki. Ki crouched low and crabbed to his right. He hugged the ground as a rider went by fast. They'd used the cover of the grass to get Jessie. Now it was his turn.

He waited, letting them move to the left, following close behind. He could still hear gunfire from the hills. A rider turned, came straight for him. Ki moved aside a few yards, then loosed a throwing star at his back. The man screamed, arching his back and clawing at the pain between his shoulders. Ki was thirty yards away before he fell. The riders came thundering through the grass, closing on all sides. Ki saw the horse's legs and the big head, the heavy mane dancing in the wind. He stood up straight, screamed, and waved his arms. The horse jerked to a stop and pawed air. The rider saw Ki and swung the barrel of his rifle around fast. Ki grabbed the man's wrist, jerked him out of the saddle, and brought his free hand down like a club to the base of his neck. The horse kicked out at Ki, trying desperately to get away. Ki clawed for the cantle, got another arm across the seat, and held on. The horse dragged him through the grass, Ki kicking blindly for the stirrup. His foot found something solid and he pulled himself into the saddle.

The riders circled him like wolves, three on one side, four bunched on the other. Ki broke free, bolting quickly out of the trap, clinging like a snake to the horse, making himself a poor target. Lead sang around him and the shots went wild. A man on a moving horse was damn good if he could hit a standing target—a lot better still if he could hit one riding the same as himself.

He saw her, then, past the others in the shadow of the hill, draped across a saddle like a sack, strawberry hair handing loosely toward the ground. A man sat mounted beside her on a big red gelding. *Copperhead!* Anger surged through his veins. He knew the man at once, though he'd never seen him before. He was a big man, broad-shouldered, and narrow at the waist. The thick chest and heavily muscled arms threatened to burst through the calico shirt. He wore his hair Indian-style, raven black and long about his shoulders. His face was a white man's face, raw-boned and hollow, a smudge of stubble on the sharp and pointed jaw. Even at a distance, Ki could see the cold contempt in his eyes.

Ki didn't hesitate an instant; he kicked the mount straight at Copperhead. A rider to his left cursed and snapped off a shot. The half-breed watched him come. He threw back his head and laughed at the sky, dancing the big gelding to one side. A blade flashed in his hand, catching fire from the sun. Ki forced his mount at the half-breed's horse. The animal tried to shy away; Ki kicked it savagely in the sides. Copperhead jerked the gelding around, leaned out of the saddle, and lashed at Ki with the heavy blade. The edge cut air, whipped back for a second try. Ki kicked out with the point of his heel. The blow caught Copperhead just above the knee, driving hard into muscle and bone. The half-breed winced, lips stretching tight against the pain. His knife hand hesitated an instant and Ki threw himself out of the saddle, buried his head in the man's belly, and dragged him to the ground. Copperhead twisted in midair, turning Ki's attack and slamming him hard against the ground. Ki cleared his head and sucked air, rolling quickly aside as the half breed's knife stabbed dirt. Ki came to his feet, drew his slim *tanto* blade, and bent low, shoulders bowed forward and both hands stretching toward his foe.

Copperhead grinned, dancing crazily from side to side, first on one foot and then the other. Ki paid no attention to his antics. He kept his eyes on the man's hands, the cords of muscle in his throat. When the cords went taut Ki moved. Copperhead's foot came forward and slammed the earth, the blade flashing

47

out for Ki's belly. Ki leaped aside and felt the sharp point slice through his shirt. Damn—the man was incredibly fast for his size!

Ki backed off, eyeing the bigger man with new respect. Copperhead charged again, cutting quick, brutal slashes, using the weapon more like a hatchet than a knife. Ki waited, letting the man throw his great strength into the blows, watching him tear up the grass with his boots. The horse bearing Jessie's limp form grazed just out of sight to his right. He didn't dare risk a look. Winchesters rattled off to the east, Copperhead's men and the hunters trading fire. Four riders rode for the *V* of the hills. There were more of the half-breed's men close by, men he'd fought in the high grass. None came close or interfered. Maybe Copperhead had waved them off, let them know he wanted this one for himself.

Ki backed away again, let the man make his moves. If the bastard were starting to tire, he was keeping it a secret. His flesh was dry as dust. Maybe he hadn't heard about sweat.

Copperhead jabbed out with his blade, stepped back, and shifted his feet on the ground, breaking his dancing, wavering stride. It wasn't much but Ki caught it, saw the split second the man was open and came in low. Copperhead brought the big knife up fast to cover his guard. Ki was already there. The slim *tanto* blade found its mark—once, twice, and then again. Ki was in and out, gone before the half-breed could stop him. Copperhead bellowed and staggered back, blinking in surprise at the three red lines across his chest. He came at Ki in a rage, the knife sweeping before him like a scythe. Ki backed off, let the steel whisper past his face, leaped straight up and kicked out with the wedge of his heel. His foot caught the half-breed just below the eye, splitting the flesh from his cheek to the corner of his mouth. The knife fell away. Ki came at him working close to the body, his blade slicing flesh like a butcher. Copperhead spit blood and lashed out blindly with his fists. A hand the size of a hammer caught Ki on the side of his head and sent him reeling. Ki rolled and came to his feet, fighting off the nausea that welled up in his throat. He shook his head, swinging the knife from a fighting crouch, ready to meet the half-breed's charge.

Copperhead roared like a bull, his face raw and ragged strips of meat. He came toward Ki, then stopped, stumbled once, and staggered for his horse. Ki's belly tightened in a knot. Too late he saw what the man was after. He came off the ground, knowing he'd never make it in time. Copperhead jerked the stubby sawed-off Remington out of its scabbard and swept the twin barrels at Ki's head. Ki stopped cold. The half-breed glared, his ruined mouth curved in a wicked grin.

"Uh-uh. Her first," he grunted. "Her first and then you, Jappo!"

"*No!*" Ki shouted in horror as the shotgun swung for Jessie's back. He leaped for the half-breed's arm, heard lead hum past his shoulder, and saw the stock of the weapon splinter, saw the gun come apart in Copperhead's hands.

The man howled and staggered back. The second shot geysered dirt at his boots. Copperhead stared, turned, and leaped into the saddle before Ki could reach him again. He dug his heels in hard and sent the horse racing off through the grass.

Ki turned and squinted up the hill. A tall figure stood in the grass, seventy yards up the slope, a rifle at his shoulder. Smoke billowed from the barrel and sound rolled over the valley. One of Copperhead's men came out of the saddle, bounced off the rump of his horse, and disappeared in the grass. The man on the hill calmly swept his weapon to the right. The rifle exploded again. Another rider slumped in the saddle and fell to the ground. The half-breed's men returned his fire. The tall figure didn't move. He fired again, dropped a gunman, and moved to another target, this time hitting a man to his left up the slope.

Ki stared in wonder as the man patiently fed fresh shells into his weapon, paused a second to aim, and patiently dropped two of Copperhead's men. The single rifleman's deadly aim was too much for the half-breed's crew. Two men bolted, then another. The men began to scatter, pour down from the hills to their horses. A sharp volley of fire swept the valley. Ki saw Silas Easter atop his big gray, leading his hunters in pursuit. The man on the hill kept firing, dropping nearly every target he found. Ki figured the riders were about two hundred yards away. Easter's men raced through the valley, adding their weapons to the fire. Men who reached their horses scattered in panic to the west. Gunmen on foot turned and fought or tried to crawl off in high grass. Easter's men sought them out and made short work of any stragglers they could find. Ki thought he saw Copperhead once, waving a rifle high in anger, trying to rally his men. There was no stopping them now. Fear had already found them and marked them for the day.

"Ki—*Ki*, is that you, damn it!"

Ki started, turned in surprise, and saw Jessie's long legs kicking the air. Good God, watching the man on the hill he'd nearly forgotten she was there!

He ran quickly to the horse, sliced the ropes that bound her, and slid her gently into his arms. "Jessie, are you all right? You're not hurt?"

"I guess," she said. She let Ki lower her to the ground while she rubbed her raw wrists and ankles. She touched the side of her head, looked at her hand, and was relieved to see it wasn't soaked with blood.

"Whatever he hit me with, I'm going to be feeling it for a week." She ran a hand through her hair and let Ki help her to her feet.

"Sure you feel like standing?"

"No, but I'm not going to sit here all day." She blew out a breath and squinted at the riders in the grass. "You mind telling me what happened? I'm kinda—Oh, *God*, Ki— that boy!" She bit her lip and closed her eyes. "I was talking to this boy from Missouri—"

"Jessie . . ." Ki took her in his arms. She backed off and shook her head. "Thanks," she said harshly, "I don't need the comfort. He's dead and I'm alive. Because *I* was talkin' to him!" Jessie looked up as Silas Easter pulled his mount up short, glanced from Jessie to Ki, and slid to the ground.

"She all right?"

"Uh-huh. She will be."

Easter squinted at Ki. "That blood on you personal or does it belong to someone else?"

"Mostly someone else." He looked up and saw the man walking his horse down the hill, the pack animal trailing behind. The man wore a Montana hat with a busted crown, denims, and a butternut shirt that buttoned to the collar. His face was lean and unsmiling, his eyes in shadow under the hat.

Silas Easter gave the newcomer a grin. "Howdy, Aaron.

50

Kinda figured that was you. Glad you dropped in when you did." Easter nodded to his right. "Ki, Miss Jessie—this feller'd be Aaron Heller."

"You pulled our hides out of the fire," said Ki. "I'd like to say thanks." He stuck out his hand and Heller shook it firmly, meeting his eyes for an instant. He glanced in Jessie's direction and nodded.

"I'm near empty," he said calmly. "You got any food handy, Silas?"

"We can find something, I reckon."

Heller nodded and walked off. Ki watched him go. He'd only looked in Heller's eyes for a moment, but a moment had been enough. If any emotion were there—anger, sorrow, regret—Ki couldn't find it at all.

Chapter 7

Eleven of Copperhead's gunmen were buried in a common grave in the high grass on the western side of the twin hills. Only two of the hunters had been killed. A man named Russ O'Brien caught a bullet in the heart. The other was Finlay James Harper, the boy from Missouri who'd been with Jessie when she was taken. Jeesie didn't learn his name until she stood beside Ki and Silas Easter at the boy's grave. She spoke to Mike Harper, a lean, veteran buffalo hunter with eyes similar to his dead brother's.

"I'm going to say it because there's no way else I can put it," she told the man. "I was talking to him when he was killed. He's dead because of me and I know that. I'm sorry. It doesn't help your grief any but I had to get it said."

The man looked at Jessie and past her. His face was heavily bearded, etched with fierce summers and harsh winters. He might be thirty or fifty, Jessie couldn't say.

"Fault ain't going to bring him back," he said soberly. "I appreciate your kindness. Don't take more on you than you need."

"I liked him," said Jessie. "He told me about Clay County and talking to Frank James."

Mike Harper almost smiled. "I'll bet he did at that. It's the truth, too." The thin smile faded. "Want to place fault I gotta take some too. He shouldn't ever ought to been out here. Should've stayed in Missouri with his ma. Christ, he wanted to be like me. That's sure a fine ambition, now ain't it?"

"He told me you were the best there is."

"Did, did he? The boy said that?"

"He did. Truly."

"Well, I ain't."

"I expect he knew what he was saying," Jessie said gently.

Mike Harper nodded, set his hat on his head, and walked off. Silas Easter took Jessie's arm. "You think these fellas blame you for what happened, you're wrong," he said fiercely. "They knew there might be trouble. We gave a good accountin' of ourselves. Two men down and a couple hurt. That's a loss, but we sure sent a bunch of those bastards to hell."

"Just *two* dead," Jessie said sharply. "We're real lucky, you figure."

Easter gave her a look. "Wasn't any luck to it," he said without expression. "A hired gun don't have to be good, just mean and lazy and lackin' good sense. These ol' boys here is hunters. Some of 'em can shoot near as good as Aaron Heller. Hell, I'm surprised we didn't get more'n we did."

Jessie looked off over the hills. "This Heller—he's not real friendly, is he?"

"He isn't going to talk your ear off." Silas gave her a grin. "Like me, fer instance."

"Ki says he never saw anyone shoot like that. Not ever."

"Uh-huh. Don't think I ever saw anything like *Ki*, for as that goes."

"What?" Jessie had been staring across the prairie.

"I got to get back to my wagons," said Silas, "get those animals headin' north." He mumbled to Jessie and walked off toward the flats. Easter hadn't seen Ki in action, but a hunter had called him over to look at the three men in the grass, one with his neck broken, and two others—the first with sharp steel points protruding from his skull; the other with the same kind of problem in his back. Most of the men had drifted over to look and rub the curious pieces of metal between their fingers. They hadn't been able to figure the man with the pretty woman, a man with a tilt to his eyes who didn't wear proper shoes on his feet. Now, they eyed him with new respect. Easter brought the *shuriken* throwing stars to Ki and dropped them in his palm.

"Reckon you'd like to have these back," he said simply.

"Thank you," Ki nodded, slipping the weapons in his pocket. If Silas were waiting for Ki to say something more, it looked as if he'd wait a long time.

• • •

53

They camped on the banks of the Powder River, bedding down early and getting up around four, the hunters and skinners eager to push hard through the fifty or so miles to Miles City. No one was worried about Copperhead trying again, having lost as many men as he had. Still, several riders circled the camp during the night, just in case. There were still ragged bands of Cheyenne and Sioux roaming about, Indians who didn't like the hollow bellies of reservation life and didn't mind running off with horses or rifles or whatever food they could find.

Before the evening fire played out, Jessie heard more than she wanted about Heller—how he was likely the best buffalo hunter around, as good or better than Hiram Bickerdyke, or Prairie Dog Dave, or Jim White and the Mooar brothers. They figured Heller had killed maybe twelve, fourteen thousand by his own gun. This figure seemed to make him a hero among the others—Jessie found the number appalling. Lord, that many! She'd never even spoken to the man and found herself liking him less and less.

Silas Easter argued about what was the finest buffalo gun ever made. He didn't give a damn what everyone else was using. He knew what he was talking about and the others were plain crazy.

"What you need is somethin' to go with your age," said one of the hunters, teasingly.

The men all laughed, and Easter assured them in no uncertain terms he could outshoot any or all of them with a damn rifle carved from a stick.

A hunter named Quirt said there'd be good hunting in the Big Horn Basin that winter, that Jim White was going over. Another said White had killed more shaggies than Heller, maybe sixteen thousand or so.

When the bottle started going around, Silas Easter launched into his tale of George Gore and his legendary hunt through the west. Everyone had heard it before, but it was a damn good story and Easter told it well. Besides, it was his right to tell it, since Jim Bridger himself had told it to Easter.

"This Gore fella now," Silas began, "whole name was *Sir* St. George Gore, by God, which is a plain mouthful, but so was this fella. Rich as God hisself, and I ain't exaggeratin' at all. Had him a couple of castles in Ireland and no tellin' what else." Easter paused to make sure he had their attention. "So one day this Gore wakes up and remembers he ain't ever gone hunting in America, and he figures he better do that. So he gets him a ship or two—hell, maybe bought hisself some for all I know. An' he gets over here, in fifty-four it was, and starts hunting up the valley of the Missouri." Easter stopped again, and the other men grinned, knowing full well what was coming.

"This Gore, now, he don't go huntin' like you and me. No, sir. This fella's got his forty servants taggin' along; he's got him a carriage, a hundred and twelve horses; he's got him twenty-one two-horse Red River carts to carry all his shit. He's got him four six-mule wagons, a couple of three-yoke ox wagons, and he's got a *gen-u-wine* brass bed, and a real purty green and white Irish linen tent to sleep in. And God knows how many wagons filled with fancy imported whiskey and wine. He's got him 'bout fifty greyhounds and staghounds taggin' along and fellas to do nothin' but just take care of his dogs."

Easter paused. Some of the hunters shook their heads and grinned. It was the finest kind of tale you could hear, something that was true yet you still could hardly believe it happened.

"Well sir," Easter went on, "Gore and this travelin' circus of his comes up on Old Gabe, Jim Bridger hisself. And since he's got the best of ever'thing else, he figures why not have him the best damn huntin' guide there is. Ol' Gabe ain't ever seen nothin' like this Gore before, and he's likely seen 'bout all there is to see. Which is what he tol' me hisself. Anyway, Bridger allows as how he'll take the job on. Well, the damn hunt lasts nearly three years. When it's over, this Gore's spent half a million dollars and trekked over six thousand miles around the west. He's been through Fort Leavenworth, Laramie, through Colorado 'fore it was even a state, up the North Platte and the Powder and the Yellowstone to the mouth of the Tongue. It's the damndest hunt there ever was, likely ever will be, either."

There was a long silence, and then as if on cue, one of the hunters piped up: "Well what'd he git, Silas? What kinda game?"

Easter gave him a solemn look. "Now that's the peculiar part. They didn't get a damn thing. Never even saw a skinny rabbit the whole trip."

The hunters roared with laughter, slapped their legs, and passed the bottle around.

"That ain't quite true," Easter added. "They *did* get 'em 'bout two thousand buffalo, sixteen or seventeen hundred deer and elk . . . and I believe it was a hundred and five bears."

"I heard a hundred and six."

"So did I," Silas said without a smile, "but old Bridger was prone to exaggerate, I'm sorry to say."

When the laughter died again, another hunter told about the Grand Duke Alexis, son of Tsar Alexander II, and how Bill Cody had guided the "Crazy Roosians" on a hunt through the west. Someone else told about General Phil Sheridan bringing a dozen of his friends out from New York and Philadelphia and Chicago, and how Cody had guided them, too. There were sixteen wagons following the hunters, mostly full of wine, and ice to keep the wine cold.

Jessie listened until her eyes grew heavy, then left the fire and found her blanket. Ki was already curled up by their belongings.

"You asleep?" she said softly.

"No. Not yet. Just thinkin'."

"Thinking about what?"

"Copperhead, I guess." He sat up and the blanket slid to his waist. Light from the fire licked at the corded tendons on his chest. "He isn't through. We both know that. He'll be in Miles City or somewhere around."

"I know."

"It isn't going to matter any to him how many men he lost today. He'll just take on some more, as many as he needs."

Jessie looked at him. "And all this is leading up to what?"

"I'm thinking maybe we could use a little help, too. That's what I'm getting at, Jessie. When we get to Miles City these fellows we're with are going off hunting in the north. We're going to be on our own." He paused and looked thoughtfully at the ground. "I don't know how to put this. Maybe I better just say it. I'll do whatever I have to do to take care of you. You know that."

"Ki—"

"Wait. Listen. Me getting killed isn't going to do you any good. It'll just make it that much easier for him. That's why I want to get help. Because Copperhead isn't going to forget what I did. He's got two things on his mind right now. The first is to find Angela Halley, get what she's got, and kill her. The other thing is killing me the minute he can. He's got to do that. I cut him up, blooded him real bad. There's only one way he can live with a thing like that. He's got to wipe out the act with another. I'm not afraid, Jessie. I don't have to tell you that. But I *am* afraid of something happening to you."

"You don't have to tell me," she said gently. "It's something I already know." She moved up to him, kissed him lightly on the cheek, and went back to her blanket. "I have a real good reason for wanting you to stay alive, old friend. And it doesn't have anything to do with taking care of me."

None of this matters, he told her silently. *My life is yours. It must not be spent for no reason.*

"And *don't* go thinking something foolish," she told him in the dark. "Something like you're thinking right now!"

They reached Miles City late in the afternoon. The town lay scattered through cottonwood groves on the east bank of the Tongue, where it emptied its waters into the Yellowstone. Jessie could smell the stink of hides long before she saw the town. When they got closer to the river she could see the stiffened hides stacked high in the great yards, awaiting shipment. Silas said a big outfit like Maxwell's might have four or five thousand on hand at a time, and there were plenty of other outfits near as big.

Jessie sat on her horse while Ki and Silas Easter guided the wagons into Easter's freighting yard. Miles City was fairly teeming with people. Hunters, skinners, hide buyers, and merchants crowded the dirt streets, pouring in and out of the crudely built cabins, stores, dance halls, and saloons. Outfits continually rode in and out of town, leaving to hunt or come back. Every man who could lift a Sharps had come up to get in on the good money. Hides had gone up as high as $2.70 each. Even local citizens who'd never shot a rat were out after their share. Rumor had it there were half a million shaggies on the broad Northern range—and half that number an easy two days from Miles City. It was a hunter's paradise as long as it lasted— and Jessie knew it couldn't last long. The Indians of the Dakotas, Montana, and Wyoming were already starved into submission. Right here, she thought, is where the hunters will finish them off. The death songs will be sung in Miles City.

"Some kind of sight, isn't it?"

Jessie turned in the saddle, surprised to find herself facing Aaron Heller. "Yes, it is," she said coolly. "Though not the kind of sight I greatly favor, Mr. Heller."

Heller nodded, as if to say he understood. It was the first time she'd seen him for more than a moment and the first time he'd spoken to her. He still wore the grease-stained hat with the broken crown and the plain butternut shirt. He didn't seem to dress like a buffalo hunter, or at least like the hunters she'd seen back in Deadwood and on the trail. He was younger than she'd thought, late twenties maybe, thirty at the most. His eyes were china-blue, his face gaunt and unsmiling.

"I hope you don't mind me ridin' over and speaking up," said Heller. "Since we didn't say hello when we met, figured it'd be the thing to do to say good-bye."

"You're leaving, then. Here at Miles City."

"Uh-huh. I got me a partner here somewhere. Fella name of Barlo Leeks. He came on with the money to buy what we need to get up on the Big Dry River."

"To shoot buffalo."

"Yeah, to shoot buffalo." He paused and looked past Jessie at a wagonload of barrels. "Silas Easter says you aren't real fond of buffalo hunters."

"I'm not too fond of what they *do*," Jessie said evenly.

"Same thing," Heller shrugged. "Man kinda is what he does."

Jessie let out a breath. "Mr. Heller, what's happening up here and what I think's right and wrong isn't going to make much difference, now is it? Aside from that, I want to thank you for what you did back there. You saved a lot of lives, including mine and my friend's."

"I was there," Heller said absently. "You folks needed a little help."

"It was *more* than a little help, I'd say."

"Yeah, well . . ." The talk seemed to make Heller nervous. He touched his hat and pulled his mount aside. "Good luck to you."

"I wish you the same," said Jessie. She tried to soften her words into a smile. "But not in slaughtering buffalo, Mr. Heller."

Heller gave her a curious look. "Don't need luck to do that." He nodded again and turned his horse away.

Jessie watched him go. Odd, she thought, that was almost the very same thing Silas Easter had said. That luck had nothing to do with hitting what you were aiming to hit. Easter had gotten a stubborn look on his face when he said it, even though he'd put his hunting days behind.

She saw Ki then, walking his horse and coming toward her across the street. She knew at once from his expression, the way he held his body, that something was wrong.

"All right," she said evenly, "I'm not going to like this, am I?"

"Come on, you can see for yourself," he said tightly. He waited until she slid out of the saddle, then took her reins and guided her quickly down the street. There was a general store and a saloon to the right, a livery after that. A wagonload of timber rattled by, then a man with a mule in harness.

"There," Ki pointed, "past the livery, one store down."

Jessie saw a flatbed wagon. A crowd gathered at the back, blocking whatever there was to see. She looked up questioningly at Ki.

"It's Pig-Eye Foley," he said flatly. "Angela Halley's friend. We're just in time for his funeral."

★
Chapter 8

Ki and Silas heard the story as soon as they entered the wagon yard. It was no big secret: Every man, woman, and child in Miles City had told it twice. Pig-Eye Foley had come to town with a breathtaking beauty—not Angela or Louisa this time, but Felicity, a name Jessie thought was an interesting choice. Foley took her to his cabin, but the girl refused to stay. She had to see Miles City, take in the town's delights. Foley gained momentary fame, then everyone forgot he was there.

Angela found every saloon and gambling den in town. At the dance halls, where local charmers charged a dollar a whirl, Angela took over the floor. Bartenders ran out of whiskey and quickly brewed up kegs of tanglefoot—boiled mountain sage and a few plugs of tobacco in water. No one noticed the difference.

Angela, following her pattern throughout the West, was ready to change partners again. The man she had at the moment was the man she didn't want. When Pig-Eye Foley tried to carry her off the floor, Angela pounded him in the face and screamed for help. A man plucked her out of Foley's arms, then shot him in the belly. A fight broke out and Angela disappeared. In the morning men saw her leaving town with a rich young Englishman named Edward Burke Montgomery.

Easter knew Montgomery, had spoken to him several times before. He owned mines and cattle and spent his time trying for big game records. He and his retinue had taken off north. There Montgomery hoped to shoot more buffalo at one single stand than anyone had ever done before.

"If everyone in town knows she's with him," Jessie sighed, "the cartel's men know it too. My God, Ki, that girl's plain out of her mind!"

"Copperhead can't get here any faster than we did," said

Ki. "Not unless he kills a lot of horses on the way. It shouldn't be too hard to find this Englishman."

"We've *got* to reach him first," Jessie said tightly. "Silas, can you—" She stopped to catch her breath. "We have to go after her and we've got to start as soon as we can. Ki thinks— we *both* think we'd better hire some men to go along, considering Copperhead's bound to recruit another army as soon as he can."

"Uh-huh. I figure he'll be anxious to see you two again," Easter said dryly. "All right, we can work somethin' out. Going to cost you plenty, though. Ever' damn fool in town figures a fortune in hides is just standing out there waiting for him to shoot it and bring it back."

"We'll pay what we have to," Jessie told him. "We've got to get her back."

"One thing," Easter grinned, "isn't any place to run to from where she's at now. There ain't any Denvers out there I ever seen. Or even a Miles City."

"Wherever she is, Silas, she's trouble," Jessie said. "Angela only needs two men to start a riot."

"Well, then . . ." Silas squared the grease-stained hat atop his head. "I'll do some askin' about. The help here can get these wagons unloaded. You figure on getting an early start, I suppose. Sunup or a little before."

"What?" Jessie shook her head in alarm. "Silas, I mean to get on the trail *tonight*. We can't waste another minute!"

"Uh-uh." Easter looked squarely at Jessie and turned to Ki. "You better talk to her, boy. Foolish to travel in the dark. Mornin' is soon enough."

"Silas, if Copperhead gets to that girl before we do—!"

"He's right," Ki said firmly. "What Silas is saying is Copperhead's the reason we can't risk riding out at night. He'll need a lot of men to hit us in open country during the day. One or two waiting in the dark, now . . ."

"Yeah, I guess." Jessie knew they were right but didn't like it. "First thing in the morning, then. And thank you, Silas. I know you're trying to do what's right."

"You're wrong," Silas said flatly. "If that's what I was doing I'd hire a couple of fellows to knock you cold and ride you clear out of the territory."

Jessie and Ki found rooms, bought tubs of hot water, bathed, and met for supper. The sun was turning the Yellowstone red when they walked past town to the river. A squat sternwheeler was tied at the dock, taking on hides for the long trip up the Yellowstone to the Missouri, and down to Bismarck and St. Louis. That route wouldn't last much longer, Jessie knew. The Northern Pacific was a hundred miles northeast of Miles City at Sentinel Butte, not ten miles from the Montana border. Next year the railroad would reach Glendive and then Miles City itself.

Real convenient, she thought grimly. Maybe they could figure some way to drive the buffalo right up into the cars, shoot 'em, and skin 'em right there.

"I'm starting to feel *old*, you know?" she told Ki. "Like Colonel Henry and Silas. I'm missing things the way they were fifty years ago in this country, and I wasn't even there."

"It can get worse than this. And it will."

"Thanks. That's an encouraging thought."

"No, but it's the truth."

"I know. But I don't have to like it." She sniffed the air and made a face. "Come on, let's get back. Everything out here smells dead."

Silas Easter had promised he'd have hands hired and waiting at the wagon yard at dawn. When Jessie and Ki arrived, horses and saddles were waiting. Two men snored under a wagon, and another leaned sleepily against the fence building a smoke. In the still dark shed, Jessie saw Silas talking to a tall, broad-shouldered figure. The men heard her and turned, and Jessie was startled to find herself facing Aaron Heller.

"Morning," said Heller; then he glanced at Ki and nodded. "Real nice day if it doesn't rain."

"Good morning, Mr. Heller," Jessie said politely, then turned to Silas Easter. "The men outside, they're the ones going with us?"

"Uh, yeah, that's them all right." Easter cleared his throat and looked at the ceiling.

"And?"

"Beg your pardon?"

"And what else? You were starting to say something else."

"Not that I can recall."

"You think three's enough?" Jessie asked, turning the question on Ki.

"Depends on how good they are."

"And if you can wake 'em up," Jessie said evenly.

"They're good men," Heller broke in. "I'll vouch for 'em."

"Oh?" Jessie eyed the hunter without expression. "You know them, Mr. Heller?"

"Guess I do. They work for me."

"What? What's that?"

"I was fixin' to tell you 'bout that," said Easter.

"Tell me what?" She glanced warily from Heller to Silas Easter. "Is this something I want to hear?"

"The thing is," Easter went on, "Aaron here's—uh—agreed to ride north with you and Ki. Seein' as how he's going up to the Englishman's camp hisself it'll work out fine."

Jessie stared. "Silas, when you said you'd hire some riders I didn't know you were considering Mr. Heller. No offense."

"None taken, ma'am," Heller said solemnly.

"I didn't have *no* one in mind," said Easter. "It just worked out that way. And it isn't going to cost you a thing. Like I said, they were going anyway."

Jessie let out a breath. "I'm grateful to you again, it seems, Mr. Heller. Please don't think I'm not. It's just that—"

"Yeah, I know." Heller chewed thoughtfully on a match. "Tell you what. I promise not to shoot more'n two, three hundred shaggies on the way."

Jessie's green eyes turned to ice. "I'd be grateful to you for that," she said stiffly. Turning on her heels, she stalked to her horse and climbed into the saddle. Without looking back she kicked the mount sharply and bolted out of the yard.

"We'll find 'em around three, maybe four, this afternoon," said Heller. "I figure they're setting up south of Big Dry Creek. Forty, fifty miles, maybe."

Jessie glanced over her shoulder. Miles City was just below the hill at her back, but the wide, rolling grasslands had already swallowed all signs of civilization. "We could make it faster than that, don't you think?"

"Yeah, I guess."

"But you don't want to for some reason?"

"I want to have a horse isn't likely going to drop, in case I have to take off kinda fast."

"All right. Your point's well taken." She swept amber hair off her shoulders and let the Stetson hang loose down her back. The sky was pleasantly overcast, cutting the harsh glare of the sun. She hadn't asked Heller to ride beside her. He took it upon himself, as soon as Ki rode out to relieve one of the riders. Heller had his men out ahead and to the sides, flanking the open prairie.

"I guess you think I'm unreasonable," Jessie said, "feeling the way I do about the herds."

"I think you've got a right to what you think."

"But it doesn't bother you at all. What you and the others are doing . . ."

"It's going to happen. With me or without me. Men are going to go after hides."

"Yes, but—"

"Miss Starbuck, look—"

"Jessie's just fine. We've been introduced."

"All right—Jessie. I think it'd be a good idea if we didn't get into this again. We both know where it's goin' to go."

"Good." Jessie shrugged. "What do you want to talk about, Mr. Heller?"

"Aaron's just fine," he said dryly. "We been introduced."

Jessie grinned. "Yes, I guess we have at that."

"We could talk about why this Copperhead fella's trying to get your hide for a trophy. I think *that's* kinda interesting."

Jessie looked right at him. "I'm sorry," she said evenly. "That's something I really can't go into right now."

Aaron shrugged. "Whatever you say."

"I would if I could, really. After all you've done." She offered him a smile. "Maybe we can talk about you instead of me."

"Now, you don't want to do that," he said soberly. "Talkin' about me'll get us back to buffalo hunting."

"I don't believe that's all there is to know about Aaron Heller."

"You don't, huh?"

"No, I don't."

"All right. I was born in Ohio on a farm. Ran away at fifteen and ended up in Kansas. Got a job haulin' buffalo hides. Only it was robes and not hides we were after when I started. You know about that, I suppose? A dealer sent some hides over to Germany. 'Bout ten years ago. A tanner there figured out a way to make 'em into good leather. Anyway, I worked up to skinner, and one day a feller let me hold and fire his Sharps .44. I found out I was better at doing that than anything I'd ever done before.

"I hunted all over Kansas, down the Arkansas, Turkey Creek, and the Smokey Hill River. Hunted out of Dodge City for a while. Met Silas Easter there; Colonel Henry, too. Silas tells me you know him. Went down to Cimmaron country, Kiowa Creek, all over. Got mixed up in that Adobe Walls mess on the South Canadian—saw all the Comanches, Kiowas and Cheyennes I ever hope to see again. What else? Fort Griffin down in Texas. The toughest damn town I ever been to in my life. Had a place called the Bee Hive dance hall there. I've seen men and women dancing together, not a stitch of clothes between 'em." Heller's face split in a grin. "Sorry, but that's what I saw. Then the buffalo ran out there and I drifted up here. See, I warned you now, didn't I? Isn't anything to tell about me except buffalo huntin'."

Jessie gave him a painful grin and shook her head in resignation. "Well, you were right. Buffalo hunting is definitely what you do. And now you're going north—to hunt *buffalo*, right?"

"I was. As of yesterday." Heller gave her a sober look. "See I gave my partner the money to get started. That'd be Barlo Leeks. I get in town last night an' find Leeks has kinda disappeared. What he did was drink and gamble away my money and his. Then he borrowed *back* the wages I'd given these three ol' boys with us now. When he spent all of that, he took off north—hired on as a hunter with this Englishman. The one supposed to have this girl you're lookin' for."

"Oh, dear . . ." Heller had told the story with a wry smile on his lips, but Jessie saw the anger in his eyes. "And you're hoping to find Barlo Leeks."

"If Barlo's lucky, I'll find him 'fore these other three do. All I want to do is kick him in the head about an hour. Those

65

boys are planning on makin' him into a hat."

Jessie laughed, not at all sure whether Heller was serious or not. Recalling his three companions, she decided Barlo Leeks had all the trouble he could handle.

Ki and the outriders came in just after two. They stopped and ate beans and cornbread and buffalo tongue roasted the night before in Miles City. Heller asked what they'd seen on the prairie, and a hunter named Odell Green said he'd spotted a small herd to the west, moving toward the Musselshell River.

"Somethin' spooked 'em," Green reported. "Couldn't tell what. Might be a couple of stray Injuns."

Heller told him to keep his eyes open, something Jessie figured Green would likely do without the telling. When they mounted up again, dark blue clouds were bunched on the western horizon, clouds the color and shape of far mountains.

"That's coming up," said Heller. "Late tonight, most likely."

Half an hour farther to the north, Green turned and high-tailed it back, waving the other men in.

"Riders," he told Heller. "Four or five, looks like. Way they're spread out I'd say they're lookin' for buffalo sign. You said come in, though, anyone at all showed up."

"Right," Heller nodded. "I don't reckon they're trouble, riding like that. Let's go out real friendly-like and see."

Jessie rode beside Ki, Aaron just ahead, and the three other hunters close by. When the other party spotted them coming, their outriders all came in, bunching around a man on a big white stallion.

"Goddamn, looky there," grinned Odell Green. "You ever see anything purtier in your life?"

"I don't reckon I have," said Heller. He glanced over his shoulder at Jessie. "We've found that Englishman of yours. Either that or ol' Custer's come back, one of the two."

Jessie saw Heller was right. The man atop the magnificent horse wore a butter-colored buckskin jacket with fringes a foot long on the sleeves and Indian beadwork on the chest. His shirt was white silk, his Stetson a pale dove gray with more bead-work on the crown. His flared riding trousers matched the hat; his legs were encased in black riding boots cut to the knees. His blond mustache and goatee were neatly trimmed, matching the thick hair about his collar.

"I'll be damned," Ki said beside Jessie. "Heller's right. It's Custer or his ghost."

The Englishman danced his horse at a jaunty angle up to Heller. Jessie saw his pale blue eyes reach out and find her and look her over with interest.

"Be best, I'd think, if you fellows would move on to the east," he said politely. "I am hunting this range myself."

"Yeah, I see you are," said Heller. Jessie saw he was making an effort not to grin. "I don't guess you'd be Montgomery, now would you?"

Odell Green snickered. The Englishman glared and thrust out his jaw. "I am *Sir* Edward Burke Montgomery, yes," he said stiffly. "And who is it I might be addressing?"

"Name's Heller. We just rode up from Miles City an—"

"Heller?" Montgomery leaned forward and stared. "Not *Aaron* Heller, surely?"

"I reckon the same."

"Well. By God, now!" The Englishman beamed with pleasure. "I am delighted. *Dee*-lighted, sir! A real pleasure, I assure you. Your reputation precedes you, Mr. Heller!" He urged his mount closer and vigorously pumped Heller's hand. "You will be my guest, of course. I shall not take no for an answer. My camp's not twenty minutes from here. We'll have a supper laid out and I have some excellent brandy. I *must* hear all your exploits, sir." He glanced past Heller to Jessie. "I, ah, don't believe I have had the pleasure, miss . . ."

"I'm Jessie Starbuck, Sir Edward. How do you do?"

"Well, now. *Edward*, please." Montgomery flushed with pleasure. "Charming. Charming. Do you, ah, hunt, Miss Starbuck?"

Heller grinned and Jessie shot him a look.

"No," she said dryly. "Mr. Heller does enough hunting for us all. Sir Edward, uh—Edward . . ." Jessie leaned forward in the saddle. "May I ask you a question, please? The matter is *most* urgent."

"Why, of course, dear lady. Of course."

"I'm looking for a girl, a young girl. We heard she might be traveling in your party."

Montgomery's smile faded. "And what is your interest in such a girl, Miss Starbuck?" he asked coolly.

67

"Have you seen her? Is she here?"

"Was here. Isn't anymore." Montgomery gave a quick, harsh burst of laughter, a laugh laced with bitterness and scorn. "We had a little skirmish with the Indians last night, Miss Starbuck. After that, the girl rode off to the north."

"What?" Jessie stared. "And—and you still haven't found her?"

"Haven't looked," Montgomery snorted. "If the bitch is in heat for the noble savage, then I say by God let them have her!"

★

Chapter 9

"I've talked to some of the men I know works for this fella," said Heller. "It's about like he told you—except the Englishman left out the interestin' parts."

"I had an idea maybe he did," said Jessie.

Heller grinned and shook his head. "Those two were at it from the minute he got her out of Miles City. This gal had the idea buffalo huntin' was something you did to pass the time on the way to St. Louis. Soon as she found out Montgomery was going to *stay* out here a couple of months, she started screaming up a storm and throwin' all his fancy dishes and stuff." Heller paused and set his thumbs in the top of his belt. It was getting close to five; the sun was still high in the west, but dark clouds had put the camp in shadow.

"Anyway," Heller went on, "Montgomery's hunters found a big herd to the west. That was last night. Remember Odell said he figured maybe Injuns were around this afternoon? Mighta been the same ones these boys met up with. Shoshonis, most likely. They were hunting the far side of the herd, and the Englishman tried to run 'em off. There were a couple of shots fired, and one of the Injuns dropped a rider. Lucky shot, but the fella's just as dead."

"Oh, dear," said Jessie.

Heller worked his mouth like something tasted bad. "Don't reckon you can guess who it was got killed."

"What?" Jessie looked puzzled. "No, I—oh, Lord!"

"Uh-huh. My old partner Barlo Leeks, that son of a bitch. He can't cheat me one way, he'll figure another."

"Aaron . . ."

"Yeah, I know. Speakin' ill of the dead. Anyway, right after this Injun business is when the girl took off. Her and Montgomery had a horrendous big fight and she got her a horse and lit out."

"And no one tried to stop her. I can't *believe* that!"

"*I* can," Heller said flatly. "The Englishman wouldn't let 'em. Turned red as a beet and jerked out that silver-plated Colt and started waving it around. Said he'd shoot anyone tried to sit on a horse."

"And they let him get away with that?"

"Damn right they did. He pays top wages, Jessie. These boys are on the gravy train and they know it."

"I don't believe this," Jessie said sharply, "not any of it!" She glared furiously at the big tent where Montgomery had laid out a sumptuous feast for herself, Ki, and Aaron Heller. There was enough food for at least twenty people—six courses and four imported wines. There was another tent close by, Montgomery's sleeping quarters. Each tent was painted in neat blue and red stripes. The British flag and pennants bearing Montgomery's family crest hung listlessly above the tents.

"He got his pride hurt, so he let that girl ride out by herself," Jessie said darkly. "He ought to be horsewhipped, Aaron."

"Yeah, he sure appreciated you telling him so, too," Aaron said absently.

"I don't care. That's exactly the way I feel." She faced Heller again. "I asked Ki to talk to you . . ."

"He did. I don't think it'll do any good but it won't hurt to try. Odell Green's going to ride out with him. We've still got three good hours of daylight, and that storm's moving in real slow. If they can pick up her trail while there's still something dry enough to follow, we can get an idea which way she headed. When they get back in, we'll take off first thing in the morning. If it isn't coming down in buckets."

Jessie clenched her fists in frustration and anger. Angela Halley had slipped through their fingers again. She was hell-bent on destruction, determined to tempt fate every way she could imagine. And fate, Jessie knew, had a way of evening up the score. "Darn that girl," she said to herself, "darn her for being such a fool!"

"Don't do anything foolish," Jessie warned Ki. "Just pick up the trail if you can and come back and get some sleep. We'll take off again at dawn."

Ki squinted at the sky and looked at Heller. "You don't think it'll hit before dark?"

"It could. I wouldn't be anywhere low if it does, I was you."

"Reckon him and me can get out of the rain," Green said wryly.

"I've seen times you couldn't find your feet, Odell."

Green threw back his head and laughed. "That was bad whiskey talking, son. I'm a changed man now."

"Well that's a delight to hear. Now get on out and get back."

Ki nodded at Jessie and pulled his mount up next to Green's. Past Jessie and Heller, he saw the Englishman standing in the shadow of his garishly-colored tent, an expression of pure disgust on his features.

They rode due north, picking up Angela's trail easy enough not half a mile from camp.

"If it was anyone had any sense we was after, I could tell you where'd they'd go," Green scowled. "Not much telling with this gal. What she'll do is keep ridin' till the horse gets tired and then stops. Try to find something to drink which she might. An' look for something to eat which she won't."

Ki nodded agreement. He'd figured it about the same way. "So what do you think she'll do? You take someone like that she'll bear off in a wide circle. Come back near where she started."

"Uh-huh. 'Cept this one's too damn stubborn. *She's* going straight." Odell spat on the ground. "She keeps her headin' she'll hit the Missouri 'bout fifty miles on—and some pretty rough country close to it. East, she'll ride through grass like this near forever." His face clouded with concern. "It's all them other directions I'm worried about. She goes for the Musselshell River she's going to find them buffalo. *And* the goddamn Injuns dogging them."

"Like you said, she's going to get real hungry before that."

"Likely didn't have too easy a night. Wonder if she knows what to do with a horse while she's beddin' down?"

Ki didn't answer. The wind had picked up from the west,

71

pushing cool air before the storm and bending the high points of grass.

"We got a couple of hours still," said Green, guessing Ki's thoughts. "You want to follow those tracks or go back?"

"Let's take it as far as we can."

"Suits me," Green muttered. "I been wet once before."

The first edge of the storm hit them half an hour later. Angela's tracks had turned abruptly to the west for no apparent reason. Maybe something spooked her, Green suggested. Or maybe she was getting tired of the game and thought she was turning back to camp. There weren't any landmarks on the prairie. One way looked much the same as the next to a girl who'd grown up in the city.

"Well, shit," Green muttered darkly, "knew this was going to happen and there she is." He squinted up at the sky as a fat drop of rain pelted his cheek. Another drummed off the brim of his hat and then they could hear the rain hitting the grass all around. "All right," he said, "let's get us some high ground while we can."

Ki nodded and kicked his horse into action. He followed Green into the wind, up the side of the hill. They pulled the horses up short, hobbled them, and jerked off the saddles. The grass bent to the ground and the rain came down in force. There was nothing to do but squat, huddle under a slicker and wait.

The slicker kept Ki dry a good minute and a half. After that the rain pounded it against him and drove in under the edges. The sound was near deafening. The sky turned black, then stark white as searing bolts of lightning lashed the earth. *There goes the trail,* thought Ki. *There won't be anything left.* He heard Green cursing under his slicker, trying to build a smoke and light it under water.

The rain didn't stop until just before the dawn. Ki got up and stomped around more than once, trying to keep his legs from going to sleep. The water washed down the hill like a river.

Odell Green emerged from cover looking miserable and mean. Without speaking to Ki, he wandered off to relieve himself and bring in the mounts. The sky was starting to lighten.

72

They ate in the saddle, dried buffalo meat and hard biscuits they'd managed to keep dry.

"Wisht I had me some pemmican," Green said. "Some folks don't like it, but I get a hunger for it. Comanches make the best there is. Dried buffalo meat cut up in strips, pounded good with fat. Then they mix in nuts and dried fruits and berries. Hell, you dip that in wild honey and it's tasty as can be, I'll tell you for sure."

"I'd like to go on a while more," Ki said. "I know there won't be a trail, but we've come this far. You want to get back or anything?"

Green shrugged. "Like you say, we come this far. Aaron and Miss Jessie was in the rain same as us. They'll figure what happened and what we're doing."

The sun came up copper-bright in a sky drained of any trace of color. Water rose in steamy tendrils from the ground. Ki wiped sweat from his face as the heat began to warm the clothing plastered to his flesh.

"We don't have any reason to figure she's still heading west," he told Green.

"Or any way to say she isn't. Not much we can do 'cept look for horse droppings. There isn't going to be any tracks."

Half an hour later, Green made a liar out of himself. They'd skirted the base of a high, grassy hill, a creek bed dry most of the year. Water and weather had leached all the soil and grass away, leaving a yellow stratum of sticky clay.

"Son of a bitch," Green smiled, sliding quickly out of the saddle. Ki joined him and climbed up the hill, bent, and ran his fingers over the deep, jagged scar in the clay.

"It's a horse and it's shod," Ki said aloud. "If it was dirt instead of clay, it'd sure be gone by now."

Green nodded. "Wonder the damn horse didn't throw her tryin' to climb a spot like this."

Ki urged his mount on, riding out ahead. The slash in the clay was old, made before the rain the day before. Still, it was something. It meant Angela was out there somewhere, heading nearly due west. Where the *hell* did she think she was going? Ki wondered. The Musselshell? The Judith Mountains, the Big

Snowy? Most likely, he knew, she'd never even heard of such places. And she sure wouldn't get that far. Not without running into trouble. She was likely getting hungry as well. The horse had plenty of grass, but there was nothing out here for people, nothing you didn't shoot. And he doubted she was doing any of that, even if she'd left with a weapon.

The land rose steadily for a mile, then leveled and stopped abruptly. Ki saw he was on the edge of a high butte, the prairie spread out far ahead until it vanished in a haze. There was a pale gray line on the horizon, maybe the Musselshell River. Closer, a dark and ragged line flowed up from the south, growing thicker in the north where it vanished behind the hills.

"Buffalo," Green said beside him. "Seven, eight hundred, maybe." He pointed back to the south. "See the buzzards circling? Been some killin' four or five miles down. Those Injuns the Englishman's boys run into. I figure this is the ass end of the herd; biggest part of it's moving up north for the Missouri."

Ki looked questioningly at Green. "The girl came this way. If she kept on going, she was past here long before the herd came by."

"Maybe." Green guessed Ki's thoughts. "An' maybe she rode right into something she shouldn't. Wouldn't be out of habit for her, now would it?"

It was late afternoon before they crossed the wide valley and came to the far side of the hills. Green had taken them the long way around, going west but dipping south. They passed the spot where the Indians had killed buffalo earlier that morning. The ground was thick with buzzards, the earth a gray-brown carpet of squawking beaks and flapping wings. Three lanky wolves watched from the side of the hill. He counted nineteen carcasses, most of them close together, the hides cut and gone, blue and red meat already growing putrid and covered with flies.

Green flapped his hat and drove away the birds to inspect the dead animals. The Indians had taken some hump and tongue and a few hindquarters and liver. Mostly, though, they'd been after the hides.

"Poor bastards," said Green. "Used to be you'd find nothing but the smell of buffalo left after a Injun got to 'em. They'd

74

take the hide and all the meat and even the innards—bones
and everything else they could carry. Make tools, moccasins,
teepees; use the sinews for bowstrings and webs for their
snowshoes. Bones is good for hoes and scrapers, geegaws to
wear. The backfat's good for grease, and the gall makes yeller
paint." Green spat on the ground. "These here is pretty sorry
Injuns. They took what they could eat and the hides to sell.
Left the rest out here to rot."

"Like the white man," said Ki.

Green looked at him. "Yeah, I reckon that's so."

Ki turned down a rifle, but Green told him he could goddamn
sure carry it whether he wanted to shoot or not. No use giving
the Indians ideas. They rode into camp, Green carrying his
Sharps .45, Ki holding the Winchester cradled in his arms. They
rode in openly, letting the Indians see them coming. There were
twenty, twenty-five in the bunch, ragtag Shoshoni wearing
mostly trade clothes. Green shook his head and told Ki he
couldn't figure what the hell they were doing where they were,
except trying to stay alive. Ki saw there weren't horses for
more than half the group.

As Green and Ki rode into camp, every man stopped what
he was doing, turned, and followed the visitors with their eyes.
There were no women and children. Only men. Green raised
his hand and pulled to a halt. A short, stocky Indian with a
nearly black face walked up to meet him.

"You talk English?" Green asked. "You understan' what I'm
saying?"

"I speak it," the Indian said without expression.

"We're not lookin' for any trouble," Green said calmly. "We
don't even care 'bout the white man you killed, couple of days
back over east." He gave the Shoshoni a broad smile. "Of
course, now, there's other whites 'round here ain't real happy
'bout that."

The Indian showed no expression at all, but Ki was dead
certain he'd gotten the message.

"What is it you want with us?" he said bluntly.

"The girl," said Green. "The white girl you got here in your
camp."

The Indian hesitated an instant. "We did not steal this

75

woman," he said plainly. "The woman came here. She rode her own horse. It was a good horse but it died. That is no fault of ours. She was hungry. We gave her food to eat."

Ki gave a silent sigh of relief. Angela *was* here, then! He and Green had figured they were right, but there was no way in hell they could prove it. If their bluff hadn't worked they could call the Indian a liar and take it from there, or ride out of camp and figure what to do next.

"We sure do appreciate what you done," Green said gravely. "We'll take her off your hands now—and we'd like to give you a gift for your kindness and hospitality."

"What kind of gift?" The Indian watched Green with suspicion.

Green held up the gold coin Ki had given him. "A twenty-dollar double-eagle. I 'spect you already know how much goods it'll buy."

The Shoshoni eyed the coin. "The money. And the Sharps rifle."

"Uh-uh. Just the money, friend. That's it." He leaned out of the saddle. "See, you didn't *steal* the lady, remember? So we ain't *buying* her or nothing like that. We just want to give you something for your trouble. While she was a guest in your camp . . ."

Ki could almost see the wheels turning in the Indian's head. He was thinking about the money, how he could kill the two men where they sat and take the coin, and maybe other coins as well. There were the Sharps and the Winchester and the horses and whatever else they might have on them. He was thinking about the other white man who had gotten in the way of a bullet, and how these two would then make three. Maybe three were too many. He had to weigh that. The white men put no value on the red man's life—a hundred, even a thousand didn't matter. But one white life, even one . . .

The Shoshoni turned and spoke rapidly over his shoulder. The tall Indian behind him stomped his foot and shouted in anger. The older man shook his head and stood his ground. The tall Indian fumed and marched stolidly past the cookfire to a cluster of hide shelters. He crawled in a shelter on his hands and knees. A shriek came out of the tent, a noise like the wail of a cat. The Indian backed out fast. He scrambled to his feet holding his cheek, stalked a few yards away, and then stopped, shouting at the Shoshoni with Ki and Green.

The Indian let out a breath. "The woman doesn't want to go. She says you are men who mean her harm."

"Angela, listen to me," Ki called out. "We're not from Heydrich. He's got men after you; I don't have to tell you that. You stick around here and they'll find you." He let his gaze rest on the Shoshoni. "And when he *does* find you, anyone took you in he'll kill them too."

The Indian frowned at Ki's words.

"You goddamn lyin' son of bitch!" Angela screamed. "Get outa here and leave me alone!"

"You speak the truth?" the Indian asked. "Men will come after this woman?"

"There's a half-breed named Copperhead after her right now," said Ki. "You ever hear of him?"

The Shoshoni's eyes went wide. "I know the name. His mother was of our people." He stopped and looked over the camp. "But I do not know if I believe you. Maybe you are from this Copperhead, as the woman says. Or maybe you only want the woman for yourself."

Green suddenly burst into laughter, startling both Ki and the Shoshoni. "Shit, *you* keep her, friend. It ain't worth all the trouble." He turned his horse in a half-circle and gave the Indian a sly grin. "How many fights you had in camp since the woman come in?"

"Three," the Shoshoni said soberly. "Three fights. But no one was badly hurt."

The Shoshoni stared at Green, then turned and shouted at the Indian by the shelter. The man's mouth fell open. He clamped his jaw tight and crawled into the shelter again. Screams erupted from inside. When the Indian stood again he had the girl across his shoulder. She beat on his back and shrieked at the top of her lungs. Long bare legs and bare feet flashed under the calico skirt.

Green flipped the double-eagle and the Indian deftly caught it. "You ought to give me back change," he said. "I'm doing you a favor."

"It may be you are right," the Shoshoni said solemnly.

★

Chapter 10

"You want to act like a human being," said Ki, "you can use your hands and feet. I don't care one way or the other."

Angela kicked out furiously and Ki stepped quickly aside. "I get my hands on you," the girl shrieked, "I'll tear your eyes out, mister!"

"Now see, that's what I'm talking about," Ki said calmly.

"Bastard! Son-of-a-bitch-slant-eyed-bastard!"

Odell Green watched the girl kicking and screaming on the ground. A low whistle escaped his teeth and he scratched his beard in wonder. "Eastern schoolin', huh? You reckon they're all like that?"

Ki squatted down carefully out of range. "I'm going to tell you this again, Angela. Try to shut up and listen. I'm not working for Ernst Heydrich. If I was, why would I tell you something different? I'd just take you on back and pick up the reward."

Angela glared through a veil of golden hair. "Lyin' goddamn Jappo," she sneered. "I wouldn't believe you if you said the sky was blue!" She jerked her head around, loosing her anger on Green. "What are *you* lookin' at, Mister? Damn, you smell like buffalo shit!"

Ki stood and walked to the edge of the creek. Water an inch deep trickled over a bed of black rocks. A patch of dead cottonwoods shaded one side of the creek. The parched leaves rattled in the late evening breeze. He looked over his shoulder and gave the girl a sour look. Odell Green had guided them north, taking them a quick five miles from the Indian camp. "In case they change their minds," Green told him, "which a Injun is likely to do."

Ki had carried the girl screaming and cursing, draped like

78

a shapely sack of goods over the front of his saddle. A mile out of camp he'd stopped to bind her legs and wrists. A mile after that, he stuffed a bandanna in her mouth.

Damned if the girl wasn't something! Foul-mouthed and loud as any drunk in a Deadwood saloon—and pretty enough to make a man cry. He wasn't at all surprised she'd left a trail of dead lovers in her wake. She was young, slender as a willow, a girl made of velvet-soft curves and lazy hollows. Her breasts poked jauntily through the fabric of her dress—even lying on her back they tilted up in a saucy angle. Her skin was a mix of honey and olive, a match for the rich golden hair that tumbled easily past her shoulders.

Still, there was a great deal more to Angela Halley than good looks. Ki was keenly aware of that. There was an aura, a wanton magic about the girl that set her apart. He'd seen prettier women, breathtaking women who'd put Angela in the shade. He knew, though, that in a roomful of beauties a man's eyes would find Angela in an instant. Every move she made, every sullen glance promised pleasure. There was a raw, animal passion about her, a quality almost impossible to define. Ki saw the way Odell looked at the girl and recognized the feelings within himself.

Green caught his expression and grinned. "There oughta be a law against that, you know?"

"They ought to put that girl in a cage," Ki muttered.

"An' do what? Lock you in with her?"

Ki didn't answer. He turned and walked back and looked at the girl. "We're going to ride a little ways and stop for the night. You want to behave, you can ride behind me sitting up. When we get where we're going you can wash yourself and eat. None of that'll be easy, if I have to keep you tied up like a sack."

Angela wet her lips. "Mind if I ask a question?"

"Go ahead."

"I read somewhere Jappos and Chinks screw their mothers. Is that true? If it is I'd like to know if—*Aaaaagh!* Stop it, goddamn you!"

Ki picked her up screaming and kicking and dropped her roughly over the saddle, trying to keep his eyes off the flash of honeyed thighs.

• • •

It was still pitch dark when Green squatted down and poked him awake. "Sun'll be up in an hour," he said. "I'd like to be on high ground 'fore it's light."

"Uh-huh." Ki sat up and stretched. The girl was awake, watching him from under a blanket a few yards away. Ki had a quick mental picture of a ferret, sharp-eyed, alert, ready to sink its teeth into a mouse. "You sleep all right?" he asked.

"I didn't sleep any," she said sullenly.

Ki knew that was a lie; he and Green had split watches during the night. They'd kept a cold camp since a fire was easy to spot on the prairie. The girl had slept fine but they hadn't. She'd refused to eat and drink and was too damn stubborn to let them risk loosening the ropes.

"I want you to untie me," she said suddenly. "I'll—I won't run away."

Ki looked at her. "Your choice. Try something just once and I'll sack you up again."

Angela stuck out her jaw in defiance. "I *said* I wouldn't, all right?" She held out her hands. Ki sliced her free with the tip of his blade, then reached down to loose her ankles. The bonds weren't tight, just taut enough to keep her off her feet during the night.

He found the dried meat and hard biscuits, offered the girl some, and took a portion for himself. She ate the food quickly like a dog, tearing at the meat with her teeth, and never taking her eyes off Ki. He gave her the canteen and she drained it. He watched the water trail down the corners of her mouth to the column of her throat, then run in small rivulets into the V of her breasts.

"Is this it?" she said flatly. "This all you got to eat?"

"This is it."

"Huh! I ate better with the Indians." She reached past Ki for another biscuit and more beef.

Green came up with the horses and grinned crookedly at the girl. "Well, we're right civilized, ain't we?"

"*Thought* I smelled buffalo shit," Angela muttered.

"Real charming, by God." Green shook his head and walked off with Ki. "We'll do like we figured last night. Keep north an' west of the herd. I reckon the main bunch is movin' north-

80

east toward the Missouri. That's where the Englishman and his crew'll be, and Aaron and Miss Jessie. We stick to this route we'll likely see 'em soon enough. And maybe this Copperhead fella if he's around."

"He's here," Ki said soberly. "He'll keep dogging the girl till he finds her."

"Yeah, well..." Green squinted into the dawn, studying the country ahead in his mind, the parts he couldn't see. "We ought to be among friends around noon or a little after. Can't be soon enough for me. I'm gettin' a crick in my neck looking over my shoulder."

Ki nodded agreement and walked back to the girl. She'd scrubbed her face clean from the canteen and smoothed out the wrinkles in her skirt as best she could. From somewhere in the folds of her dress she'd found a brush. Gritting her teeth against the pull, she vigorously worked the tangles out of her hair. The hair was thick and rich. It tumbled like raw spun gold about her shoulders. Ki glanced quickly away. The girl caught him and grinned.

"Like m'hair, do you?" she smiled.

"Looks some better than it did," Ki said shortly. He wrapped up the last of his gear and tied it securely on the skirt of his saddle. Without looking at the girl, he swung his leg easily over the mount. "Come on, get up behind me. We got to get moving."

"Oh, sounds like *fun!*" She gave a mischievous little laugh that set Ki's nerves on edge. He offered a helping hand and she took it, placed one foot in the stirrup, gripped the cantle, and sprang lightly up behind him. He was acutely aware of the pressure of her body against his own, the long line of her legs, the sharp points of her breasts. Snuggling in close, she molded herself to fit, taking all the time in the world to get settled.

"There now. How's that?" she said finally, wrapping her arms tightly around his waist. He could smell her hair, feel her breath on the back of his neck. "I don't want to fall off. Case you get to ridin' real *hard.*"

"Yeah, that's just fine," Ki said dryly. He kicked the horse harder than he'd planned and bolted off after Green. Angela pressed her head against his shoulder, and Ki tried to pretend she wasn't there.

81

There was a clear, well-defined line on the prairie; south of that the rain had soaked the land, bringing a lush green color to the grass. To the north the hills were dry and parched, the grass as dry as paper.

"Kinda what I figured," said Green. "That's why the herd's moving fast. They knew we was hittin' dry country. Isn't much water at all clear up to the Missouri."

Green rode on, keeping to the flank of the hill. The herd was spread out to the right, thousands upon thousands of the animals, their pelts thickening up as summer pushed into fall. Some of the late calves were still a dull red ochre; the others were turning a silky shade of brown. Odell Green said the herd was strung out in maybe three or four parts. The northernmost bunch was likely twenty miles away. The Englishman, he figured, was somewhere between here and there.

Ki decided he was getting nowhere with the girl. "I don't know what to tell you," he said darkly. "Heydrich didn't send me—you can trust me or not, Angela. I can't force you to believe me."

"Huh!" Angela said at his back. "Wouldn't trust *anything* a man had to say. A man can't open his mouth without spittin' out a lie."

"Maybe you've been hanging around with the wrong men," Ki suggested.

"Shit. There isn't but one kind!"

"Oh, is that it?"

"That's it."

"You don't see any difference between me and, say, Ernst Heydrich?"

"Should I? You something special?"

"I'm not trying to kill you," Ki said flatly. "I haven't offered fifty thousand dollars to the man who'll bring me your head in a sack. *That's* some difference."

Her body stiffened against him. Angela tried to cover her reaction with a laugh. "Guess I'm supposed to be scared, right? Well, I'm not. You might as well quit trying."

Ki made a noise in his throat. "For God's sake, girl, will you stop it? If you're *not* scared you're plain stupid. You've been running from Ernst Heydrich for six months. I know who Heydrich is and I know about the list and what's on it. I know what Copperhead'll do if he finds you. He'll have you 'bout three or four minutes and you'll tell him about the list and where it is—then you'll beg him to let you tell him something else, everything that's happened since you were born. You'll say whatever you can to make him stop. Only Copperhead won't. He'll keep on at you till you're crazy with pain. Then he'll stop and let you rest and start again. Angela, I *know* why you're running. I'm not a damn fool."

Angela let out a long breath. "Who—who the hell are you, mister?"

"We through playing games?"

"I asked you a question."

"My name's Ki. You've heard Green say it so that's nothing new. I work for a lady named Jessie Starbuck. You ever heard the name before?"

"Yeah, I've heard it. You work for her? Is that true?"

"Yes, it's true, Angela."

"And what is it this Jessie Starbuck wants with me?"

"You said you know who she is," Ki said tightly. "What do you think she wants, girl? She wants that list, the names of the people on it. She wants to stop the cartel from taking over this country, and that list will slow them down. She'll take care of you, Angela, see that you're not harmed. You can change your name and disappear if you like. Go anywhere in the world and start over. South America, wherever you want. The cartel won't be able to touch you."

Angela was silent a long moment. Green guided his mount down the side of the grassy slope and Ki followed. Angela began laughing to herself.

"What's so funny?" he said sharply. "I can't think of anything to laugh about."

"I was just thinking," Angela said lightly, "what that Green fellow said. 'Bout me causing these Injuns to fight. Honest to God, now!"

Ki felt the heat rise to his face. "Are you out of your mind! Don't you understand what's happening here, what you—"

"Sure I do. You and me are ridin' along nice and easy. I'm

83

wondering whether Green'll maybe give me a drink of whiskey. I know he's got some on him. And *you're* wondering if I really slept with every one of those Injuns. To tell you the truth, mister—"

"Angela, where's the list?" Ki demanded. "Did you hide it somewhere or what?"

"What list?" Angela said absently. "I honestly don't know what you're talking about, friend."

The breeze picked up and blew a hot, dry wind across the prairie. Dead grass rattled against the ground. The girl's hair brushed Ki's cheek like a feather. The sun was straight up when Green eased back his reins and brought his mount abruptly to a halt. Ki stopped and waited. Green sat for a long time without moving. Finally he motioned Ki to him.

"I heard something," he said. "I don't know what. Hold my horse a minute; I'm going to walk up to the top of that slope and have a look."

Ki took his reins. Green came stiffly out of the saddle and stalked toward the top of the grassy rise.

"I'm going to get down and stretch," said Angela.

"No, you're not," Ki told her.

"Why? What's wrong with that?"

"Nothing. Just sit still."

"Maybe I have to do something," the girl suggested.

"If you do, it better wait." Ki became suddenly alert as Green turned and bounded back, running as fast as he could. Closer, Ki could see his face was drained of color.

"It's fire," Green blurted, "comin' fast on the wind. Not two hundred yards over the hill. That's what I heard—heat explodin' seed tops on the grass. You can bet some bastard started it just for us. Shit, *look!*" Green pointed, and Ki saw white smoke rising swiftly toward them over the crest. "Christ, once those shaggies smell it—"

"What are we waiting for?" Angela gasped. "Let's get the hell out of here!"

"Get the hell *where*, girl?" Green turned to Ki, his eyes narrowed to slits. "That fire's coming faster'n a train. I seen one eat up half of Kansas 'fore you could spit. Come on—we got one chance and we'd better take it." He pulled himself in

84

the saddle and kicked his horse down the rise, heading straight for the head of the herd.

"What are you doing?" Angela cried out. "Are you *crazy?*"

"Shut up," Ki snapped, "hang on and don't talk."

He glanced back over his shoulder; his heart nearly stopped at the sight. The fire was racing over the slope in a fury, the wind driving a wall of white smoke on ahead. In that instant the buffalo smelled the smoke. The herd turned at once, thousands of shaggy backs shifting and moving, bolting in alarm and bellowing out their fear. Angela buried her head in Ki's back. Ki saw Green leap off his horse up ahead, grab the big Sharps rifle, and slap his mount away. The herd came toward him, thundering ahead of the flames. Green fired at a big bull on the edge of the pack. The animal snorted and folded. Green calmly reloaded, aimed, and downed another. He turned, saw Ki, and frantically waved him forward. Ki slid to the ground, grabbed the girl, and guided her through the choking smoke.

"Let the horse go," Green shouted. "Come on!"

Ki reluctantly loosed his reins. The horse's eyes went wide. It trembled and bolted free.

"No," Angela shrieked. "Damn it, we're dead without that horse!"

Ki held her to him, forcing her to the ground. He soaked a bandanna from his canteen and slapped it across her face. Green bent to the first big bull, ripped open the carcass with a single stroke of his knife. Plunging his arms inside, he tore out the entrails and spilled the wet mess on the ground.

"Get in with the girl," he shouted to Ki. "Pull the hide around you tight!"

"What about you?"

"I got two, didn't I? The other one's for me. Now git in, damn it!"

Ki pulled the girl to him. She backed off in horror, pounding his face with her fists. Ki clipped her lightly across the jaw. Angela went limp. He bent to the ground and rolled her into the carcass, the smell making him retch down his shirt. He crawled in behind her and pulled the wet hide as tightly as he could. He felt the herd coming, pounding hooves nearly lost in the roar of the fire. He bent close to Angela, pressing her hard against the sickening flesh. The herd thundered around the carcass, bellowing insanely with fear. Ki closed his eyes and gritted his teeth, certain a ton of meat would crush his skull at any moment.

★

Chapter 11

Aaron turned in the saddle and waved her forward. Jessie rode up the slope and Aaron grinned and pointed down the valley.

"My God," she gasped, "what a beautiful sight! There must be thousands of them—*hundreds* of thousands!"

"Close to it. It's a fair big piece of the northern herd."

Jessie stared at the dark mass choking the valley floor. The buffalo stretched from north to south as far as the eye could see. In places the herd was a good three or four miles across. From her position atop the bluff the mass changed its shape like shifting shadow, one part flowing into another before her eyes, as if there were only one beast instead of thousands.

Glancing at Aaron Heller, she saw an expression in his eyes she couldn't define. There was a sense of awe and wonder, like a man who'd seen a vision. Jessie realized with a start that Heller looked at the herd the way a man looked at a woman, with the same hunger and need. She flushed at the thought and turned away, filled with a sudden, unreasoning anger. She'd forgotten for the moment who he was and why they were there. The lust in his eyes was a lust for killing, nothing more. Some of her anger was directed at herself, at the feelings Heller's hunger brought to light. She found herself both attracted and repelled at what she saw and didn't like the sensation at all.

"What is it?" Aaron asked. "You all right?"

"I'm fine," she said shortly. "Why wouldn't I be?"

"Beats me. Just wondered." He gave her a curious look and moved his mount idly about.

"What happens now?" Jessie asked tightly. "You just line up and start shooting or what?"

Aaron didn't miss the razor edge in her voice. "You really asking or what?"

"I'm asking."

Heller nodded to his right. "The Englishman's boys'll work their way a couple of miles against the wind, find 'em a quiet spot. That grass thins out a ways yonder, so they'll likely crawl up with gunny sacks over their backs the last quarter mile, helps blend them with the dirt. They'll get about two hundred or so yards off, the closer the better."

"My God . . ."

"Told you you didn't want to hear it."

"Go on."

"Jessie . . ."

"Aaron, just *tell* me, all right?"

Heller let out a breath. "I told you this is all one herd, maybe three or four parts. Might be fifty or sixty miles long. Maybe even more. The hunters will find the head of this piece, locate a good stand, and drop the leaders. Do it right and you don't spook the herd."

"And then you just—keep killing."

Heller ignored her. "One hunter will use two Sharps rifles usually. They get real hot and you got to let them cool. Barrel starts expanding, and when it does that the bullet's likely to go all wobbly. Hell, use one too long and she'll explode right in your hands."

"Ahd then what?"

"What d'you mean?"

"After it's over."

"After it's over, the skinners come in with the wagon teams and go to work."

Jessie squinted past the herd. "How many will they kill, Aaron?"

"How the hell do I know how?" he said sharply. "Depends on how good he is, how the herd sits."

"How many do you think?"

"I don't think a goddamn thing. Jessie, what are you doing? You don't want to hear this."

"You're right," said Jessie, "I don't."

"Then what are you asking for?"

Jessie didn't answer. She turned her horse in a wide circle and rode off alone. Heller probably thought she was crazy, and maybe she couldn't blame him. She wanted to purge her feelings, make herself hate him for what he was, for what she'd seen in his eyes. Only it hadn't worked, damn it—it hadn't worked at all. She didn't hate Aaron; all she'd managed to do was punish herself.

"I'm sorry," she told him later. "I had no business doing that. I was—worried. About Ki."

"Well, yeah, I know that."

It was only half a lie. Her concern for Ki had been there all along, but it had nothing to do with Heller. Ki had left with Odell Green late Tuesday afternoon. She'd expected him back that night, but then the storm had hit hard and Aaron told her Ki and Odell would hole up and wait, that both men had better sense than to try to ride in that kind of rain. But then the storm had moved swiftly to the east, and still they hadn't returned. That afternoon, Wednesday, Montgomery's scouts had found the main body of the herd and they'd broken camp and moved west. Jessie was certain they'd meet Ki and Green on the way. Only they didn't. She was anxious, but it didn't make sense to go riding off trying to chase them down. Aaron Heller agreed; Ki and Green could take care of themselves. If they weren't back now it meant they'd likely found the girl or picked up her trail.

"Or they ran into Copperhead," Jessie had suggested. "You forget about him?"

"No, I haven't forgotten," Heller told her. "Only you're forgetting, Jessie. Copperhead isn't going chasing after Ki. What he'll learn in Miles City is that the girl went off with Montgomery. He'll come looking for her here, not somewhere out on the prairie."

"Only he hasn't. And he's had plenty of time."

Heller gave her a curious look. "You real anxouis to see that bastard again?"

"You know very well what I'm saying," she told him. "I'm waiting for the other shoe to drop. And yes—I'd rather know where he is than just wonder."

Heller hadn't answered. The look on his face told her nothing at all. She'd told Montgomery their problem as soon as they got to his camp, told him what had happened south of Miles City and that the men who wanted Angela would try again. She owed him a warning, she explained. As long as

Copperhead thought the girl was here, every man was in danger.

The Englishman had laughed. By God, let the beggars try, he'd told her. He had close to thirty good men. Why, he'd give this Copperhead fellow what for if he showed his face.

What's the matter with everyone? Jessie wondered. Was Montgomery such a fool he couldn't hear a word she'd said? And Aaron—she'd thought he had good sense, but now she wasn't sure.

And now it was Thursday close to noon. Ki and Green had been gone over forty hours. Not all that much for two days, maybe—they *could* have picked up Angela's trail or even found her.

Jessie stared out over the herd. Montgomery's men were working their way north. The shooting, the killing, would start any moment.

"I'm going after Ki," she said suddenly. "You don't have to come."

"Hey, you know I won't let you ride out there by yourself," he said soberly.

"You think I've got reason to be worried. Don't you, Aaron?"

"Didn't say that. But I'd kinda like to see 'em ride in. I'll get C.L. and Bobby. I want us to have a little help out there if we're going. We'll get a bite to eat and go have a look."

"Thank you." She bit her lip and swept hair off her shoulders. "I didn't mean to act like a fool."

"I don't think you did. Makes good sense to be worried when there's something to worry about. Person has to—" Aaron stopped, cupped his hand under his brim, and squinted curiously to the south. "Goddamn it," he snapped, "that sure isn't going to do us any good."

"What?" Jessie followed his eyes. "I don't see a thing but sky and clouds."

"Yeah, well that isn't exactly a cloud," he said tightly. "It's a fire, Jessie—a prairie fire. Maybe twenty, thirty miles south, right on the tail end of the herd and comin' fast from the looks of it." He jerked his reins and turned his mount in a half-circle. "I got to tell the others, case they haven't seen it."

Aaron spurred his mount and threw the horse into a run. Jessie watched him a moment and followed his dust. They wouldn't be riding after Ki. All they could do was get out of the way, get out and let what was coming have its day.

Ki huddled inside the carcass, holding the girl close against him. She groaned, stirring in her sleep, still out from the blow he'd delivered to her jaw.

The earth thundered around him as the maddened herd fled the raging flames. More than once, a crazed animal struck some part of the carcass, then veered aside at the last instant. The smoke was getting worse, so thick around him now it covered the terrible stench of the animal itself. Ki pressed his nose in the crook of his arm, fighting for a breath of fresh air. The girl came awake, coughing and gasping for breath. He held the wet bandanna against her face. She fought out blindly, struggling and screaming her fear, suddenly aware of where she was.

"Hold still, damn it!" Ki shouted into her ear. The girl was too frightened to listen. She tore at his grip, trying to rip the wet cloth from her face. Ki held on grimly, pressing himself against her to keep her still.

He was suddenly aware the noise was gone—not gone but not the same. The thunder of hooves had disappeared. In its place now was a roar like an oncoming train, the howl of a tornado sweeping everything in its path.

Fire!

The girl cried out beneath him and Ki realized he was digging his fingers into her arms. The flames raced through the dry valley, burning with a white-hot fury. The fire fed on itself, gathering strength from the driving wind. The rush of flame and heated air was no longer simply a fire—it was a *firestorm* now, a wall of roiling destruction that whipped across the prairie at an awesome, incredible speed.

Ki heard the howl of the flames and the roar of the wind as the firestorm suddenly struck. At once the carcass became a furnace. Flames licked at the shaggy hide; Ki cried out as the heat of burning flesh scorched his back. The heat turned his skin red and raw. The force of the storm sucked air out of his lungs, leaving him gasping for breath. Angela went limp beneath him; her mouth fell open and her eyes rolled back in her head. Something stung Ki's cheek and he flinched away from the pain. The smell told him it was fat, sizzling off the buffalo's flesh and dropping onto his face.

Ki drew scalding hot air into his lungs, choked, and fought to keep the darkness from pulling him under. He tried to find his canteen. It was caught between his legs, a hundred miles away. Hot entrails and blood seared his back and ran like molten metal down his sides. He wiped the girl's face with the cloth, moved his hands from her shoulders, and tried to slap her awake.

"Angela—*Angela!* Wake up," he shouted. "Damn it, girl—!"

Ki stopped, shook his head, and listened. The sound was moving away; the wind and the flames no longer howled overhead. Maybe it was over. Maybe the thing was gone.

To hell with it, he told himself darkly. Anything was better than sucking air in a dead beast, waiting for its guts to boil you alive.

He reached out blindly, tearing at the hide, and felt a brief, terrible moment of panic as the flesh refused to give. The flaps of skin had burned together, trapping them inside!

Ki beat at the hide with all his strength, kicked out with his feet, and ripped the flesh apart. Gasping for air, he rolled into the open, taking the girl with him. The earth burned his flesh and he staggered to his feet. The girl was limp in his arms. He opened the canteen and splashed her face. She groaned, choked, and went still. Ki gave a silent sigh of relief. At least she was still alive. For a moment he'd been certain she was gone.

He stood where he was, fighting to get his strength. A pall of white smoke drifted lazily over the ground. The earth had turned black as far as the eye could see. The fire blazed toward the north, already a mile away. Dead buffalo lay in twisted, charred heaps all around. Ki could see a dozen from where he stood. The hair on the carcass beside him was singed to the hide.

He looked to his right, searching through the drifting veils of smoke. He saw the dark, awful shape and knew in an instant what it was. An angry, helpless cry escaped his throat. He held the girl in his arms and stepped closer to make certain he was right. Green's big Wilson knife was still in his hand. He'd managed to rip the animal's belly and start pulling the entrails aside. Then something had happened. More than likely the smoke had overcome him. Or one of the maddened animals had struck him down. It didn't much matter how it happened. He'd gotten Ki and the girl to safety and left no time for himself.

Ki looked at the body once more and turned away, moving as fast as he could and keeping low. There was no time to bury Odell Green, even if he had the shovel to do it. Someone had started the fire to kill them—whoever they were, they'd want to see if the job was done.

He kept to the near side of the valley, moving from one narrow gully to the next. There was no more cover; the grass was black stubble, an inch above the earth. When the girl opened her eyes he stopped and laid her gently on the ground. She looked up and suddenly remembered. A cry started in her throat and Ki stopped it with his hand.

"Take it easy," he said softly. "You're all right now. Here, take some water." She nodded, let him bring the canteen to her mouth, gripping her hands tightly over his. She drained the canteen quickly. He didn't tell her that's all there was.

"My God," she gasped, eyes going wide with fear, "did that—did that really happen?" She trembled and tried to breathe. "Yeah, I guess it did." She leaned up and looked past him. "Where is he, where's Green?"

"He's dead," Ki said flatly.

"Oh!" Her face fell. "Oh God, I'm sorry."

Ki didn't answer. The smoke was nearly gone. The afternoon sun beat harshly on his back, stinging the skin the buffalo's flesh had burned raw. He peered down the gully, searching for motion over the dark ground beyond.

"Lord, you look awful." Angela made a face. "You're all red and covered with blood and I don't know what!"

"So are you," said Ki. "Sit still and keep your head down."

"What for?" Angela's eyes went wide with alarm. "Who are we hiding from?"

"I don't know. Whoever started the fire."

"Someone—someone started it?"

"Just keep quiet and stay right there. I'll be back."

"What?" Angela sat up straight and gripped his arm. "Where you going? You're not *leaving* me here!"

"I'm going about four feet away, all right?" he said irritably.

"Think you can handle that?" He turned away and crawled to the end of the depression. Rising slowly, he saw them. There were five of them, sitting on their ponies a hundred yards away. The sight filled him with rage. It wasn't Copperhead or any of his men. It was the Indians, the Shoshonis, the ragged and hungry bunch who'd had the girl. Ki knew he'd never have the slightest idea why they'd done it. Maybe they were mad about the girl. Maybe they simply wanted to kill some whites, try to even the score a little. Maybe they didn't have a reason at all.

What difference does it make, Ki thought bitterly. *It's over and done.*

Chapter 12

He sat in the burned-out ravine, watching the Shoshonis and waiting. They guided their horses slowly up and down the broad valley—north then south, tracing their path again and again. Ki finally figured out what they were doing. They were curious, but not curious enough to cross the charred path of the fire. For some reason they shied away from that. Instead they kept riding back and forth along the edge, hoping they'd see what they hadn't seen before.

"Go on, go on," Ki muttered beneath his breath. "Get the hell out of here!"

The afternoon sun was white-hot in a copper sky. His flesh was scarred with burns; his shoulders, neck, and upper back were raw with open sores where the intense heat of the carcass had seared his skin. He was coated from head to toe with ash and dust, the buffalo's blood and entrails. It had all dried quickly in the sun, then cracked and opened the wounds still farther. His shirt was stuck to his flesh; he didn't dare try to take it off. He glanced back at the girl. She didn't look a hell of a lot better.

"We going to stay here all day?" she asked miserably. "God, I can't *stand* this shit all over me much longer!"

"We'll stay until they decide to go away."

"You don't *know* they started that fire," she said. "You didn't see 'em do it."

"What?"

"Maybe they're just looking for us. Trying to help."

"Oh, well sure," Ki said soberly. "That's probably it."

Angela stuck out her jaw defiantly. "Well, you don't. You don't know everything. They—they didn't seem mad or anything to me."

Ki turned away and watched the Shoshonis. They rode up and down another ten or twenty minutes, then trailed off down to the south. Ki waited to make sure, then nodded to the girl and started walking north up the gully. He didn't turn to see if she was there.

A quarter-mile ahead, the land to their left turned to slabs of eroded red stone. Ki crossed to the shelter of the rocks. Angela protested, but he made her climb to the top. The land on the other side was green, untouched by the fire. Ki guessed it was three, maybe four miles away. He breathed a sigh of relief and started back down to the narrow valley. Far off to the right, he could see the distant smoke of the fire, still racing to the north. Straight ahead, trees began to follow the base of shallow hills.

"We'll try over there," he told the girl. "It's only a few miles. It's good cover, and it'll keep us out of the sun. Maybe we'll even find some water."

Angela gave him a puzzled look. "Aren't you even going to look for the damn horses? I'm getting real tired of all this walking."

"Angela—" Ki ran a hand across his face. "Angela, the horses are twenty miles from here if they're alive. Most likely, they got caught in the fire."

"That's silly," she protested. "Horses can run faster than a fire."

Ki shook his head and started walking, leaving the girl muttering to herself on the burned-out prairie. He remembered the scene he'd come upon in Texas, people and horses roasted like meat, a man and a woman sitting straight up in a wagon, an inch or two of reins still clutched in the man's hands. There were five families, twenty or so people. They'd all figured anyone could ride a lot faster than a fire.

The shade brought blessed relief from the heat. Ki let himself relax. The Indians had gone back south and he didn't expect to see them again. There was always Copperhead, but it was pretty unlikely he'd send a large party this far west. Ki didn't intend to get careless. He'd gone after the girl and he'd found her. Now all he had to do was get her back.

"You mind me asking," Angela said behind him, "is it too

much trouble just to tell me where we're going?"

"North," said Ki. "Montgomery will follow the herd, and Jessie's with him. That's where we're going."

"Christ!" Angela made a face and ran her fingers through the crusty strands of her hair. "I don't *want* to go there. I can't stand that son of a bitch!"

Ki repressed a grin. "Last I heard, he isn't real fond of you."

"Is that so?" Angela's eyes flashed in anger. "You think I care what that silly bastard thinks? Do you? God, men make me sick!"

"That isn't what I hear," said Ki.

Ki didn't see her stop or hear anything at all until the blow hit him solidly across the back. It struck the raw flesh and the pain shot through him like a lance. He went to his knees, shook his head, and brought himself shakily to his feet. He saw her as she vanished through the trees. He picked up the stick and saw it was part of a rotten branch and a good four inches thick. It had broken in two when it hit his back. If the thing had been solid instead of dead . . . He muttered under his breath and started after the girl.

He found her some fifty yards into the trees, hiding behind a rock. She faced him, blue eyes dark with contempt.

"Go ahead," she said boldly, "do whatever the hell you're going to do. Kill me, I don't care."

"Why did you do that?" Ki asked. "I'm trying to keep you alive. Don't you understand anything at all?"

"You shouldn't have said what you did 'bout me and men."

"You figure that's good enough reason to break my back?"

"Say you're sorry."

"What?" Ki stared at the girl in disbelief.

"Say you're sorry, or by God I'll try it again. First chance I get!"

Ki knew she wasn't bluffing. "All right. I'm sorry. And you're right, Angela—what you do is none of my business. Now, you hear this good: You try anything like that again and you'll wish to hell you hadn't."

"I won't if you won't," she pouted. "And I'm sorry I hit you with a stick. Here, help me up." She stretched out her hand. "I'm sittin' in a patch of goddamn nettles."

Ki turned and stalked off down the path through the trees.

• • •

They found a stream in a thick grove of cottonwoods. It was shallow and narrow, twenty feet wide and barely knee deep, but it was the finest sight Ki had ever seen. Angela Halley shrieked and ran headlong into the water, sat down with a laugh, and splashed the cooling liquid in her face, scooping water into her mouth until she choked. Ki drank his fill and lay back, letting the stream wash away the coated filth and the pain. He closed his eyes, basking in the pleasure. The breeze rattled pale green leaves overhead. He could feel the water loosening the crust around his burns. His shirt would come off in strips and he wondered what he'd do about that. His back wouldn't take the open sun. He'd have to cover himself with something.

He let his breath out slowly, allowing his body to sink into the water. When he surfaced again and rubbed his eyes, he saw Angela standing naked by the shore. She was ankle-deep in water, facing the other way, stretching on her toes to spread her wet dress on a branch.

Ki's mouth went dry at the sight. His eyes followed the long, slender columns of her legs past the firmly rounded bottom and the narrow curve of her waist. He was working his way back down when she turned quickly and caught him.

"Uh-huh, thought so," she said evenly. "See anything you haven't seen before?" She looked right at him and set her palms on the points of her hips.

"I'm, uh—beginning to understand a couple of things," Ki said solemnly.

"Yeah, like what?"

"Like how you get in so damn much trouble all the time."

Angela threw back her head and laughed. Yellow shafts of afternoon sun pierced the branches, patterning her skin with coins of light. Bright pearls of moisture danced on the hard tips of her breasts and jeweled the feathery nest between her legs.

"I guess that's some kinda compliment, right?" She cocked her head and raised a critical brow. "It *better* be, mister."

"Angela, it's a compliment," he assured her. "You're a very beautiful girl. That's all I was trying to say."

"And that's why I get in trouble all the time."

"Let's not get started again, all right?"

"I won't if you won't," she said firmly. "Just watch the way you talk. Shit, I've got feelings you know."

"I won't say another word."

"Good."

Ki wondered what to do next. Angela was making no effort to turn away, cover herself, or do anything other than what she was doing—standing bare and lovely not ten feet away. Her slim young body was enough to drive a man crazy. The sight of her sent a sharp surge of hunger through his loins. She was fashioned long and sleek, all lazy hollows and satiny curves. Every inch of her promised pleasure, from her taut little upturned breasts to the wanton tilt of her mouth. God, she was a riot walking around waiting to happen!

She caught his eyes and gave him an impish grin. "I bet you were hell on candy when you were a kid."

"What?" Ki gave her a puzzled look.

"I can tell," she said dryly, "by the way you're working your mouth."

Ki felt his face color. "I—Angela, I wonder if I could ask you a favor?"

"Yeah, and what'd that be?" she said warily.

"I'd do it myself if I could. I got burned pretty bad in that carcass. My shirt's still stuck in a couple of places. I don't want to pull it loose and make it any worse than it is."

"Oh God, do I have to?" Angela made a face. "I just *hate* things like that!"

"No, you don't have to do a thing."

"Oh, all right," she sighed, "sit up and turn around. Let's get it over with."

Ki turned. Angela waded to him and gingerly touched his back. He couldn't see her, but he was acutely aware of her body only inches from his own. Her hands were surprisingly gentle. She'd protested loudly enough, but now that she set to the task she went about it quickly and with skill. He could feel her working the fabric free of his burns, softly laddling water with her hands to soothe his flesh.

"That feel better?"

"A lot. Thanks. You have good hands."

"Yeah, I know."

Ki kept quiet.

"That was awful, lyin' in that—in that *thing*. I don't remember it much—except wakin' up and knowing where I was. I've never been so scared in my life!"

"Only one thing worse," Ki said soberly. "Being out instead of in."

Angela guessed his thoughts. "Look, I'm real sorry about your friend."

"So am I. He was a good man."

"I guess you did me a favor. Poking me in the jaw like that. I *damn* sure wouldn't have crawled in myself." Her fingers trembled slightly against his flesh. Ki held his breath as the tips of her breasts lightly kissed his shoulder.

"There's nothing much left of the shirt. What are you going to do?"

"Just peel it off the best you can," he told her.

"You're going to need something on," she said firmly. "Couple of those places will get infected. I cleaned 'em out as well as I could but you probably got buffalo shit and God knows what ground in. Hey, I can tear off some strips from my dress. That'll help you to—"

"Angela," Ki said suddenly, "I've got to ask you something."

"What?" As ever, he caught the wary undertone in her voice. It was always there, hidden most of the time beneath the brash, bolder Angela Halley, but it was there all the same.

"I just want to know if you've decided to trust me."

Angela hesitated. "Some, maybe. I don't know. You're all right, I guess."

"You guess. You don't know."

"Well 'course I don't know!"

He felt her hands go tense. "I'm not from Ernst Heydrich. You've got to believe that."

"I don't *have* to believe anything of the kind," she said curtly.

"Yes, you do," he said calmly. "You're going to have to decide who's with you and who's against you. Heydrich wants you and he wants that list. You've been lucky so far. I hope you're not fool enough to think that luck'll hold forever. It won't, Angela. Let Jessie have the list and we can take some of the steam out of Heydrich. Make *him* run for cover and hide. He won't have a hell of a lot of time to look for you."

"Sure sounds real good."

"I'm glad to hear you say it."

"Sounds real good if it's true."

Ki let out a breath. "Angela, it's true. Just trust me, all right?"

Angela gave a burst of nervous laughter. "Now where the hell have I heard *that* before? Look, friend—it doesn't make any difference if you're lying or if you're not. I haven't *got* any damn list. I don't know what you're talking about!"

"Angela, stop it."

She stood suddenly, walked around him in the water and faced him, slammed her hands against her hips and planted her feet boldly apart. "You see any *list,* mister? I've only got a couple places to hide it. You want to check, go ahead." Her eyes blazed with a wanton challenge. She thrust her lovely silken mound at his face, daring him to touch it, taunting him with the rich, woman-scent of her body. She let her hands slide slowly to her thighs; she stroked herself lightly with her fingers.

Ki loosed a ragged sigh between his teeth, stood, and turned toward the shore.

Angela laughed at his back. "God, what kind of a man are you, anyway?"

"A man who's got somewhere to go," he said tightly. "Get dressed and come on." He didn't look back. He could hear her loosening the dress from the branches, hear the rustle of the fabric on her skin.

"You ever had a woman?" she yelled, her voice full of scorn.

"No," Ki said calmly, "I just look at girls in creeks."

"I believe it. Maybe you're one of those sissy fellas, huh? I knew a Frenchy once in Paris—"

"Angela, shut up." he said wearily, "we've got a long way to walk. I don't think I can take the sun and you both."

"Well, don't then," she shrieked. "Just go *on,* you son of a bitch. I don't need you. I don't need a goddamn—"

"Angela, get down!" Ki blurted out the words as a man stepped from cover and raised a rifle to his shoulder. Light exploded and lead clipped bark at Ki's head. He leaped aside and scrambled for cover, crawling frantically through the trees along the shore as the rifle stitched dirt at his feet. He rolled

and came up in a crouch, ignoring the searing pain in his back. The rifle roared again and he saw the man coming right at him, stalking along the shore and firing the gun, levering one shell after another. Ki's fingers closed on a round river stone as big as his fist. In one quick motion he slammed his right foot to the ground and stepped from cover, letting the rock fly in a blur. The man flinched and instinctively brought the rifle up to his face. The rock struck metal above the trigger and drove the barrel into the gunman's face. He howled and stumbled back, jerked the rifle to his waist, and fired wildly at Ki. Ki lowered his head and closed the distance between them. The man lost his footing, levered another shell in the chamber, and fired pointblank at Ki's belly. The rifle clicked empty. Terror and surprise froze on his features. He tossed the rifle at Ki and clawed for the pistol at his belt. Ki thrust his leg out like a piston and hit the man solidly in the throat. His head snapped back and he fell limply to the ground.

Ki didn't look at the man twice. He grabbed the pistol and disappeared into the trees. Where there was one, there might easily be another. If the man had a friend, he'd heard the shots and wouldn't be sitting sucking his thumb.

When he came out of the trees he led a gray spotted mare with a black mane. Angela was staring at the man on the ground, her hand pressed flat against her breasts.

"Is he—did you kill him?"

"He's dead," said Ki. He handed Angela the reins, bent to the gunman, and started working on the buttons of his shirt.

"What—what are you going to do?" she gasped.

"I'm going to get me a shirt. He doesn't need it and I do."

"God, that's *awful!*"

"What is?"

"Wearing a dead man's clothes."

Ki turned the man over and pulled the sleeves off of his limp arms. "Girl, you've got some really funny ideas about what's awful and what isn't."

"What's that supposed to mean?"

Ki slipped on the shirt, walked to the horse, and stuck his hand in the saddlebag. "I went through his stuff back there in the trees," he told her. "Here. Guess this fella was an admirer of yours."

Angela looked puzzled. She took the small piece of cardboard from Ki, gave a short little cry, and let it fall to the ground.

"My God..." Her face was pale as chalk. "That's a—a photograph of me. Why would he have a picture of *me!*"

Ki gave her a long and sober look. "Why don't you think about that? Give you something to do." He turned and grabbed the gunman under his shoulders and started dragging him to the cover of the cottonwood trees away from the creek.

★

Chapter 13

He kept to the trees as long as he could, following the creek and letting the sun lengthen shadows to his left. He was anxious to get to the north but he knew it was foolish to try the open country again. Not until dark. It was clear, now, what Copperhead was doing. He'd led his main party out looking for the Englishman's camp—Ki didn't doubt that for a minute. But he was also sending men across the land, covering his bets on every side. Maybe the man he'd killed had found the Shoshonis and given them something to make them talk about the girl. Or maybe he'd found Green and gotten curious, then followed their tracks cross country to the creek. Ki figured they were lucky. The man was alone, and no one would miss him for a while.

"I'm getting hungry," Angela complained. "We going to ride forever or what?"

"We're going to ride until the trees run out and then we'll stop and get some sleep. When it's dark, we'll head north again."

"I'm hungry now," Angela snapped, "not sometime next week!"

"There's more of the jerky and hard bread in the saddlebag," he told her. "'Course it's dead man's food. I wouldn't eat it if I were you."

Angela muttered under her breath. In a minute he heard her rummaging around behind him. She thrust some jerky and bread up under his nose. Ki grinned to himself and took it.

"Where'd you have that photograph taken?" he asked her. "You looked real pretty. Like you were going to a ball or something."

104

"Ernst had it done," she said shortly. "He was crazy about having my picture taken. You ought to see some of them," she added wryly. "Some of 'em *without* pretty gowns or anything else. You're so fond of just looking you'd probably like them."

"Yeah, I guess maybe I would. Like you say, looking's what I do best."

"Huh!"

"What's that for?"

"Nothing. Just trying to figure you out. God, this meat tastes awful."

"Don't eat it."

"Well I can't just starve, can I?"

"I don't guess."

"Shit. You sure are fun to talk to."

Ki laughed and kicked the horse ahead along the stream.

An hour before sundown he turned up the hill and found a thicket under trees and told Angela to get down and wait, that he'd be back before it got dark. He left her the gunman's pistol, knowing it was likely a bad idea. She might get scared and shoot at shadows, or worse still, take a couple of shots at him on the way in. All he was sure about Angela was you couldn't be sure of a thing.

He rode back south, pushing the mount hard, crisscrossing the creek and up the hill and back until he was sure no one was on their trail. Finally he cut a wide loop to the west, came north again past their camp, and scouted out the land they hadn't crossed. As he'd guessed, the good cover thinned out to nothing less than three miles ahead. The country they'd cross after dark was open prairie. There'd be a moon, and the sky was clear. They could see anyone who was about—and anyone could see them too. Still it was the only game there was.

He came in easy, walking the horse, hobbling it north of the camp and coming through the trees without a sound until he could see what the girl was doing. Standing safely behind a tree, he called to her softly.

"It's me, Angela. I'm coming in."

Angela let out a squeal, jerked around, and pointed the pistol into the dark.

"Will you put that down please?"

She lowered the gun with a sigh. "You don't have to scare me to death," she snapped.

"No, I could come in stomping down the hill and get my head shot off." He reached out and took the Colt and stuck it in his belt.

"You don't trust me any, do you?"

"Nothing I trust more than a woman who whacks me 'cross the back with a log."

"It wasn't a log; it was a stick. An old rotten stick."

"Yeah, right. I forgot." He tossed her the blanket from the gunman's bedroll. "You'll need that. It'll get a little cool and we can't risk starting a fire."

"What are you going to do?"

"I've got his slicker. I'll lay on that. Doesn't make much difference, I sure can't sleep on my back."

"Oh, yeah." She bit her lip in sudden concern. "Does it hurt a whole lot?"

"It hurts a whole lot."

"You want me to pour some water on it or something?"

"Thanks. I mostly want to leave it alone. It'll be a lot better tomorrow." He watched her curl up in the blanket, her hair dry and clean now and tumbling like gold over her shoulders. "It's about eight, I guess. We'll get some sleep and ride out maybe ten or eleven. It isn't much rest but it'll help."

"You think the man Ernst sent after me, this Copperhead—you think he'll head up to Montgomery's camp?"

"I know he will. That's where you're supposed to be."

"Uh-huh." Angela hesitated a moment, then turned to face him, resting her chin in her hands. "Then if you're so all-fired anxious to *help* me, like you keep telling me you are—why the hell are you taking me right straight where those bastards can find me?"

"Fair enough question," Ki nodded. "First, I can't take care of you forever out here. If there'd been more than one of those fellas back at the creek, that whole business might have ended up different. If we try to get back to Miles City or up to the Missouri, someone's going to spot us. Especially riding double. That's why we're going where we're going. Montgomery's got a lot of men. Besides I'll leave you somewhere while I go in— talk to Jessie and see if everything's all right."

106

Angela gave him a cautious nod of approval. "You've thought it all out, haven't you?"

"As well as I can, yes."

"Great." Angela shook her head and turned away. "Now all you've got to do is make it work."

Ki felt the color rise to his face. "Damn it all," he snapped, "you got a better way to save your hide, you let me know. You haven't done all that well so far!"

"I was doing just fine."

"Oh, sure you were. You did everything but put up signs: This way to Angela Halley."

Angela pulled the blankets about her shoulders. "I'm doing *real* good now, though." she said sweetly. "Since I met you, I've hid out inside a damn buffalo and like to got burned to death in a fire. Oh, yeah—and nearly got shot in a creek."

"No one shot at you," Ki reminded her. "It was me they were shooting at, case you forgot."

"I'm tired of talking now," she yawned.

"I'm sure pleased to hear that."

Angela didn't answer. In a moment he heard the slow and easy breathing that told him she was asleep. *Well, why not?* he thought irritably. *The girl doesn't have a care in the world.*

When he turned on his back he woke quickly, jerking up from the sudden pain. He closed his eyes and let the breath pass slowly through his teeth. The night breeze helped, and in a moment the white-hot wires in his back eased to a dull and throbbing ache. The wounds worried him more than a little. He could work his hand close enough to tell him that his flesh was hot and swollen. An infection that wasn't treated quickly could lead to blood poisoning—and blood poisoning could kill a man fast. If he didn't get some help . . .

It might make sense to risk a fire, heat up some water, and let Angela try to draw out the infection with hot cloths. No, he decided, not now. Not until he got her back safely. A few more hours wouldn't change things all that much. First, get Angela in safe hands. Maybe she'd talk to Jessie, tell her about the list.

Ki shook his head in irritation. He was convinced, now, she didn't have it with her. He'd checked her shoes when she'd made a trip to the bushes, looking carefully to see if she'd stitched something into the leather. No, she'd stashed the list somewhere else. Somewhere between Chicago and Kansas City and Denver, Deadwood and Miles City and the prairie. Just half the country. That narrowed it down a lot.

He eased himself down on his side, looking up at a sky full of stars. He guessed it was nine, maybe later. A couple of hours sleep and the rest would help his back. He heard the girl sit up, heard the blanket rustle against the grass. When he turned she was sitting up watching him through a veil of tousled hair.

"You all right?" she asked sleepily.

"I just woke up is all."

"Your back's hurting," she said firmly. "That's what I thought."

"It'll be all right."

Angela didn't answer. Instead she tossed the blanket aside and came to him, easing herself down and crossing her legs on the edge of his slicker. She wore a thin cotton chemise and nothing more. The flesh of her shoulders and legs was a pale, dusky ivory against the dark. She touched his back gently, her fingers soothing and cool against his skin.

"Uh-uh. That's not good. You feel a fever or anything?"

"No, not yet."

"You will if you don't do something for it."

"I'll make it till we get where we're going."

"You're going to be a big brave man, right?" she said scornfully.

"Right. Unless it hurts too bad. Then I'm going to scream and have a fit."

Angela grinned. "Women can take a lot more pain than a man. They have babies."

"Say, I heard about that."

"Don't be funny."

"Okay. And you're right. I expect that hurts more than my back."

"Yeah, well, since you aren't real likely to have a baby, I guess your sore back'll have to do."

Without warning she turned her head to one side and kissed him softly on the mouth. It was a long, lingering kiss, all the

108

more sensuous and delightful because her lips scarcely touched him. When she was through she leaned back and gave him an impish grin. "Surprised you, right?"

Ki had to laugh. "I didn't even think we *liked* each other, Angela."

"Who said we did?" She closed her eyes and came to him again, touching his cheeks lightly with her hands. Ki relished the scent of flesh, the clean smell of her hair. Her lips were soft and warm, alive with hunger and excitement. He explored each moist and secret hollow of her mouth. She met his tongue with her own; the rapid little thrusts were a bold imitation of a man entering a woman. Ki let his lips trail the column of her neck to the cleft between her breasts. Angela gave a quick little sigh, brought her shoulders together, and let the straps of her chemise slip down her arms. Ki slid his hands down her throat over the curve of her breasts. Hard little nipples sprang up to meet his touch. The tight, pouty tips seemed to swell under his gaze. He cupped the firm and lovely mounds in his palms, kneading them gently as he rubbed the taut nubs with his thumbs.

"Oh, yeah," Angela sighed. She closed her eyes and rolled her head in a lazy circle. "I reckon I was wrong. You *have* had a woman before. Maybe even *more* than one."

"I swear," Ki said soberly, "you're the first. I'll just do the best I can."

Angela laughed, reached down, and slipped her hands under his. Squeezing her breasts together, she stroked the nipples between her fingers. "In that case, I'll try to help you out. Just bend your head a little and put one of these in your mouth. These hard little tits of mine are just achin' for a kiss!"

"In my mouth, huh? That's the way you do it?"

"Yes," she said gently, "that's the way you do it. Think you can remember that? You just—*Ahhh*, God, you've got it, all right!"

Ki drew her breast firmly into his mouth, letting the pliant flesh slip moistly between his lips. The musky taste assailed his senses and swelled his already rigid member as hard as iron.

"I think we're going to be friends after all," Angela whispered. "Damned if we're not!"

Ki grasped the narrow curve of her waist and lowered her

gently to the ground. She pressed her body against him, sighing with the pleasure of his touch. Her breasts were hot points of fire against his hands. She reached down and slipped the thin chemise over her hips, baring her body to his eyes. Ki sat back and quickly peeled off his trousers. She spread her legs wide to welcome him in, arching her back to thrust her treasure up to meet him. Her hands snaked past his belly to seize his erection. She circled his shaft firmly, kneading the swollen tip against her flesh. She carressed him with the moist folds of her pleasure, grinding her silken mound against his member.

Ki drank in the beauty of her body, the haunting, wanton swell of her belly, the lean flanks of her thighs. Under the pale moon, her flesh seemed to throb with a light of its own. Her eyes caught the diamond points of the stars; she watched him intently as she stroked herself languidly with his shaft. Once more he took her breasts between his lips, drawing the swollen nipples into his mouth. Angela cried out, jerked her firm mound up to meet him and thrust his rigid shaft into her body. Her hands found his back, then quickly drew away, remembering the pain that was there.

Angela stroked him with her flesh, drawing him deeply within her, then softly releasing her hold. She moved her pelvis in a slow and lazy circle. The downy nest teased him, urged him to find release, to spill himself inside her.

Ki sucked in a breath and held it. Suddenly he realized he was losing all control. The girl was unbelievable, a master of the higher arts of love. She could do whatever she liked with the moist little petals between her legs, the velvety muscles of her thighs. The silken wall around his member was a honeyed mouth, a stroking tongue. He fought to hold her off, to make the pleasure last. Angela laughed with delight at his efforts. Ki gave up and laughed with her, pounding her relentlessly, slamming himself against her again and again. Angela bared her teeth, gripped her own breasts, and squeezed them in a quick frantic motion.

Ki felt the fires race through his loins, a churning heat so intense Angela gasped as each new spasm entered her body. For an instant their mingled pain and pleasure was too much to bear. Angela gave a hoarse cry of release, matching Ki's deeper bellow of delight. Her body trembled against him an-

110

other moment, then she gave a final cry and collapsed in his arms.

Ki bent to kiss her, the sweat of their bodies a delicious sensation between them.

"I guess I like you a little," she grinned. "Hell, I'm real sure I do."

"I kinda thought you did." Ki shook his head in wonder. "Lady, you are some kind of woman. You could drive a man crazy with tricks like that."

"You're not so bad yourself," she said, bringing her mouth hungrily against his own. "Especially for your very first time with a girl."

Ki laughed. "Just trying to learn the best I can."

Angela gazed solemnly into his eyes. "Mister," she said without expression, "you were *born* knowing how to make love like that. It's one way you and me are just the same."

He slept an hour longer than he'd planned, waking to find Angela's slender form tucked neatly against his chest. She moaned and protested, then followed him naked down to the creek. Ki sank in up to his neck, the cool water bringing him relief. Angela muttered about the cold, poked a slender foot in the water, and jerked it back. Finally she lowered herself quickly below the surface, gasped for breath, and ran up the hill to find her dress. Ki watched her slim white figure disappear, the sight of her bringing new pleasure to his loins.

The stars told him it was well after one in the morning when they left the cover of the trees and started northeast over the prairie. Almost at once Angela started complaining again. The jerky had gone bad and the biscuits were too hard to chew. The water from the creek tasted funny. She was cold, wanted fresh clothes and a decent breakfast. It was clear as glass to Ki that the only way to keep the girl happy was to throw her on the ground and spread her legs. It wasn't the worst job a man could have, but even the best lover in the world would have to stop now and then for a rest. And when he did, Ki was certain, Angela would be on him in a minute, telling him what he wasn't doing right.

"I don't think you know *where* you're going," she said darkly. "I think you're plain lost is what I think."

"I'm not lost," Ki said patiently. "They'll be where we're riding, Angela. Northeast or thereabouts, where the head of the herd was going."

"Huh! *Thereabouts*. That could mean anything!"

"It could but it doesn't," said Ki. She went blessedly silent at his back, eating the uneatable jerky, and drinking the bad water. He guessed it was getting on five or six in the morning. The land to the east was growing perceptibly brighter. The idea of morning made him nervous. Somehow he'd hoped they'd find the camp before light. They'd covered a good many miles in the dark, following the unmistakable path of the herd, the burned-out land that still smelled of fire.

Where the hell was Jessie, the camp? The Missouri wasn't far; it couldn't be more than a good hour. Ki urged his mount forward, one wary eye on the pale strip of sky. In a moment the sun would rise over the Great Plains; they'd be exposed, vulnerable, out in the flats with no place to hide. And when the harsh light of day started heating up his back . . . He hadn't told the girl, but his wounds were getting worse by the moment. His flesh was throbbing with heat, spreading down his back and into his arms. His throat was bone dry, and he could feel the hot surge of fever in his head. If he didn't get help, didn't find the camp soon . . .

"You all right?" she asked. "Hey, you're not, are you?"

"No, I'm not real good," he admitted. "I feel like hell, Angela."

"Maybe we ought to stop or something. Give you a chance to rest."

"What I'd better do," he sighed, "is try to sit this horse until we get to where we're going."

"Till you fall on your face, you mean."

"Angela—"

"All right, I'm *sorry*. It's just that it doesn't *look* like we're getting anywhere at all, you know? You're getting sicker every mile and the sun's coming up and—Christ, what's *that?*"

"Huh?" Ki pulled himself straight in the saddle and shook the cobwebs out of his head. "What, Angela—what is it?"

"There," she pointed, "where the light's starting to show. It's either buffalo or cattle or something else."

"Oh my God..!" Ki groaned as his eyes swam into focus.

112

The hair rose up on the back of his neck and he jerked the horse to a halt. "Get down," he snapped, "fast!"

Angela obeyed and Ki slid to the earth, kicking and cursing as he forced the horse to its kees. The mount protested, but finally let Ki take it to the ground and roll on its side. He pulled Angela to him, pressing her flat against the prairie, holding the horse's head and trying to gentle it with his hands.

"It's not buffalo, right?" Angela said shakily.

"No. It's Copperhead. Got to be. Twenty or thirty riders." A cold, helpless rage caught in his throat. The men would pass right by and the sky was growing brighter every minute. They'd have to all go blind to miss them lying out in the open on the black, burned stubble of the prairie.

Chapter 14

Aaron Heller rode hard down the hill toward the point of the herd. Jessie followed, glancing back at the ominous gray mass rising swiftly to the south. The sight had changed drastically in only a few short minutes. Now there was no mistaking it for a ragged bank of clouds. Even from a distance it was clear that a terrible, awesome force was approaching, a force that would consume anything that dared stand in its way.

Jessie caught up with Aaron as he pulled his mount to a halt in a shallow ravine. A dozen men stood about, shading their eyes against the sun, watching the cloud to the south. Past them, a thousand yards to the west, Jessie saw a puff of smoke appear against the dark line of the herd. An instant later, the harsh boom of a Sharps reached her ears.

Aaron frowned at the hunters and nodded to the west. "Anyone ridden out to tell him? You just goin' to sit there?"

A man with a grizzled beard looked up at Heller. "Figure the man's got eyes. Ain't all that hard to spot. Even for a English fella."

The other men laughed. Heller's expression didn't change. "Who's out with him?"

"Lansdale and Shiner's with him at the stand," the man answered. "Howard and ol' Chad's thereabouts."

Heller looked annoyed. "They all got sense enough to leave. What the hell's keeping them?"

A gaunt man in greasy leather spat tobacco on the ground. "Aaron, the son of a bitch ain't all that easy to talk to. What I figure is, they told him what's coming and he told *them* any man wants to run can pick up his pay. There's a quarter million buffalo in that herd, and the Englishman don't figure on missin' more than two."

"Shit." Aaron gave the man a withering look. "Well, *I* don't work for him." He yanked his horse around toward the west.

"Lansdale and them others'll get him out."

"I been huntin' with Lansdale before," Heller said shortly. He turned and rode off toward the herd. Jessie brought her mount up beside him.

"Why don't you stay here?" he asked.

"Why would I want to do that?"

Heller didn't answer. "That old man's right. I ought to mind my own business."

"Why don't you, then?"

"'Cause I've got no patience with fools," Heller said. He glanced meaningfully at Jessie. "I got caught in one of these things once. Don't let it put you off 'cause it's way the hell south right now."

"I hope Ki's not anywhere near it," Jessie said.

Heller laughed. "Odell Green's not as dumb as Lord Fancypants. I don't figure Ki is either."

Montgomery had chosen a slight, brushy rise for his stand, some two hundred yards from the herd. Two of his men were crouched beside him, while two more sat idly by in the grass. The Englishman was using three guns, each gun mounted with a telescopic sight. One gun cooled while the hunters with Montgomery kept busy reloading the other pair. The ground was covered with empty brass shell casings. Montgomery stood, swiveling his rifle in the crook of a Y-shaped rest.

Heller eyed the sight with open disgust, knowing Montgomery's rifle was made to load and fire eight times a minute. The gun would throw lead for five miles. No one ever shot that fast or that far—one or two times a minute at a decent range was good enough. With the hunters handing the Englishman fresh rifles, he was getting off four, maybe five shots a minute. He was an excellent shot, Heller knew—but what he was doing now was no test of an expert's skill. With telescopic sights at two hundred yards, killing wasn't any big challenge. A buffalo had a keen sense of smell but its weak, tiny eyes weren't worth a damn. It didn't understand the sound of a bullet; it'd jump a little maybe and shy off, then settle down again. As long as a hunter kept well into the wind, shot quietly and carefully, dropping every buffalo that started to wander away, the others would cluster around eating grass, wandering through an ever-growing pile of their own dead.

The killing didn't bother Aaron Heller; hunting was the way he made his living. But Montgomery wasn't shooting for money. He didn't give a damn whether his skinners got the hides or let them rot. He was killing for the numbers, to see how many he could get. He could crow about a record shoot over whiskey at his club. That angered Heller, it made no sense to him at all.

As Jessie and Aaron approached, one of the hunters half stood and francially waved them off. Heller ignored him, slid out of the saddle, handed his reins to Jessie, then walked off up to the stand.

The Englishman turned, his rifle clutched in his hands, and stared in disbelief. "Damn you," he snapped, "get off my shoot, you bloody fool!"

"One of us is, all right," said Heller. "Don't guess it's me." He looked at the muzzle. "Point that somewhere else," he said tightly. "Right now, mister."

Montgomery's face turned scarlet. He lowered the weapon and glared at Heller. "I know about the damned fire. Is that what this is about?"

"Uh-huh, that's it."

"Fine. You've done your duty. Now get out of here, please."

Heller looked at the hunters; the other pair had now drifted up curiously from the brush. "You know better," he said evenly. "What are you sticking around here for?"

One of the men looked narrowly at Heller. "Man wants to shoot a few buffalo, Aaron. I reckon we can handle it without you."

Aaron showed him a wicked grin. "Well hell, Lansdale— if you're runnin' this show I'm not worried about a thing."

The man's fists doubled at his sides. Aaron nodded to Montgomery. "Good luck. Been nice talking to you." He turned, walked back to his horse, and mounted. An old hunter with silver hair followed him from the stand.

"Aaron, I'd be obliged if you'd give me a ride back," he said soberly.

"There's a man makes sense," said Aaron. "Climb on up, Chad."

"You leave and you can forget about your pay," the Englishman raged. "Do you *hear* me, fellow!"

"Can't spend wages in hell," Chad told him. "Sorry, mister."

Montgomery cursed his back. Heller turned and kicked his mount off to the east. "Waste of goddamn time," he said darkly.

"I guess," Jessie sighed. She glanced to the south again. The gray cloud was rising rapidly into the sky.

She stood beside Aaron with the rest of the hunters. Heller glanced at the herd without blinking.

"You never seen it before, doesn't look like anything at all," he told her. "That's what Montgomery's thinking now—that the fire's maybe fifteen, twenty miles off and he's got all the time in the world. The other fellows, now, they haven't seen it before they sure as hell know someone who has. There— look!" He raised his hand suddenly and swept it to the south. A huge, irregular mass appeared in the sky, black, inky fingers etched against the rising smoke. As the mass grew closer it spread, separating now into countless thousands of birds fleeing the fire.

"My God . . ." Jessie said under her breath.

"He better git his ass out now," one of the men muttered beside her.

"If I was you I'd get some horses moving, friend," Aaron suggested.

The man nodded and walked off down the draw.

Jessie knew what was coming. She caught herself holding her breath, remembering a moment with her father, five or six years before. They were driving a herd of longhorns north to market over the Goodnight Trail. The world had stood still and held its breath, then exploded in a fury without warning. That was the thing Heller knew, the thing Montgomery didn't understand. The fire was maybe a good hour away, but the danger was only minutes, maybe seconds down the valley. The moment the fire had started, fear began to ripple through the herd. It would move like lightning from the south, faster than a person who'd never seen it could imagine. When it reached the dark mass to the west, the lazy, slow-moving beasts would suddenly bolt, move in the blink of an eye, turn as one creature in a mindless stampede that would destroy everything in its path. When it happened, if Montgomery and the others were still there . . .

"Jessie, listen—" Aaron gripped her arm so hard she winced. She heard it, then, a sound like rolling thunder. Squinting into the west, she saw four tiny figures running toward them, about a thousand yards across the prairie. The man with a string of horses raced to meet them.

Jessie caught her breath. "It's going to be close, Aaron—close!"

"They'll make it." He grinned from ear to ear. "Goddamn, that English fella sure can run."

The thunder grew to a sound that shook the earth. Movement rippled through the herd as if some giant wind had bent the shaggy backs. The buffalo bolted in a panic, one cresting wave to the north, another in a dense black line to the east. The hunter with the horses finally reached the fleeing figures. The men left dusty clouds in their wake, racing for the safety of the high, eroded bluff. Jessie, Aaron, and the others were already there.

Three men made it—Montgomery and two of the hunters. The fourth, Lansdale, jerked his horse in the wrong direction twenty yards from the top of the bluff. The horse spilled him from the saddle and galloped wild-eyed up the hill. Lansdale tumbled to the bottom, caught himself, and broke into a run, bounding up the steep grade like a squirrel. At the top he kept going and wouldn't stop. Two men caught him and pulled him down. Heller laughed until his belly started to hurt.

Below the dark tide of fury reached the bluff, scraped reddish-black hides against the wall, and thundered away. The seething mass followed the furrows of the land, finally swerving back to the north.

Lord Montgomery ordered his men to break camp and move north at once after the herd. The fire, he reasoned, would burn itself out at the Missouri, only a few miles away. The buffalo would then turn east or west or find some spot to cross the

118

river. Whatever they did, he'd pick up the trail and resume the hunt.

The hunters nodded without comment and went about their business. Only one told the Englishman the truth, that the fire might indeed cross the river. With a strong enough wind filling the air with bright sparks and burning brush, the firestorm could spread its awesome fury for hundreds of miles in any direction. And even if it didn't, if it burned itself out and the herd turned away or crossed water, they likely wouldn't stop running for days. It was possible they could follow the panicked herd clear to Canada before it settled down again.

The hunter had failed to measure the Englishman's fury. Montgomery seethed with anger. Every man in camp had watched him running like a fool before the herd. He cursed the hunter soundly and sent him packing without a dollar of his pay.

The party moved north, watching the fire rage to the west. Throughout the afternoon smoke blackened the sky and shut out the sun. Aaron told Jessie there was no use starting after Ki and Odell, not across the burned out land. They'd wait until dark and leave then.

Jessie couldn't argue. Looking for Ki would be hopeless on the devastated prairie. Wherever he was, he certainly wouldn't be out there.

"I don't know Ki," said Aaron, "but I know Odell like a book. He'll know what the herd's going to do, and he'll figure we're heading north. If I was him, I'd go to the river and turn back east, thinking I'd sure run into someone along the line, or close to it."

"You think so? Really?" Aaron's words were reassuring; Jessie felt more hopeful than she had in days. "Lord, I'm ready to go—I may be crazy, but I don't feel all that protected in this place anymore. I sure don't trust our host. If Copperhead did show up, Montgomery's just as likely to ask him to tea as he is to run him off."

Aaron grinned. "My feelings exactly." His smile faded a moment. "You know we could miss 'em, Jessie. Ki and Odell. We could take off and go looking and they could show up here."

119

"No," Jessie said firmly, "it's not going to happen that way."

"'Cause you don't want it to, right?"

Jessie shot him a challenging look. "Yes, that's it exactly. Because I don't want it to. I want to get out of here, Aaron, and I want to find Ki."

It was nearly dark when they reached the Missouri and made camp. The land along this stretch of the river was mostly badlands and deep canyons. The herd, they learned from two lone hunters, had turned abruptly west along the banks, heading back for the Musselshell River and points beyond. The news didn't please Montgomery at all. Still he was determined to have his way. If that's where the beasts were headed, then that's where he would follow.

"Shit," one of the hunters confided to Aaron, "those buffalo could be clear to the Judith River—or maybe they found some shallows across the Missouri and ran on up past the Bear Paws. We got more chance of findin' another herd *behind* us than ahead. Back down to the Big Dry and the Yellowstone."

"You're right as rain," said Aaron. "You ought to pass on this enlightenin' information to your boss. I expect he'd appreciate the help."

"Uh-uh." The man shot Heller a dark look. "I'll keep my big mouth shut is what I'll do. Damn fool pays better wages than I can make chasin' skins. Reckon I can stand the irritation."

Jessie watched the river with Aaron as the night set in. The lights of a sternwheeler passed, the boat low in the water and heavy with hides. It was moving downriver from Fort Benton to the west, starting the long trip south. At one time, the thirty-five days from Fort Benton to St. Louis were the fast, safe way to get to Montana. Now, Jessie knew, she was likely seeing some of the sternwheelers' last days. The railroad had already crossed into the territory south and was poised on the border to the east. Next year traffic on the river would begin to die fast.

The long day had drained her, and when they walked back from the river Jessie left Aaron and carried her blanket to the far edge of the camp, determined to get an hour or so of sleep.

Aaron promised he'd call her when he and C.L. and Bobby got packed and ready to go.

Jessie was certain she was doing the right thing. She wasn't all that worried about Ki—just eager. As Aaron kept saying, *they* were the ones likely sitting in the middle of trouble—right where Copperhead was certain to look. Getting away from Montgomery was reason enough to take off. The man was totally unpleasant, a tyrant and a big spoiled child. Lord, the way he treated his men! He knew they'd put up with nearly anything he wanted. Aaron said he was paying close to triple wages for the job. A man could swallow a lot for that.

Sleep was just beginning to overtake her when she heard heavy footsteps moving toward her through the grass. Jessie closed her eyes and made a face.

"I just *got* here," she moaned. "Go away, Aaron. Give me a couple more minutes, all right?" The footsteps stopped. Aaron didn't answer. "All right," Jessie sighed, tossing the blanket aside, "you win, I'm coming. Wouldn't hurt you any to—*hey, stop that, damn it!*"

She flailed with her fists as he grabbed the folds of the blanket and wrapped it tightly about her head, pinning her arms to her sides. Flopping her rudely on her stomach, he slipped a cord tightly around her waist, then lifted her off the ground. Jessie kicked out with her legs and tried to jerk herself free. She cursed him soundly but the blanket muffled her cries.

"Damn you, Aaron," she screamed, "this isn't funny anymore. Put me down or you're going to wish to hell you had!"

She could hear him laughing deeply to himself. Jessie kicked out again in a fury. What did he think he was doing? Had he lost his mind or what? It struck her, then, that he wasn't joking at all—he had something else in mind and this was the way he figured to get it done. If that was it she'd kill him. Of all the fool—

"*Uhh!*" She gasped for breath, shaken, as he dropped her roughly to the ground. His hand found her throat and cut off her cries. The awful sound of a sharp blade ripping fabric reached her ears. Cool air hit her face once more.

"There," he whispered close to her head, "you're a bloody fine looking woman, but I don't think we need any talking, now do we?"

Jessie stared up in horror. *Montgomery!* His lips were close to her face; she smelled the foul odor of whiskey on his breath, saw clearly in his eyes that the drink had done its work.

"Just lie back and enjoy it, love," he said gently. "You've been wanting me to take you from the start, you can't deny that. By God, you're going to get your wish now!"

Chapter 15

The sharp blade gleamed in Montgomery's hand. Jessie felt it slice the blanket away, leaving only the strip beneath the cord that bound her hands to her sides. He straddled her just below her thighs, making her legs useless.

"Now you're going to have to help," he told her calmly. "You keep squirming about it's going to be a bit of trouble getting you out of those trousers."

Jessie shouted through her gag and tried to pull her head off the ground. Without warning the Englishman slapped her hard. Jessie felt her ears ring. The blow stunned her for a moment; the pain numbed her cheek and her jaw. Montgomery slipped the tip of his blade in the V of her shirt and deftly ripped it to her waist. He laid the knife aside and tore the rest of the garment away, then cupped her breasts roughly in his hands.

Jessie went stiff as his fingers caressed her flesh. He tweaked her nipples and chuckled to himself, then bent to take the pliant buds between his lips. He moaned in delight, crooning like a child, rubbing his bearded face across her breasts. Jessie's flesh crawled. She struggled to free her hands; the more she moved the more the cords cut harshly into her skin. Montgomery eased himself back down her body, resting heavily on her knees. Jessie felt his fingers working frantically at her belt. She heard him laugh as he found the little ivory-handled derringer nestled behind her buckle.

"Charming toy you have here," he said, "charming!" Jessie gasped as he pressed the twin barrels against her belly, then slid the weapon teasingly over her flesh. He tossed the gun aside, clutched the waist of her denims, and tore the buttons away.

"Ah, yes, *yes!*" he said softly. Jessie saw the flesh go taut around his mouth, saw the joy of anticipation in his eyes. His fingers slipped under the cloth, slid to the curve of her hips, and tugged the trousers past her thighs. His hands caressed the slight swell of her belly, touched the downy nest between her legs. His fingers trembled and his eyes went wide. Jessie heard the cry catch in his throat and then the shadow came down swiftly without warning and lifted him off the ground. Montgomery bellowed in surprise as he struck the earth. He came to his knees and Aaron kicked him in the ribs. The Englishman retched whiskey and fell on his face. He tried to crawl off and Aaron kicked him savagely again.

"You even breathe, you son of a bitch," he warned, "I'll kill you right here!" He leaned over Jessie, concern in his dark eyes. "You all right?" He stared at her ruined clothing, the bare flesh of her body. "My God, Jessie!" He loosened the gag and cut her bonds. Jessie drew in a breath.

"I'm scared clean out of my wits, Aaron. Other than that I'm just fine." She laughed, without knowing it was coming, a high, nervous little sound on the edge of fear. "Nice night, don't you think? Plenty of stars out and—"

"Quiet," he told her gently. He stripped the warm leather jacket off his arms and draped it over her shoulders. "Should've known that fool'd maybe get around to you. Been drinking hard all evening, giving everybody hell. Come on, let me help you up."

"Thanks, I'll—*God, Aaron!*"

The gun exploded with a burst of light and sound. Heller cried out in pain and threw Jessie roughly aside. Montgomery came at him, Jessie's derringer trembling in his hand. Aaron hit him hard, driving him back on his heels. The second load exploded in the air. Aaron straddled the Englishman's chest and pounded him in the face. Montgomery shrieked like a cat, clawing desperately at Heller to fend off the blows. Aaron swept his arms aside. His fists cut the Englishman's face to ribbons. The bones in his nose snapped and blood ran down his chin.

"Aaron, don't!" Jessie yelled, "You'll kill him!"

Aaron didn't hear. Men from the camp came out of the dark,

lanterns lighting the night. Three men tore Aaron to the ground, fists still flailing the air.

"Jesus God," a man breathed, lowering a light to Montgomery's face, "get him out of here. See what you can do." The hunter looked at Jessie, saw the torn shreds of her shirt, the jacket held tightly about her shoulders. No one had to tell him what had happened. The men let Aaron go. He sat back and held the point of his shoulder. Blood ran down his arm over his chest.

"I know you're fixing to leave," the man told Aaron. "I'd go ahead and do it, I was you. Soon as you get that arm fixed up." He nodded over his shoulder. "There's a couple of sorry bastards in this crew might figure on making a little bonus when that Englishman comes around."

Aaron's eyes blazed with anger. "You *tell* those sorry bastards I'll be down at the river if they want to find me!"

"I'm just sayin' what is," the man shrugged.

"You said it," a voice spoke from the dark. "Now git."

Jessie looked over her shoulder and saw C.L. and Bobby.

"Get the horses and wait east of the camp," Aaron told them. "I got to clean up some."

"You all right?"

"I will be. Just go on."

The two men disappeared. Jessie went to Aaron carrying the strips of her shirt. She saw the derringer on the ground and stuck it in her belt.

"Glad you weren't carrying something bigger," Heller grinned weakly.

"I'm glad that bastard isn't as good with a pistol as he is with a rifle." She helped him to his feet and picked up one of the lanterns the men had left. "Come on, you're bleeding like a pig. I've got to do something about that."

Heller didn't argue. He let her wrap his belt tightly around his arm and then followed her down to the river. She helped him over the steep bank to the shore and hung the lantern on a branch of a dead tree. Pulling his shirt gently aside, she saw the slug had gone through the fleshy part of his arm, just below the shoulder. The lead was still visible under the skin, trying to force itself out.

"It's not too bad," she said, "could've been worse. Here, give me your knife."

"What for," he said narrowly, "you a doctor or something?"

"Come on," Jessie grinned, "give it here." She took the knife and lit a dry stick from the lantern and cleaned the blade. He flinched as she deftly punctured his flesh and let the bullet fall to the ground. "Here," she said, handing him the lead, "you can keep this to remember me by."

"I can remember you just fine," he said shortly and tossed the lead toward the water.

She went to the shore and soaked a piece of her shirt. When she returned Aaron reached into the pocket of the jacket he'd loaned her and pulled out a small bottle of brandy. "Here," he said, "pour some of this on it 'fore you bind it."

"Where'd you get this?"

"Out of my pack. Been carrying it around awhile. I was coming to find you and offer you a wake-up drink. Found you already had an engagement."

"That's not even funny."

"Don't use all that up. It'll do us a lot more good inside than out." He took the bottle from her, downed a healthy slug, and offered it to her. Jessie decided this was one of those times when she could definitely use a drink. She brought the bottle to her lips and made a face.

"God, Aaron, that's awful!"

"I know. But it's cheap."

"I'd never have guessed."

He glanced at his shoulder and worked his arm. "You're not too bad a doctor. That ought to do just fine."

"It'll likely stiffen."

"Well, if it does, it does."

"I didn't thank you, did I?"

"You don't have to. Not for that."

"All right. I *want* to, then. I'm grateful, Aaron. I'm glad you happened by."

Heller shrugged off her thanks. "Looks like leaving this place is turning out to be a good idea."

Jessie shuddered and hugged her arms. "I guess I'm surprised—and not surprised, either. He hits that bottle pretty hard."

"Isn't any surprise to me," Aaron said darkly. "Hell, he's had his sights on you since we rode in. Probably figured he was doing you a favor. The son of a bitch is used to getting his way."

"I thought you were going to kill him," she said evenly.

"Wouldn't have been any big loss." He pulled himself erect, his features tightening in sudden pain.

"Hey, take it easy." Jessie grasped his hand and pulled him gently down again. "We can hold off a minute longer. Bobby and C.L. will wait."

"Didn't figure it'd hurt this much," Aaron grumbled. "Must be the poor doctorin' I got."

"Yes, that's it," Jessie grinned. She leaned back and studied the dark waters of the Missouri. "Aaron, there's something I want to tell you. Something I feel you ought to know. You've been real patient and I appreciate that."

"Jessie, you don't have to tell me more of your business than you want."

"I do want to, though," she said firmly. "You've put yourself on the line for me more than once. You're getting ready to do it again and I think you deserve some answers." She told him, then, about Angela Halley and Ernst Heydrich—why Angela was running and why it was so important to find her. She told him about the Prussian business cartel, and how she and Ki had faced them more than once. Finally she told him the story of how they'd murdered both her mother and her father.

Heller listened without expression until she was finished. He looked thoughtfully at the ground a long moment, then shook his head in wonder. "By God, lady, you've bitten off a fair-sized piece of trouble, looks to me."

"I didn't bite it," she said ruefully. "*It* bit me."

"Yeah, but you could've walked away and let it be."

"No, I don't think I could have done that, Aaron. Lord, there's nothing I'd like better, believe me. But I can't. Not until it's over. And finding Angela, getting that list, it could be a big step in setting the cartel back on its heels. They've spent *years* getting their agents into high places. Years, and a small fortune. There's no way to guess how many lives have been ruined, how many have died so the people the cartel own could move up another rung on the ladder. With that list in our hands they'll have to start over from the bottom. And this time, I think, we'd make it a lot harder for them ever to get to the top again. It hasn't been easy, but I've managed to convince some folks who count that the cartel is *real*. Not many, but some."

"We'll get the girl," Aaron said firmly, "and that goddamn list." His eyes narrowed and he stared out over the water. "Ki and Odell will try to come back along the Missouri. It's the surest way of running us down. After that, I can get us good and lost—west and south to the Little Belt Mountains and the Big. Cross the Missouri again and trail along the Divide. Won't anyone be able to follow where I'll go. We can keep you out of trouble till you get the girl safe. Then—"

"Aaron . . ." Jessie gently laid a hand on his chest, leaned in, and kissed him lightly on the cheek.

Heller blinked, looked startled then pleased. "Damn, tell me what I said. I want to say it again."

"You got it for being you. Taking on my troubles and listening to me tell you what's wrong with huntin' buffalo."

Heller gave her a wary look. "Now don't tell me you're going to stop doing that."

"'Course I'm not going to stop. I'm right and you're wrong. And I have my pride to think of, friend. I've *got* to bring you around to my way of thinking."

"You were off to a good start there, you know."

"What?"

"That little peck on the cheek just then. It got me to thinking, Jessie. If we were to get into that a little *further* now, why I might promise to give up huntin' all together."

"Aaron!" Jessie tried to look appalled. "Why, that's shameless. It's bribery is what it is."

"I'm just a buffalo hunter. Shows you how much I need help."

"What *you* need," Jessie said firmly, "is to quit sitting by the river watching the moon. I don't think that's good for a man in your condition at all. Come on." She stood and put a hand under his shoulder. "I expect C.L. and Bobby are ready to go and then some."

"Make a wounded man get on a horse," Aaron complained. "That's sure going to make me feel better."

"Stop complaining. A little ride'll take the kinks out of your arm."

"Don't know whether I'd rather have a doctor that knows his business, or a pretty one doesn't know a damn thing. It's a—" Heller stopped abruptly. His eyes darted quickly across the night.

"Aaron, what is it? What's wrong?"

"I don't know. Something. Bird took off real fast across the water. Frogs stopped talkin' all of a sudden. Jessie, douse that lantern—come on, do it now!" Jessie moved away from him and turned out the lamp. "Just back up slow," he said calmly, "let's walk real quiet down to the shore."

"Aaron—"

"Just stay close and do what I say, all right?" He moved back to the shore, Jessie at his side. He held the pistol in his good hand, the barrel sweeping the dark. The sound came quickly, suddenly, across the night—squeaking leather, horses splashing through the shallows. Aaron and Jessie went to the ground, dropping behind the cover of driftwood and brush. An instant later they saw them, riders hugging the shore. Water sprayed silver along the bank. Aaron touched Jessie's shoulder and pointed. Keeping low, she followed him into the river. The water was slightly cool, sluggish, and muddy on the bottom. Driftwood was jammed in a narrow crescent twenty yards out into the river. They pulled their way along, waist high, until there was no place else to go. Jessie could see the riders now, the long column coming out of the shadows and climbing the bank where they'd been.

"You wondered where Copperhead was," Aaron said between his teeth. "There he is."

"My God," Jessie gasped, "they won't have any warning at all, Aaron. The men in camp won't have a chance!"

"If I fired off two or three rounds you and me'd be dead," he said flatly. "And it wouldn't help any of them."

Jessie didn't answer. She knew it was true, but that didn't help the chill that surged through her veins.

An instant later, the first shot rang out from shore. In a moment, it was hard to tell one burst of fire from the next.

★
Chapter 16

Light and sound exploded through the tall grass like a terrible storm come to ground. Jessie tried to shut out the horror, to make it go away. A riderless horse burst into the open, jerked to a stop along the shore, and then fearfully galloped back up the bank. Aaron gripped her shoulder hard. She turned, staring blindly into his face.

"Jessie—"

"Yes, I'm all right."

"Look, I need your help. I'm trying to work this log out of the jam. I can't do it with one hand."

Jessie pushed a limp strand of hair out of her face. He showed her what he wanted. The log was tangled underwater. She took a breath and went down and worked at the brush, came up for air, and tried again. The log was snagged on a cluster of roots and she borrowed Aaron's knife to cut it free.

"I think that'll do it," she whispered. "We're all right."

"Good." Aaron studied the shore. His gunbelt and holster were wrapped around the broken stub of a branch. The gunfire in the camp stopped abruptly. He didn't look at Jessie. They both understood the sudden silence.

The log began to drift into the current, slowly at first, then faster, turning them around in dizzying circles. This stretch of the Missouri looked placid on the surface, scarcely moving at all, yet she could feel the swift water just below, cold, tugging at her legs.

Aaron let out a breath beside her. "The farther we get downstream, the better. They'll be coming, that's for certain. They'll ask people questions in the camp and they'll get whatever they want. They already know about the girl—that she's not here and you are. They'll want you if they can get you, Jessie."

"I know. I know what they'll do." She flinched as several

evenly spaced shots rang out on the shore. "They'll kill every-one, Aaron. They won't leave anyone alive."

"There was nothing we could have done to stop it. We'd be just as dead if we had gone back there with the others."

Jessie didn't answer. She kept seeing the faces of the different men in camp. "Are you all right, Aaron? Your arm . . ."

"I'll make it," he said. "Jessie, they know we've got to be out here; they'll search along the shore, know we couldn't run far on foot, and figure we've got to be in the river. They can't cover every inch of the shore. We've got all night and the Missouri's full of logs and brush. They'll play hell figuring which pile's ours. We'll be out and long gone before dawn."

"I know. We'll make it." Anger blurred her eyes. "Damn it all, this wasn't their fight. They didn't even know why they died! You got any sense, you'll swim off and leave me floating down the river by myself!"

"I can't," he told her.

"What?"

"I can't," he said, the weary trace of a smile creasing his features. "I only got one arm workin' good."

They heard the shots an hour later, a mile or so back along the shore. Aaron told her they were shooting at shadows or maybe some animal in the river. Not long after, they spotted the riders along the bank, riding fast, passing them, heading east and following the river.

"They'll wait downriver, won't they?" said Jessie. "Try to spot us as we pass."

"Maybe," he said. "They're not going to have a lot of luck. There's a ferry a few miles down if I remember. Some of 'em might cross in case we try for the north bank."

"Will we? Would that be a good idea?"

"What, come out on the other side? Maybe, I don't know. Right now we're better off out here. Wouldn't bother me at all to float all the way to St. Louis."

"Uh-uh. Hanging on with one arm." Jessie studied the dark shore. The land was much the same as the country around their camp. There were flat places to land, but plenty of high bluffs and rugged canyons. *Good,* she told herself. *It's harder going for them than it is for us.*

131

She kept trying to tell herself Aaron was right—that there was more shoreline than the riders could possibly cover. She and Heller could pick their own time, their own landing spot. And then what? she wondered. They'd be on foot and vulnerable again. No horses. One Colt, a derringer, and a knife. And Aaron Heller with a stiff arm. She decided the hunter made sense—the longer they stayed in the water, the better.

At close to midnight the bright lights of a sternwheeler appeared downriver. It passed less than thirty yards away, thrashing through the water and churning up mud from the bottom. Jessie and Aaron stayed clear. They couldn't risk shouting over the noise of the engine and the paddle; no one aboard would ever hear them, but their voices might carry to the shore. Jessie watched helplessly from the cover of their log. She could see the captain's shadow in the wheelhouse, the orange glow of his pipe.

"Yeah, well, I didn't want to ride on *that* boat anyway. It smells to high heaven," said Jessie.

Heller grinned. "You're out of luck then. They're all going to smell like that on the Missouri. Once they've hauled hides downriver, the stink never goes away."

Jessie looked closely at Aaron. Even in the dim light of the moon she could see his features were strained, his lips stretched painfully back from his teeth. The wound in his arm, grasping the log with one hand, was quickly draining him of his strength.

"We're going to have to get to shore," she said tightly. "If you fall off, I'm not real sure I can hold you."

"That's a hell of a thing to be thinking about," he muttered.

"Maybe not, but it's true. Your wound isn't all that bad, Aaron. But you can't keep treating it like this and keep going. You ought to see your face."

Heller nodded. He didn't try to deny she was right. "I've been looking. A little farther down, Jessie. Better . . . cover along shore, I'm thinking."

"A little farther," she said sternly. "But not much." It had to be soon, she knew. Her own arms were nearly numb. She could imagine how it was for Aaron. The weight of trousers and boots pulled you down, draining you all the more. She was still wearing Aaron's leather jacket, the garment he'd given

132

her after the Englishman had sliced her shirt to ribbons. The jacket was heavy with water but she didn't dare let it go. Boots and clothing were a burden for the moment, but they'd need them desperately when they got ashore, when the sun came up and baked the land.

The dark shore seemed to glide by faster than it had the moment before. The current caught them up and brought them dangerously close to the south bank. Jessie and Aaron could do nothing but keep low and hope no one was there to notice they weren't part of the log and its stubby branches.

The moon's dim ribbon of light seemed to Jessie as bright as day. She peered into the night, straining to see the stretch of water just ahead. Aaron hadn't spoken for some time. His eyes were half closed and she knew he couldn't make it much longer. She was afraid to look away, certain he might suddenly let go, slip under the dark water, and disappear.

The sky above suddenly shrank down to nothing and she knew they were coming to a bend. The current tugged at her body; the log turned in a circle and picked up speed at an alarming rate.

"Aaron, *Aaron!*" She came close to him, rubbing her hand across his face. "Aaron, for God's sake don't go to sleep on me now!"

"Huh, what?" He blinked, looked at her with glazed eyes. "I'm—all right—fine."

"No, damn it, you're not *fine* at all. Aaron, just hold on. Do you hear me? We're coming to a bend. It's going to get a little rough."

"Little—rough. All right . . ."

Jessie gritted her teeth. Holding on with one arm, she reached down and loosened the buckle of her belt, then struggled to pull it through the wet loops. When she had the belt free, she ran the tip through Aaron's belt and pulled it tightly around her buckle. Then she wrapped the free end around her hand.

Great, she thought soberly. *If he slips off and sinks, I can hold on and let him pull me to the bottom.*

Still it seemed like the thing to do. It was something.

She heard it before she saw it, the sound of rushing water. The noise nearly stiffened her with fear. Then an instant later she saw the dark shadow above the line of foaming water and

nearly cried aloud with joy. It wasn't fast water as she'd feared—
it was a jam, a great tangle nearly twenty feet high reaching
out from the northern bank. The snag would stop them, let her
work their log to shore and out of the river. The water wasn't
all that fast; the stronger current swept past the snag to the
center of the river.

Jessie felt a great sense of relief as the log began to slow,
bobbing gently as it drifted behind the great natural dam.

"It's all right, Aaron," she said softly, "hold on. Hang on
a little longer."

The big jam loomed overhead. Jessie could see the stark
white bones of great trees, some most likely from as far as the
Southern Rockies, the Madison and the Jefferson that fed the
Missouri.

She held onto Aaron as the log edged into slow water. She
could see that getting ashore might be easier than she'd imag-
ined. The water before the jam was thick with dark stones,
smoothly rounded rocks a foot high and a yard or so wide.
There were hundreds of them, clustered ahead of the tangle.
Maybe the rocks were the reason the jam had started, she
decided. At any rate they'd make the passage to dry land fairly
simple. All she had to do was get Aaron onto one of the rocks.
She could help him to shore from there.

Jessie let the log drift easily through the water. Closer, she
was suddenly aware of a terrible, overpowering odor. She shook
her head and nearly retched. Lord, something had crawled into
the jam and died! The cloying smell of death and decay was
unmistakable. She choked and tried to breathe through her
mouth. It helped but not much. Aaron groaned beside her,
lifted his head, and made a face.

"What—what's that?" he muttered.

"I don't know," Jessie told him. "Nice, isn't it? Come on,
we're getting out of this place."

Jessie let go of the belt she'd attached to Aaron, crooked
her arm firmly around the log, and reached out to pull herself
to the nearest rock. The surface of the rock was slick. She let
go and grabbed it with both hands. The rock suddenly moved,
bobbed in the water. Jessie cried out, jerked her hands away,
and retreated to the log. She stared in horror as the rock slowly
turned on its side. A stink even worse than before assailed her

senses. Four stiffened legs rose into the air. A great distended belly turned to face her, taut white skin swollen with the gases of decay. The corpse rolled again and she saw the wet fur she'd mistaken for moss, the head with yellow horns, the eyes and nose eaten away, the swollen tongue forcing the mouth open.

"My—*God!*" Jessie closed her eyes, trying not to gag. Only the thought of Aaron beside her kept her from clawing in panic through the water, swimming blindly for the clear current of the river.

"Jessie . . . what the . . . hell!" Aaron's eyes went wide. He stared right through her. Something was wrong; he was too tired to think about what it might be.

"Least the smell got you up," Jessie said grimly. "Hang on and don't breathe."

"I never smelled anything worse in my life!" Aaron moaned.

Jessie paddled with one hand, guiding the log slowly toward the shore. "You're the buffalo hunter," she said, "not me. You ought to feel right at home. There's got to be least a hundred head in here."

"You sure do carry a grudge, lady."

"Hang on," she said, "we're almost there."

Aaron muttered something she couldn't understand. Her feet touched bottom and she said a silent prayer. She worked the log as close to the bank as she could. Aaron didn't look as if he could go an extra foot. The bank was steep here, not like it was upriver. She made sure he was secure, then clamored out herself, braced her feet on a dead tree, and helped him out. Aaron grasped her hand, one arm hanging limply by his side. He stumbled past her and fell, lying on his back and gasping for air. Jessie left him and slipped back into the water, remembering the gunbelt and holster looped to the stub of a branch.

"Damn, *damn!*" She pounded her fist against her leg.

"What . . . what's wrong?"

"Nothing, everything's fine." She'd tell him later that the gunbelt was gone, that it had slipped off somewhere in the river. It wouldn't do him any good to know now.

The bluff was nearly thirty feet high. It wasn't too steep, but Jessie guessed it took a good half hour to get Aaron to the top. Stunted trees lined the ridge, and the land below was a series of steep gullies, eroded badland country. Even in the dark she could see there was no way they were going any farther, not until Aaron got some rest.

She left him sleeping on a patch of sandy ground and walked east along the bluff. At least, she decided, luck was leaning a little in their direction. The terrain was high and rugged, full of blind gullies and hard going for anyone on a horse. A hell of a lot better than open prairie. Maybe the awful stench would keep everyone away. It wasn't as bad now with the bluff between herself and the mass of floating bodies, but she could smell them well enough. She was sure she'd probably smell them the rest of her life.

Jessie found what she wanted fifty yards down the ridge. It was farther than she liked, a long walk for Aaron, but there was nothing any better on the way. Thick scrub whiskered the bluff in a low line, masking eroded channels in rocky soil. One was large enough to crawl inside, halfway closed at the top, and seven feet or so square inside. All she had to do now was get Aaron on his feet—keep him awake a few minutes and get him down the path and inside.

She picked up sticks and rocks and tossed them in the hole, hoping the noise would encourage any rattlers or other tenants to go away. There was no way to tell if the place was empty. The hole harbored a small patch of moonlight near the back. The rest was black as pitch.

Walking back down the path she studied the stars and guessed it was close to three in the morning. Good, Aaron would have time to rest up. A little time, at least. She'd get him out of his wet clothes, try to get him warm and dry. A fire would help a lot, but she knew she couldn't risk it. Not until daylight, anyway. Then, maybe, if everything were clear...

Jessie stopped, frozen in her tracks. She heard a man laugh and then another man answered. She saw them in the gully just below and to her right, two men on horses riding straight for her up the ridge.

★

Chapter 17

Jessie went to her knees, pressing herself flat against the bluff. *The whole Missouri River,* she thought darkly, *and we've got to land right in their laps!*

She could see Aaron Heller, sleeping where she'd left him. He was fifteen, maybe twenty feet away. Jessie was in shadow but Aaron was in the open. If the men kept coming, all they had to do was glance to the right and they'd see him.

Jessie took a deep, calming breath. The first man turned in the saddle and spoke to his companion. The man muttered an answer. Jessie hefted a small rock in her hand, then tossed it into the brush. It landed a foot in front of the first rider. His horse shied, backed up, and shook its head.

"What the hell's the matter?"

"Don't know—something spooked him. Snake, maybe."

The man in front looked over his shoulder. Jessie threw the second rock hard, striking the horse just behind its ear. The animal bolted, backing up and kicking out at the horse behind. Both riders cursed and struggled to bring their mounts under control.

"Shit, go on back down," the first man growled, "I ain't going to break my neck for some damn snake!"

Jessie waited. When the riders moved back down the trail, she bellied to the edge of the ridge and watched them as long as she could. They kept riding east, paralleling the ridge on a lower trail. Jessie decided they weren't intent on searching the bluff. Maybe they weren't Copperhead's people after all. She sat back on her knees and let out a breath. It didn't make much difference who they were—she couldn't take a chance on being seen. Not now, not by anyone.

• • •

She got him to the hole in the ridge, certain he wouldn't remember the trip. He mumbled something and fell back exhausted. Jessie pulled off his boots, took off his socks, and rung them out. Opening the buttons of his shirt, she managed to lift him enough to remove his arms from the sleeves. He groaned once when she touched his wounded arm. Jessie laid her palm gently against his skin. As she'd guessed from the start, the wound was clean. There was no fever at all. Shock and hanging on to the log half the night had drained his strength.

The early morning air was slightly cool, so she decided wet trousers would do him more harm than good. Working at his belt, she pulled the clammy garment over his hips and past his feet. Finally she struggled with her own wet boots and socks, peeled down her denims, and slipped out of Aaron's leather jacket. Crawling to the end of the rocky funnel, she squeezed all of the clothes out flat. She hoped that when the sun came up they'd dry quickly on the rocky surface.

Feeling her way back through the hole, she found the naked flesh of Aaron's leg. She jerked her hand back, then silently laughed at her reaction. When the sun came up, they'd both be jaybird naked in the hole. Which wasn't any different from being naked in the dark. She could lie down beside him and keep a prudent space between them—or make them *both* more comfortable and get a little sleep.

"All right, Aaron Heller," she said quietly, "looks like you and me are about to get better acquainted. Whether you know it or not."

She turned her back to him and snuggled into the curve of his chest. Aaron muttered happily in his sleep and snaked his hand along her side to the curve of her breast. Jessie grinned and moved his hand back down to her waist.

When she woke, a pale and almost luminescent glow touched the rocky walls. A patch of early morning sky filled the round hole directly above. She moaned sleepily to herself and burrowed into the warmth at her back. A hand brushed her shoulder, lingered there, and slid down her arm. The hand felt good and she groaned again, stretched her arms lazily over her head, and twisted fully to press the length of her body against him. A mouth met her lips in a long and lazy kiss. Jessie opened her eyes and came fully awake. She drew back, startled, pushing her hands against his shoulders.

"Uh—good morning," she said soberly, "how long has this been going on?"

"Two or three seconds," Aaron smiled. "You haven't missed a thing."

"I haven't huh?"

"Nope. I was sleeping nice and easy and this naked lady turns over right in my face. Hell, I didn't know what to do next."

"Oh, I'm sure of that," Jessie bit her lip and gave him a sheepish grin, feeling a flush of color rise to her face. She was pressed firmly against him, her breasts flattened on his chest. She could feel the hard length of his body, and there was no mistaking the touch of his rigid member. She had to admit, it wasn't the worst way to wake up in the morning.

"Jessie," Aaron said evenly, "I don't much want to get up for breakfast."

"I don't much either. Seein' there isn't any."

"That isn't what I meant."

"I know what you meant." She let her hands slide from his shoulders to circle his neck. "We've got a good start, Aaron. I—don't think I want to stop, do you?"

"Not a whole lot, no." He buried his hands in her hair and brought her lips to his again. Jessie closed her eyes and relaxed in the circle of his arms. When his mouth touched hers, a quick surge of pleasure swept through her body. She parted her lips to welcome the probing thrust of his tongue. Aaron's body tensed, drawing her close against him. Jessie opened her mouth, matching his hunger with her own, drinking in the taste of his kisses. Aaron stretched the pliant corners of her mouth, exploring every hollow of delight. His kisses smoldered in her belly, seared the hard points of her nipples.

Aaron let his mouth trail slowly down the ivory column of her throat to the swell of her breasts. Jessie sucked in a breath at his touch. Pulling out of his grasp, she swept amber hair off her shoulders, arched her back, and cupped her naked breasts in her hands. She watched his dark eyes drink her in, saw a vein pulse rapidly on his brow. She offered her breasts lovingly to his mouth, heard the sharp cry catch in his throat as his bearded face ground roughly against her. She moaned as his tongue caressed her nipples, swelling the dusky circles into satiny points of pleasure. She felt his body tremble, hardening with the tension that sang between them. His intense maleness was a hot and burning brand between her thighs. She squirmed beneath his touch, grinding her silken mound against him.

"Get inside me," she cried, "get—*deep* inside me, Aaron!"

Heller growled within his chest; her words seemed to drive him to a greater peak of hunger. She threw back her head and gasped for breath. Aaron suddenly gripped the slender circle of her waist and slid down the length of her body. Jessie cried out as his tongue found the hollow of her belly, trailed to the soft downy line below her navel. She spread her legs in loving invitation, shuddered as his tongue moved in a slow, lazy circle past her curly little nest. His hands caressed her thighs while his tongue explored the sensitive flesh between her legs. He taunted her relentlessly, letting his hot breath touch the sweet and honeyed places. He paused to kiss the long planes of her thighs, returned to brush her treasure with his lips.

"Aaron," Jessie said sharply, "I can't—take any more of that. Get in me, *please!*"

"You're sure in a hurry to get going," he said, "for a lady without breakfast or a horse."

"This doesn't have—anything to—do with horses or breakfast, damn it!"

Aaron laughed and slid his fingers gently inside her. Jessie gasped and raised her bottom off the ground. His fingers opened her like a flower, baring the coral folds of flesh to his gaze. His tongue stroked the moist and silky petals, teased the hard little pearl that glistened within.

"Oh, yes, *yes!*" Jessie cried aloud. She clawed the earth with her fingers, thrashed her head frantically from side to side.

Again and again Aaron caressed the lovely hollow, thrusting his tongue even deeper. Jessie felt the sting of sweat on her brow. Each stroke of his tongue was an agony of delight. She squeezed her eyes shut; bright sparks exploded across her vision. His lips closed firmly over the hard, swollen pearl, flicking the little bud with the tip of his tongue.

"Now-now-*now!*" Jessie whispered between her teeth, beating her fists against the ground. Aaron gripped the swell of her bottom and drew the swollen nub into his mouth.

Jessie gasped, her features contorted in a mix of pain and delight. Heat filled her body, liquid heat that surged from her belly to the rigid points of her nipples. Her body jerked uncontrollably against him. She exploded again and again, letting the hungry fires devour her. The orgasm raced through her loins once more, lifted her in a final spasm of joy, and dropped her limply to the earth.

"Oh, Lord," she sighed, sucking hungrily for air, "that was some kind of loving, mister. Just about as good as you can get!"

Aaron took her into his arms. "I'm pleased if you are, ma'am," he said dryly.

"Now aren't you the gentleman, Mr. Heller." Her eyes suddenly narrowed in concern. "Aaron I—never even thought to ask. Are you okay?"

He reached out to touch the tip of her breast. "Never felt anything better in my life."

"That's not what I meant and you know it," she scolded, slapping his hand playfully away. "I *know* you're not crippled—that's pretty obvious. But are you truly all right? The wound's not infected is it?"

"It's stiff is all," he told her. "That's a problem I've been having all over this morning."

"*Aaron!*" Jessie tried to look shocked, but his solemn expression sent her into a fresh burst of laughter. She trailed her hand along the hard planes of his body and grasped his member in her fingers. "Oh, my—looks like you *do* have a problem. What are we going to do about that?"

"I was kind of hoping maybe you already knew."

"Who, me?" Jessie showed him an impish grin. "Well, we could do *this* maybe . . ." She slid her fingers from the base of his member to the tip. "That help any?"

"Not—not any at all," Aaron groaned. "Makes it a lot worse, as a matter of fact."

"Well, maybe I'd better stop. I'm probably doing something wrong."

"Now, don't do that," Aaron said quickly, "just—just keep trying, you'll get it right."

"I sure do hope so," Jessie sighed. She held him lovingly

141

in her hand, stroking the hard flesh in a long, easy rhythm. Aaron closed his eyes and let a lazy sigh escape his lips. She pumped him a little harder, feeling him swell even more. When she was certain he'd explode she pulled away, touching him gently again. She rubbed her fingertips like a whisper over the tip, then slid one hand to the base of his shaft and cupped him in her palm. She could feel his body tremble, see the cords of muscle in his belly go taut as a spring.

"That any better?" she teased. "Am I helping your problem, Mr. Heller? If I'm not just—*Aaron!*"

Jessie cried out as he thrust his hands beneath her and flipped her roughly on her belly. She laughed and kicked her long legs helplessly in the air. He kneeled between her thighs and grasped her waist, then thrust his shaft inside her without warning. A long, ragged cry escaped her throat. He gripped the curve of her back and thrust himself against her again and again. Jessie spread her knees wide and raised the lovely swell of her bottom up to meet him. The sharp, animal scent of their pleasure assailed her senses. She squirmed against him like a snake, stroking his flesh intently with her own.

"All of me," she urged between her teeth. "Take *all* of me, Aaron!"

Aaron gripped her hips hard and slammed himself against her. Each stroke sent the breath from her lungs. His manhood seemed to devour her. The strong, savage thrusts were no longer confined to the treasure between her legs; her whole body was now a vessel of desire, a cauldron of liquid fire. She was certain he'd burn her to a cinder with his passion. The storm churned within her, an agony of pleasure and pain. Still her body begged him for more. Her teeth brought the copper taste of blood to her mouth. She thrust her warmth against him, the roiling furnace in her loins driving her to a frenzy. She could feel her passion mounting, surging through her veins. The satiny walls of her pleasure spasmed around him, tightening agan and again about his member. She heard him cry out behind her; his body went rigid as he loosed himself inside her. Jessie gave a ragged shout of joy and let her own release burst free. Her body shook without control; the flesh went taut about her mouth. Every muscle went limp and she slid on her belly with a sigh.

Aaron took her into his arms. She could feel his eyes drinking her in, tasting every sleek curve of her body. She returned the gesture in kind, boldly studying his hard and slender frame with grinning approval. He watched her inspect the corded muscle of his arms, the light matting of hair that trailed down his chest past his belly. His member was still nearly rigid, only beginning to relax in a curve across his loins.

"You keep starin' like that, you're going to get yourself in trouble again," he told her.

"Now that's the kind of threat a girl likes to hear," Jessie grinned. She touched a finger to his lips. "You'd just love me to call your bluff, now wouldn't you? Figure you could rise to the occasion?" Aaron looked pained and Jessie laughed, suddenly aware of what she'd said. "Oh Lord—bad jokes before breakfast?"

Aaron muttered to himself and sat up. "I'm empty as a barrel and you're talking about breakfast." He gave her a bleary look. "This end of Montana's real shy of nuts and berries. You got any good ideas?"

Jessie gave him a look. "You're the hunter, not me."

"Huh!" Aaron peered up at the lightening sky. "You're going to have to fill me in some. I don't remember a whole lot about getting where we are. I was kinda—" He stopped and stared straight at her. "Hey, wait a minute. We've still got a Colt. I remember that much. Maybe I can find us a rabbit!"

"Aaron," she said soberly, "it's gone. We lost it in the river."

"Oh, great." Aaron scowled. "That means we start playin' Injun with snares. Or catching catfish in the Missouri."

Jessie stood and moved past him to the high angle of rock at the end of the hole, where she'd spread their clothes. Feeling in the pocket of her denims, she brought out the ivory-handled derringer. In another pocket she found three loose shells.

"It's not a Sharps rifle," she said, holding the weapon in her palm, "but it's all we've got, I'm afraid."

Aaron forced a grin. "If we find us a rabbit fast asleep, you can poke that thing in his ear."

"Yeah, well..." Jessie tossed him dry clothes and boots and began pulling her own denims over her legs. When they were dressed, she told him about the dead buffalo in the river and where they were on the bluff. Finally she told him about the riders and what had happened.

Aaron sat up and showed interest. "Well now, things are looking up some, Jessie."

Jessie paused in the struggle with her still-wet boots. "You think that's *good* news? Lord, Aaron, those two could be camped close by, down on the other side of the ridge."

"I hope to hell you're right," he said plainly. "If you are, we won't have to walk too far for breakfast."

Chapter 18

"I wish we'd had some money or something to leave," said Jessie. "I know we had to do it, but it doesn't sit right, Aaron."

Heller shot her a look. "Walkin' and going hungry doesn't sit right either. They've still got a rifle and plenty to eat. They're hunters—they'll be madder'n hell but they'll be just fine." He caught her expression and shook his head. "Look, I don't hold with stealing. But no one's trying to kill those two. You can't say the same for us."

"Yeah, I guess." Jessie kicked her mount and urged it up the slope. She'd chosen the gray gelding, and Heller had picked the black mare. The whole thing had been absurdly easy—as if Lady Luck were trying to even up the score. They'd found the camp in a gully half a mile to the east. The horses were saddled and ready to go. There were blankets and saddlebags and provisions, two Sharps rifles and a Winchester. The two men were scrubbing their eating gear in the shallows, well out of sight of the camp. Aaron quickly stuffed hard bread and dried beef in one of the saddlebags, took one of the Sharps rifles and the Winchester, and filled his pocket with shells. In a moment they were gone, heading north away from the camp, then bearing back east along the river.

The men were clearly hunters, not Copperhead's men as she'd feared the night before. The Sharps rifles, brass shells and powder, plus primers and patch paper and extra ripping and skinning knives told the story.

Jessie was relieved. If the men had belonged to Copperhead, they would have had to take some action besides stealing. They couldn't afford simply to let the pair go to sound the alarm. That meant tying them to a tree where they'd likely starve, or killing them in cold blood. Murder wasn't an option, but tying

145

them up was about the same. She was glad there'd been no need. Too many men were dead already—good and bad alike.

They kept to the northern bank, using the bluffs to screen them from the river. Now and then Aaron edged back to the Missouri for a look. It was a tricky business at best, Jessie knew. Copperhead's killers were almost certainly watching the river. If she and Aaron found riders or a camp, they'd have to make a decision from a distance. And how would they manage that? One bad guess was all they'd get.

She caught herself gripping the reins hard and tried to relax. The whole business was going sour, getting worse instead of better. Riding east, she was getting farther from Ki every mile. And if Ki were all right, he was riding east as well trying to find her. Right toward the camp Copperhead had turned into a slaughterhouse. Jessie thrust the thought aside. The list, Angela Halley—Ki's life was too heavy a price to pay for either one.

"Jessie, come over here, quick!" Aaron's words broke into her thoughts. She rode to his side and followed his eyes to the river. Through the sparse grove of trees she saw a brassy expanse of water, and on the banks closer by, a small cluster of tents and makeshift shacks. A crude landing wharf extended into the river. Barrels and stacks of hides crowded the shore and the rough-hewn dock. Jessie could see maybe two dozen men milling about.

"It's a hunters' camp," Heller explained, "run by one of the big hide buying outfits like Maxwell's. The sternwheelers stop here sometimes going up and downriver."

Jessie shot him a wary look. "Aaron, Copperhead's people are bound to check out a place like this."

"Course they are. But we don't have a lot of choice, now do we? We can't keep hiding out in holes."

"I know we can't. I just—"

"Yeah, I know." Aaron caught her expression and forced a grin. "Hey, these ol' boys are hunters. I recognize about half of them from here."

"And what if one of them recognizes these horses?"

"We'll have to take the chance and hope our luck holds. I can always say I bought 'em. Besides, those fellas were ridin'

146

toward this place, not from it. Maybe they haven't been here before. Come on, might as well get at it."

Jessie waited in the shade with the horses while Aaron talked to the hunters. She still wore her big leather jacket which fit her like a tent. She'd tucked her fiery hair under her hat and pulled the brim as low as she could. Now she sat hunched over in the saddle, hoping she looked like a sack. After a moment it was clear the ruse wasn't working. The hunters didn't care if she was ugly as a fish. She was a woman, still breathing in and out. Every man at the landing found a reason to look her over, then turn and come back the other way.

Aaron ducked out of one of the lean-to shelters and walked toward her through the trees. "Get down and come inside," he told her. "They've got beer that's been coolin' in the river and I've rustled up some steaks. One of these ol' boys loaned me a few dollars."

"I'm ready," Jessie said soberly, sliding out of the saddle. "I've been stripped down and raped about fifteen times."

"I'm not real surprised." Aaron tried to hide a grin behind his hand. "They don't mean any harm. Just looking."

"Oh, sure."

Aaron took the horses and looped the reins over a rail. Jessie stepped into the lean-to and glanced around. The structure was ten feet square, a dirt-packed floor, and two barrels and a plank for a bar. There were small boxes to sit on and two bigger boxes for tables. The room smelled like buffalo hide, whiskey, and sweat. Three hunters were leaving as Jessie entered. They nodded, followed her with their eyes, and stepped outside.

Jessie pulled up a box and Aaron brought them cool beers. In a moment she heard buffalo steak sizzling out back and smelled the delicious aroma.

"I found out a couple of things," Aaron said quietly. "One, nobody's come here asking questions. That doesn't mean they won't. An old boy I talked to just came from across the river, south down by the Big Dry. He's seen riders that don't belong, and I figure it's Copperhead."

Jessie repressed a shudder. "Lord, Aaron, there's no telling how many men the cartel has riding!"

"Yeah, well, they don't have enough," he said tightly. "They can't cover all of Montana." He reached out and gripped her hand. "The other thing is, there's a sternwheeler due downriver any minute. Out of Fort Benton. Old Rafe who runs this place says it's the *Missouri Pearl*. If it is, I know the captain." Jessie started to protest, but Aaron cut in, "I know what you're going to say and you're right. They'll be checking all the boats downriver, wherever they're scheduled to stop. But not too many people are going to know about Rafe's landing. I'm betting on that."

Jessie bit her lip in thought. "You're right—one man and a woman on horseback following the river. Someone's going to spot us sooner or later..."

"Right. And I don't intend to *stay* on the boat, Jessie. Just get somewhere we can get off and get us some help. Trouble is," he added sourly, "we're in the wrong end of the territory. There's nothing much here. No railroad, no forts—just buffalo, a few settlements on the river, and Indian reservations. If we were south, or over in the west, we could get help fast. Hell, I'd take us south or back upriver if I thought we could make it."

"And where will we be when we get downriver?"

"I don't know," he said honestly. "Out of here, that's all. Out of Copperhead's hands."

"Damn it all, Aaron!" Jessie's green eyes blazed. "I don't want to keep running. I don't like it at all!"

"I don't either," he told her. "It doesn't go down good with me. Only we're going to have to run 'fore we turn around and fight, Jessie."

She knew he was right. But that did little to quell the anger and frustration that was tying her stomach in a knot.

The *Missouri Pearl* pulled in at three that afternoon, the boat riding so low in the water Jessie was certain it would settle to the bottom any moment. At first glance it looked as if an enormous dirt bluff had broken free and floated downriver. The boat was piled high with hides; nothing below the roof of the hurricane deck was visible to the eye. Aaron said he was certain there were at least ten thousand hides aboard.

"And we're going to ride on *that?*" Jessie sniffed the air

148

and made a face. "I can smell it from here, Aaron."

"Wait till you get aboard," he told her.

"Get aboard where? There isn't any place to *get* that I can see."

Moments later Jessie discovered she was very close to right. There was nothing but narrow tunnels through the hides—tunnels to the engine and the boiler, tunnels forward and aft, and a crawlway that led up to the hurricane deck and the wheelhouse. Bile rose to her throat and she was certain she'd throw up her steak. The odor was a nearly visible pall. Great clouds of flies swarmed over the stinking hides, adding to her discomfort.

"This is really a great idea," she told Aaron, pressing a bandanna against her mouth. "You see what I mean about killing off the herds? Buffalo don't *smell* this bad when they're alive."

Heller grinned at her logic. "I could argue that but I won't." He led her to the hurricane deck and up to the captain's wheelhouse. Two men were standing together, smoking cigars and looking over the river. One was a lean, red-faced man in his fifties, wearing a captain's cap and a worn blue jacket with tarnished buttons. The other was a portly young man with watery eyes and a ragged mustache. The captain looked up at their approach, recognized Heller, and laughed aloud.

"By God," he roared, "what have we got here? If you ain't a sight to see, boy!" He grasped Heller's hand and pumped it enthusiastically. "Now don't tell me these are *your* hides I'm haulin' downriver. Just come aboard to see 'em safely to Bismarck, did you?"

"Yeah, they're mine, Cap'n," Heller said soberly. "Shot 'em all before breakfast last Tuesday."

The captain laughed and let his eyes dart past Heller to Jessie. "Captain Josh Carter, this is Miss—Maryann Greenleaf from St. Joseph," said Aaron.

"I'm charmed, miss," said the captain. He touched the bill of his cap. "This is my first mate, Mr. Taggert." the young man shook Aaron's hand and gave Jessie an oily smile.

"Pleasure," he mumbled, and looked at his boots. Jessie disliked him almost at once.

"Mr. Taggert," said the captain, "make ready to get underway. We are wasting precious time at this place." The first mate nodded and scurried below.

At once Carter's easy smile faded. "I've known you since you were sixteen years old," he told Aaron. "You got something on your mind besides a ride on a stinkin' boat."

"You're right," said Aaron, "I do." He glanced at the belching gusts of smoke from the twin stacks forward. "The lady and me have got some troubles. Big troubles, Josh. We need to get downriver, get ashore, and get some help."

"Done, then, of course," Carter said at once. "What else can I do?"

"I reckon that'll be plenty," said Aaron. "That, and forgettin' you ever saw us."

"Goes without saying," Carter said gruffly.

"Captain," Jessie spoke up, "have you seen anything unusual on your trip downriver? Riders, for instance. Men along the shore."

"I have," Carter told her. "Past Judith Landing near the Breaks. Eight or ten riders. They followed us 'bout an hour and disappeared. Took on wood some time after that and I saw 'em again. Watching from the bluffs."

"Watching to see who got off," Jessie said under breath.

"Might have. I couldn't say that." He glanced thoughtfully from Jessie to Heller. "If you two got troubles like that, I'd suggest you stay out of sight when we get underway. Take Cabin Two. It'll be pretty stuffy, but it will keep you hidden." He paused, then continued. "We'll hit Wolf Point 'fore sundown. You know it, Aaron? Little settlement sprang up about two years ago. Nothing much there, but some army fellas hang around sometimes. I can't stop, but I can slow down and let you off somewhere right before or after. Don't know how much help you'll get. Sounds to me like you need a lot more'n they got."

"We'll likely have to take what we can get," said Aaron.

"Might be best if you was to stay aboard. Wait till we get a little farther on down."

Aaron looked at Jessie and shook his head. "I can't say a lot more, Josh. And it isn't a matter of trust. I don't have to tell you that."

"Didn't ask, did I?" Carter said.

"The thing is, Captain," Jessie said, "we're not just running. We're—" she gave him a weary grin—"I guess you'd say we're getting *out* of trouble so we can get back in. That's why we can't stay aboard any longer than we have to."

"Christ a'mighty." Carter frowned and shook his head. "All right, get on below. Let me do some thinking. Might be able to come up with something useful." He gave Jessie a wary eye. "You ought to watch what kind of fellows you hang around with, miss. Man like Heller here's nothing but trouble. I know him."

Jessie laughed. "Captain, you're likely right about Aaron— but this time I'm afraid it's the other way around."

The *Missouri Pearl* ran into trouble less than an hour downriver, sandbars that had shifted since the last trip up. Captain Carter knew his business and spotted the problem in time. With a load such as his boat was carrying now, going aground would have been a disaster. The Missouri River was littered with sunken remains of captains' mistakes. The sternwheeler polked along at a snail's pace, crewmen wading ahead or rowing the boat's dory, probing the bottom with poles for a safe passage. The sun was nearly gone when the boat got underway once more.

Carter joined Jessie and Aaron for a moment, a cabin boy trailing behind with their evening meal on a covered tray, and a canvas sack he laid on a chair.

"Little touch of spirits here, too, if you'd like it," Carter announced, setting an amber bottle on the table. "This delay's bad for me and good for you. We'll be passing Wolf Point 'bout three hours late. That means it'll be pitch dark. Won't anyone know we even slowed to let you off. You still want to chance it here, do you?"

"It isn't St. Louis," Jessie sighed, "but I think we'd better try. We can get more horses there and ride south all night till we find some help or some telegraph poles."

"Good luck to you," said Carter. "I hope you find the end of this trouble of yours. Wish I could do more for you folks." He looked narrowly at Aaron. "There's provisions in that sack the boy brought. And take the whiskey with you. Never can tell when you'll need a little snakebite medicine."

• • •

The *Missouri Pearl* slowed nearly to a stop, thirty yards from the north bank of the river. Jessie and Aaron stepped off into the shallows and waded ashore in the dark. Aaron carried the two saddles he'd borrowed that morning, and Jessie brought the provisions and the two rifles.

The settlement of Wolf Point was a quarter mile east. They watched the lights of the sternwheeler disappear, then walked along the shore toward the town. There were few people about, a light in the small saloon and the dim glow of a lantern before the livery.

"I don't see any reception committee," Aaron said softly. "Guess that's a good start. Come on, let's go."

Jessie followed him past the darkened buildings, avoiding the main street until they came to the back of the livery. Aaron laid his saddles down outside, took the Winchester from Jessie, and quietly levered a shell into the chamber. He slipped through the door, Jessie at his back. There were stalls to the left, a hayrack on the right. Two dim lanterns hung near the stalls.

"Nobody around," Aaron whispered. He muttered under his breath. "Hell, if I got to go pokin' around town trying to wake some kid . . ."

"He's bound to be around here," said Jessie. "I'll look up front and you—"

"Drop it right quick or you're dead, mister!" The voice spoke harshly from the dark.

Aaron bent his knees and made a quick quarter turn.

"Don't try it!"

Aaron froze, stood straight, and let the Winchester hang limply at his side.

"Drop it nice and easy. You too, lady."

Jessie gritted her teeth in anger and let the Sharps fall to the floor. Aaron laid his rifle on the ground. Jessie heard a man step from the darkened stall behind her. He made a wide berth around Aaron, then faced them and stopped, holding the double-barreled shotgun just above his waist. He was a big, heavyset man in butternut trousers, a faded yellow shirt, and a dark Stetson. His heavily-browed eyes flicked from Jessie to Aaron and back again.

152

"Well now," he grinned, "what have we got here? Henry, what do you think?"

A lean, sandy-haired man in a dusty black suit appeared at the front of the livery, stopped and eyed Jessie a long moment but said nothing. Jessie caught sudden movement behind him. A round pudgy face peered cautiously into the livery, grinned at Jessie and Aaron, and stepped into the light.

"Aaron!" Jessie gasped in surprise.

"You little son of a bitch!" Aaron doubled his fists at his sides. Josh Carter's portly first mate stepped back at Aaron's anger.

"You can yell at me all you want," he said boldly. "You're done for, mister—an' I'm the one that caught you!"

Chapter 19

"Shut up!" Henry snapped, "get out of the way!" The riverman instantly obeyed. Henry studied Jessie a long moment. "Take off your hat," he said flatly. "Drop it on the ground."

Jessie didn't move. The man cursed under his breath, stepped forward, and tore her Stetson away. Strawberry-blond hair tumbled freely about her shoulders.

"Shit, it's not her, is it?" the heavyset man growled. "It's the other one."

"You're Jessie Starbuck," said Henry. "Where's the girl, Angela Halley? Where have you got her?"

"Who?" Jessie said curiously. "Sorry, mister. I don't know what you're talking about."

Henry gave her a nasty grin. "I expect it'll come to you, lady."

"What is this!" the riverman blurted, "what d'you mean it isn't her? I get the re-ward, don't I?"

Henry glared. "Will you shut up, fella?" He turned to the man with the shotgun. "Get these two out of here, Charlie. Real quiet and easy."

"You mind if I ask a question, mister?" said Jessie.

"What is it?"

"That little bastard over there—" she nodded at Captain Carter's mate. "What'd you do, listen at the door while we were talking to Josh? Hear we were leaving at Wolf Point?"

The man grinned broadly at Jessie's attention. "Well, sure I did. I knew right where he'd slow down, too. Got off about a mile sooner and beat you here. Pretty good, huh?"

Henry caught Jessie's expression. "Lady, if it hadn't been him it would have been someone else. The word's out on you and that damn girl all along the river and half of Montana."

"This son of a bitch was workin' with you folks all along?" asked Aaron.

"Him?" Henry made a face. "Hell, no. He probably talked to one of our boys in a saloon somewhere. Fort Benton, I guess. Isn't hardly anyone around hasn't heard there's good cash bein' paid for information. See this?" He pointed at a bright blue bandanna wrapped around his wrist. "There's men with one of these in every two-bit hole in the territory. All you got to do is look around. Like this fella did."

"My God! . . ." Jessie looked appalled.

"Now what?" Heller's voice sounded hollow and empty. "What happens next?"

"Next you two get a nice long ride down south. There's a man real anxious to see you." He glanced idly at Aaron and turned to the man with the shotgun. "Charlie, we need this one at all? Nobody said a thing about him, 'cept he was likely with her."

"Take him along," Charlie shrugged. "Might be something extra in it for us."

Henry nodded. He seemed to remember something and turned to Josh Carter's mate. "Where you goin' to spend all that money?" he asked. "A thousand dollars'll sure buy a heap of fun."

"I got plenty of ideas," the man beamed.

"Well, I just bet you do," said Henry. He walked to an empty stall near the front of the livery and stooped to pick a saddlebag off the floor. "Here's what you're waiting for, friend. Take it and get out of here."

The man almost ran to the stall. He reached for the saddlebag draped over Henry's arm. Something silver flashed between them in a blur. The riverman jerked up straight, stared in disbelief, and fell limply to the ground. Henry kicked him roughly into the stall, bent to wipe his blade on straw, then turned and looked at his friend.

"What are you standin' around for, Charlie? We got a hell of a long way to go."

The sun came up the color of brick, hidden in a veil of low-lying clouds. Ki forced himself to stand, willing the strength into his legs. Pain lanced through his back and shoulders. He could smell the sweat of fever on his face mixing with the sickeningly sweet odor of death. The black-winged carrion birds waddled out of his way, turning their naked heads to squawk angrily in his direction.

She wasn't there, he was sure of that now. Her body wasn't among the dead, and Aaron Heller was missing too. He made himself believe that had a meaning.

They could both be free . . . they don't have to be in Copperhead's hands . . .

He clung to that hope, praying his logic was sound. He had good reason to think she might have gotten away. They'd bound two of the men before they killed them, the Englishman and a man who'd worked for Heller. That had to mean they wanted answers: Where was Angela Halley? Where was Jessie? He understood, now, where the riders were going, the men he and Angela had seen just before first light. They were coming from this camp and they were heading back west, where he and Odell Green were likely to be. If that were true, and if he were right about Jessie getting away, there'd be other riders as well, heading in another direction.

He walked out of the camp, back down the draw where he'd left the girl with the horse. Angela came a cautious step forward to meet him.

"Are you all right? God, you look awful!"

"No. I'm not all right." He raised one foot to the stirrup, gritted his teeth, and gripped the saddlehorn. Pain ripped through his body as he stretched his leg over the saddle. "Come on," he said, "let's go. Try not to touch my back if you can help it."

Angela carefully mounted behind him. Ki urged the horse down the gully away from the river.

"Are they—are they all dead? Everybody?" Ki caught the quiver of fear in her voice.

"Every one who was there. They're all dead," he replied.

"Oh, Lord! And—Jessie Starbuck? The lady you—"

"She's not there. I don't know where she is. I don't think they got her."

"What are you going to do?" Angela said.

"Try to find her."

He circled the camp, finding the tracks where Copperhead's

riders had come up from the south. The tracks split, and he saw how they'd worked around the camp, sending one party to the river while the rest came from below. They'd caught the camp in a crossfire; Ki doubted if any of the men inside had gotten off more than half a dozen shots.

He found what he was looking for east of the camp, close to the banks of the Missouri. Men had set out riding hard, a party nearly as large as the one that had ridden to the west. He eased his mount to a stop and squinted down the river. That had to be it. There was no other answer he could see.

"What is it?" asked Angela, "What are you thinkin' about?"

"Jessie and Aaron Heller," he said, half talking to himself. "I think they got away downriver. I don't know how—it isn't likely they had a boat or anything but that's the way it happened. The raid was sometime late last night." He bit his lip in thought. "If they did go downriver, there's no way of telling how far they'd get. Or how close the others were on their tail." The pain and the fever clouded his reason. He closed his eyes and took a long, deep breath, trying to drive the hurt away as his samurai training had taught him. The fever, the poison in his body didn't exist, not if he willed it away, not if he didn't want it to be.

"Hey, what are you doing?" Angela sounded frightened. "What's the *matter* with you!"

"I'm fine. I'm better now."

"You sure could've fooled me."

Ki reined in the horse by the river, found a patch of shade, and eased himself painfully out of the saddle. "Get down for a minute," he told her. "We've got to talk."

He sat in the shade of the bluff; Angela joined him, a question in her eyes. "There's something I've got to do," he explained. "You're not going to like it. I don't much like it myself but I don't see any other way." He paused and looked over the river. "We're going to make a fire and heat some water, and you're going to put hot cloths on my back and drain out some of that poison. I found some kind of ointment in the camp. A couple of hours of hot packs and grease, I ought to be in better shape."

Angela gave him a narrow look. "Yeah, and then what? There's more to it than that. The part I'm not going to like."

Ki showed her a weary grin. "All right. There's plenty of food in that camp. There are tents, blankets, everything you'll need. Copperhead's boys weren't looking for loot; they left nearly everything behind."

"Hey now, look—"

"I'm going to fix you up a place a few miles downriver," Ki went on. "Back in the bluffs in a safe spot. Somewhere no one will ever find you. You'll be comfortable and you'll be all right until I can—"

"Oh now *wait* a minute!" Angela exploded. Her eyes sparked with sudden anger. "You're talking about leaving me behind, right? Out *here?* You are plain crazy if you think I'm going to do that!"

"Angela, listen—"

"Uh-uh. *You* listen. I am not staying alone. I–I can't do that."

"Yes. You can do it," Ki said firmly. "You have to, Angela. It's the only way we've got. I don't know where Jessie is. I can't look all over Montana Territory trying to find her. There's no time for that and I haven't got the strength to even try. I've got to get help and I can't risk taking you with me. Copperhead's people are thick as flies. If they see you, you're dead. I can't stop them. Not now. Do I have to tell you that?"

"No, but—" For an instant, the stubborn look of defiance disappeared. "Listen, I know you're tryin' to help. But I can't do that. I can't stay here. I'd rather go with you and take my chances. Besides," she added, "you're not going to make it alone. You think you can ride like that? You ought to see yourself!"

"I'll be a lot better after you fix me up and I get a little rest."

Angela laughed harshly. "You need a hospital, friend—not hot packs and a can of smelly grease."

"I haven't got a hospital," he said calmly. "I have you."

"Huh!" Angela let out a breath. "Where do you think you're going? Not that you'll ever get there."

"Miles City. I figure it's a—"

"*Miles City!*" Angela's eyes went wide. "My God, how far is that from here!"

"I'm guessing a hundred miles. I think I can get some help

there. And there's nothing else closer that'll do us any good."

"You're going to ride to Miles City," she said scornfully.

"There are plenty of loose horses around here now. Nobody's going to be using them. I'll take me two or three and ride them hard and switch off. I can make it that way in fifteen hours tops. I'll be there tomorrow morning by three."

"Either that, or you'll be dead of blood poisoning," she said flatly.

"That's not going to happen." He reached out and touched her hand. "You're going to fix me up real good, Angela. I'm going to make it, and I'll be back for you before you know it."

"You'd—you'd better. You just damn well better . . ." She stood quickly and turned to hide her tears. "Come on, I want your back lookin' real good when you fall off your horse and drop dead."

At one forty-five in the morning, Silas Easter grabbed his 10-gauge Remington and padded down the stairs in his faded longjohns. He waited without moving until the noise came again, then felt his way to the back and slipped silently outside. The wagonyard was empty; the moon cast long chalky shadows on the ground. He picked out the square shape of the shed, a coil of old rope, and a broken wheel. He let his eyes sweep the familiar yard, looking for something that didn't belong.

Nothing. A dog barked across town. A horse blew air in the stable. The sound came again and Silas jerked up straight, a chill running up the back of his neck. Damn—whatever it was, it was right under his nose! He eased back the hammer of the shotgun as quietly as he could, then inched around the side of the building. Silas stared, bringing the weapon halfway to his shoulder. The horse stood there looking at him. He could see its lathered flanks in the pale light. He took a step forward and then stopped. The man lay on his face in the dirt. Silas ran to him, laid the Remington on the ground, and turned him over.

"Damn," he muttered under his breath. Ki's features were so contorted in pain, Easter had to look twice to make certain who it was.

•   •   •

159

Less than an hour after Ki collapsed at Silas Easter's door, a flatbed wagon came to a halt on a grassy slope some twenty miles north of Miles City. Almost at once three armed men appeared and leveled their weapons at the wagon.

"Take it easy," Henry said calmly, "it's me and Charlie Gates."

"Henry? What the hell are you doin' here?" a voice said shortly. "You're supposed to be up on the river."

"Not with what I got," Henry stepped down from the wagon. One of the riflemen started forward, then stopped. A tall, broad-shouldered man stalked hurriedly past the three guards and loomed over Henry.

"What is it?" he demanded, "what do you have in the wagon?"

Henry's easy smile faded under the big man's gaze. It was all he could do to keep from turning away. The man's face was a horror, the flesh cut deeply in half a dozen places. One eye was nearly closed; the skin from the corner of his mouth to his cheek was an ugly wound, painting his face with a broad and terrible grin.

"I got the woman, Copperhead," Henry said evenly. "Jessie Starbuck. There was a man with her and we brought him, too. Uh—just in case you want him," he added quickly.

Copperhead didn't look at him again. "Bring them," he said shortly, then turned and walked back down the hill.

Jessie's skin crawled. She'd only heard the voice once but she knew it in an instant.

"Take it easy," said Aaron, "it's okay."

Jessie started to answer. Charlie came around the tail of the wagon and cut the bonds at their hands and wrists. Jessie sat up and lowered herself shakily to the ground, groaning as her legs started waking up again.

"Down there," Charlie muttered, "in the draw."

Charlie stayed behind. One of the men with a rifle led the way, Henry at his side. Another followed in the rear. A path was worn in the shoulder-high grass. In a moment, Jessie saw a cluster of tents, a dozen horses in a small grove of trees in a rope corral. The guards stopped before one of the larger tents. A lantern glowed dimly inside.

After a long moment Copperhead stepped out of the tent. He glanced at Jessie without expression. Jessie drew a breath and shrank back at the sight of his face. Copperhead stepped aside and another man walked out of the tent to stand beside him. He was a short, slightly overweight man in a blue silk robe. Thinning hair lay plastered neatly in dark strands over his skull, as if someone had painted it on. His eyes looked owlish behind thick-lensed glasses. He blinked at Jessie, his eyes darting about in a quick, nervous little motion.

"Who is that?" he asked, growling at Heller.

"He's the man who shot at us down south," Copperhead said evenly. "I told you about him."

"Get him out of here. I want to see the woman."

"I'm not going anywhere, mister!" Aaron protested. A rifle butt slammed into his belly. Aaron gasped in pain and folded. The short man nodded past Jessie's shoulder. A gunman grabbed her arm and tossed her roughly into the tent. Jessie cried out and sprawled on the ground. The man in the robe stood above her. His face showed no expression at all. The hanging lantern glinted off of his glasses and turned his eyes to golden coins.

"I am Ernst Heydrich," he said calmly. "Tell me where she is. Where is Angela Halley?"

"I don't have the slightest idea," said Jessie.

Heydrich nodded, as if he understood her answer and accepted it. "Then I am going to hurt you," he said simply. "I'm going to hurt you very badly, Miss Starbuck."

Chapter 20

The world was no longer silent and empty.

A bright, searing red line licked at the gray horizon. Thunder shook the earth and he looked up and saw them, a million hump-backed beasts as big as mountains, beasts with blood-red eyes and silver horns, their shaggy fur alive with white-hot flame. He screamed and tried to run but nothing happened. He looked down at his legs and saw they were gone.

"All right, boy, easy. Just take it easy now."

Ki opened his eyes and stared. His heart pounded wildly against his chest. Silas Easter pressed him gently back on the pillow.

"No," said Ki, "I've got to sit up. Give me a hand. Please..."

Silas protested, but Ki eased his feet shakily to the floor. At once he felt light-headed and empty. His back and shoulders still hurt, but the pain was considerably dulled. His body smelled of sour sweat; the fever was gone but the odor was still there.

"Glad to see you back among the living," Silas said shortly. "I sure wouldn't push it if I was you."

Ki ran a hand through his hair. He squinted at the painfully bright light of the open window. "What time is it? How long was I out?"

"You got here sometime after midnight. It's three or so in the afternoon now."

Ki closed his eyes. "That's—too damn long."

"Not long enough, you ask me." Easter stood and shook his head. "Don't reckon you remember, but Doc Cuppscott worked on you half the night. Poultices and heat drawed out a lot of the poison, but you came close to big trouble." He gave Ki a curious look. "You feel like telling me what the hell happened out there? You did a lot of ravin' and carrying on, but I ain't real strong on Japanese—or whatever it was you were jabbering."

Ki gripped the brass bedstead and brought himself erect. "I can tell you some—my part of it. I'll have to guess the rest." He told Silas Easter about looking for the girl with Odell Green, meeting the Shoshonis, the buffalo stampede, and Green's death. He didn't say they'd actually found Angela Halley. He trusted Silas completely, but knew every man would break under the right kind of pressure. Finally he explained what had happened on the Missouri, the massacre of Lord Montgomery's men.

"Christ a'mighty . . ." Silas ran a hand over his chin. "And you figure Miss Jessie and Aaron got away?" He shook his head and frowned. "I see your reasoning, son, but you're slicing it pretty thin. I hate to say it, but Copperhead could have 'em. There could be some other reason for that party searchin' out to the east."

"There could be but there isn't," Ki said bluntly. "They're alive. I know it." He let go of the bed and walked across the room on his own, pushing back the pain and the weakness. There was no more time for that now.

"I'd like to wash up if I can," he told Silas. "I could use a change of clothes if you can manage."

"I've taken care of that," said Silas. "Threw the stuff you had on away." He looked thoughtfully at Ki. "Now what, boy? I figure you're going to do something, but I'm damned if I know what it is. I wouldn't count on talking the law in Miles City into riding clear up to the Missouri, if that's what you're thinking. They wouldn't get real excited about that."

"No, I wasn't looking for any help there."

"The army's a couple of days away. You might get help and you might not. They got plenty to do, keeping the Injuns from running off the reservations lookin' for food." Easter made a face, then looked straight at Ki. "You get any help here, it's going to be folks I know and friends of Aaron. There's some of both around."

"I was counting on that," said Ki.

"Uh-huh. And where the hell are you goin' to take 'em if you get them? You studied on the size of Montana Territory lately?"

"Silas, I've got to do *something!*" Ki blurted.

"Yeah, I know that. I sure can't fault you, either." Easter pulled himself erect and hitched up his belt. "Go ahead and wash up and get dressed. There's cornbread and stew on the stove. I'm going out and see who's hanging around town. Looks like a good day to count how many friends a man's got."

"Thanks, Silas. I'm grateful."

Silas shook his head. "If I was you I'd try to get myself some rest. I don't figure you will but that doesn't mean it ain't good advice." He jammed his worn Stetson on his head and stalked out of the room. A moment later Ki heard the back door open and slam shut.

He found the basin and a bucket of cold water in the corner and cleaned himself up as best he could. The denims and the plain cotton shirt Silas had brought him fit well enough. He couldn't remember where he'd lost his rope-soled sandals, but he didn't need them. After clean clothes and a good meal, he felt a great deal better. Silas was right—some of the poison was still in him and he was wobbly on his feet. Even the little exertion of getting dressed and walking around had drained his strength. He needed rest for certain, but couldn't afford the luxury now.

Jessie was in trouble. He could feel it, almost see her at the edge of his thoughts. It was not some wild imagining, he knew. He trusted his sixth sense, as he had so many times before.

Angela Halley suddenly came into his mind. Ki gave a short, impatient sigh. He'd left her safe, well hidden. She had food, water, shelter, and a weapon. All she had to do was stay put until he returned to her.

It sounded just fine until he remembered who it was he was thinking about. Reason and good sense weren't exactly Angela Halley's top cards. If she took it into her head to do something foolish . . . Ki shrugged off the thought. There wasn't a thing he could do about it now. He had to get help, go after Jessie. He told himself he'd find her, keep her from the cartel's killers. The vow he had taken to protect her was as strong that moment as the day he'd spoken the words to Jessie's father.

He opened his eyes and knew he'd fallen asleep in the chair. The shades were drawn and the soft yellow light that filled the room told him the day was fading fast. He started to move, pull himself to his feet to see if Silas had returned. He'd likely be back, maybe down below.

Suddenly every nerve in Ki's body shouted a warning. The cords in his shoulders went tight and he gripped the arms of his chair.

"Just hold it right where you got it," the voice said softly. "That'd be the smart thing to do, mister."

"All right," Ki said calmly. "You're holding the cards. What do you want?"

The man stepped out of the shadow to Ki's right, then walked a few paces so Ki could see him. He was a sandy-haired man with eyes the color of broken glass. He held the shotgun in a loose and easy grip, a man who clearly felt at home with his weapon.

"Listen real good," the man said, "I'm only goin' to say this once. The old man's in the wagonyard. A friend of mine's down there with him. We got no cause to hurt him. That's up to you. I won't kill you 'cause I need you alive. What I *will* do now is shoot off part of your foot. That won't keep you from sittin' a horse." He showed Ki an easy grin.

"What's your name?" Ki said bluntly. "Who are you?"

The man looked surprised. "Why the hell you want to know that? We ain't going to be close friends."

"I like to know who I'm talking to."

The man grinned. "It's Henry," he said. "That make you happy?" Henry didn't wait for an answer. "I don't need to ask yours; I already know it. You're Ki, and you work for the Starbuck woman. We've got her. Her and a hunter named Heller."

Jessie! Ki shot the man a withering look to mask his feelings. "That's easy enough to say. How do I know whether you have her or not?"

"Fair enough question. They figured maybe you'd ask." Henry removed one hand from the stock of the weapon. The shotgun didn't waver. His fingers went to his pocket, found what he wanted, and tossed it in Ki's lap.

He grasped the coil of strawberry-blonde hair in his fist. His belly tightened in a knot. "All right. What do you want from me?"

Henry's smile faded before the cold, deadly anger in Ki's

165

eyes. "You've got the girl," he said flatly. "Don't waste time saying you don't. We talked to that bunch of raggedy-ass Shoshonis and we know you took her from 'em. We also figure you're smart enough to tuck her away somewhere. What you got to do is give her to us. Jessie Starbuck for the girl, even trade. The girl, and the information she's got with her. Ride due north at sunup. Don't worry about where you're going, we'll find you. Don't bring anyone with you. That'll get the lady killed real quick."

Ki shook his head. "No deal, mister. I'm not a damned fool."

"What are you talkin' about?" Henry stared at Ki. "Mister, you know what you're saying? You want me to bring you the Starbuck woman's *head?*"

Ki laughed aloud. "I'd sure give you what you want then, now wouldn't I? Uh-uh. What I'll do is this. I'll ride out and I'll *talk*. That's all. You don't get the girl or the list. Not until I see Jessie alive."

"Goddamn it!" Henry's face went dark with anger. "You aren't callin' the shots here, fella. We are!"

Ki looked right at him. "That's the way I'm playing it. Take it or leave it alone."

"We've got the woman," Henry snarled. "You're talking her into a grave, friend!"

"No, I don't think so," said Ki, forcing the calm into his voice. "Jessie Starbuck's all you've got to trade."

The man looked at Ki a long moment, then backed to the door of the room. "A smart man knows when to throw in his hand," he said evenly. "I'd think on that if I was you. You *be* there, and you bring the girl."

"I'll think on it," said Ki.

The man backed up another step, turned, and disappeared. Ki heard the back door slam behind him and moments later heard the sound of horses in the wagonyard below. Silas Easter began to curse at the top of his lungs. Ki breathed a sigh of relief. They hadn't hurt him, then. The thought had crossed his mind that they'd simply cut his throat to make their point, or just because killing an old man was an easy thing to do.

Ki didn't move out of his chair. Henry was right. He was holding a busted hand. The people who'd sent the men here knew exactly the kind of answer Ki would give. He wouldn't ride in with the girl and make it easy. He'd come in alone and try a bluff, buy a little time. He'd try it because there was nothing else to do. *And in the end, it won't make any difference at all,* he thought grimly. They wouldn't have the girl or the list but they'd have him, and they knew that was enough. All they had to do was touch Jessie, let him watch them hurt her. He'd tell them where Angela was because he wouldn't be able to stop. And when they got the girl they'd make her tell them about the list and then they'd kill her. Then he and Jessie would die as well. Whatever he did now it was wrong. If he waited, didn't leave at dawn as they'd asked, they'd simply come to him again. Only next time they'd bring him a finger or an ear. Ki was certain they knew him better than that, knew he wouldn't wait for that to happen.

When they brought her back and tossed her into the tent she cried out, biting her lip to choke back the bile that rose to her throat. At first she thought he was dead. His face was a mass of bruises and swollen flesh; his shirt was gone and his back was flayed raw. Her hands and legs were bound and she crawled to his side as best she could. Aaron heard her, opened his ruined mouth, and tried to talk.

"Don't," she told him, "just lie still, Aaron. It's all right."

"Jessie..." Her name was a harsh, grating sound in his throat.

She raged, "Damn them—damn them for doing this to you!"

"Yeah, well..." Heller showed her a ghastly smile. "Seems like they...kinda remembered me from that little business before. Some folks sure do...hold a grudge."

"Aaron, rest. Don't talk."

"You—you all right?" he asked her. "When they took you in there..."

"I'm all right. I'm just fine."

"Good...that's good..." His lips moved, then he drifted back into sleep.

Jessie watched him, helpless to do anything at all to ease his pain. They'd worked him over good, taking out their anger for the day he'd stood on the hill and wreaked havoc among them with his rifle. He was still alive, she knew, because Ernst

Heydrich wanted him alive for some reason. Jessie shuddered at the thought. It was as simple as that: Aaron was alive so they could hurt him again.

Her first look at Heydrich surprised her—a squat little man going bald, a man with a bulbous nose and no chin and that ridiculous lock of hair plastered flat across his head. Was this really Angela Halley's lover, the cartel's most important agent in the country? Lord, he looked for all the world like a store-keeper, a teller in a bank!

The moment she heard his voice, she forgot Ernst Heydrich's appearance. A cold, unreasoning fear reached out and seized her in its grip. There was nothing at all behind the bright, owlish eyes—no feeling, not the faintest trace of emotion. Jessie knew at once if she laughed or cried or screamed in pain it wouldn't matter. Heydrich would hear noises and nothing more, noises other people made, sounds that meant nothing to him.

When he asked her about Angela and she said she didn't know anything, Heydrich had said he'd hurt her. The words carried no anger at all. It was a statement, a fact. Something he'd told her he'd do. She'd waited, then, steeling herself for the moment as best she could, knowing it had to come. And Heydrich had simply looked at her and blinked and called Copperhead in from outside. The half-breed entered at once, his big form towering over the shorter man.

"Put a gag on her please," Heydrich said calmly. "I expect she'll make a fuss."

Jessie shrank back, trying desperately to drag herself over the ground. Copperhead whipped a bandanna from his pocket, bent to her, and swiftly stuffed the wad of cloth in her mouth. He turned, then, and sat down hard on her knees, facing her feet, pressing her legs painfully to the ground. Jessie's blood ran cold as she felt the half-breed pull off one of her boots and remove her stocking.

Heydrich walked to her side and bent his head slightly. "Miss Starbuck, where is Angela Halley? I will ask you once again. What have you done with the girl?"

Jessie shook her head from side to side, cursing him through the gag.

"Yes, all right," said Heydrich. He reached up and plucked a shiny object from the silken lapel of his robe, held it to the light, and showed it to Jessie.

"This is very simple and effective," he told her. "It's a needle, nothing more. Copperhead here will insert it in the soft tissue between your toes. Let me know when you wish him to stop."

Jessie went cold all over. Heydrich passed the needle to the half-breed. Copperhead gripped her bound ankles in one hand. She felt his fingers touch her foot and then a hot, agonizing pain rushed up her leg.

Jessie screamed. Her body went rigid and she jerked uncontrollably off the floor. Heydrich studied her curiously over his glasses. Jessie glared contemptuously through her tears and Heydrich nodded at Copperhead again. The pain seared her like a white-hot wire. Jessie cried out against her gag, begging him to stop. Heydrich turned away and ignored her. He glanced at her foot with no interest at all.

The pain suddenly went away.

Jessie opened her eyes and gasped for breath. Another man stood beside Heydrich. Jessie had never seen him before. He was tall, middle-aged, with a brush of gray at his temples. His dark, English-tailored suit looked curiously out of place in the middle of the Montana prairie.

"That's enough," Heydrich said quietly, "remove the gag, please."

Copperhead stood, turned, and yanked the bandanna from Jessie's mouth. Heydrich dismissed him with a nod and the half-breed stalked out of the tent.

"There will be no need for further questions," Heydrich told Jessie. "I have learned where Angela is."

"Oh? And where is she then?" Jessie said, spitting out her anger.

"Your friend has her. The Oriental. It seems that he rescued her from the savages." Heydrich's lips curled slightly in distaste. It was the only time Jessie had seen him give way to any feeling. He turned and walked out of the tent without a glance. The other man followed. He hadn't spoken a word in her presence. A moment later the guards came and took her back to Aaron.

Heller still slept. Jessie listened to the slow, ragged sound of his breath. Light was beginning to show through the tent. She'd tried to sleep, but sleep wouldn't come. Strangely, she felt no pain in her foot. The half-breed's torture had no lasting effects. Once the needle was removed, the pain was gone. The pain, but not the memory of how it had been. That, she was certain, would never leave her. She shook her head and looked at Aaron. Lord, whatever she'd suffered it was nothing compared to the beatings Aaron had endured!

She heard the camp begin to stir. A man coughed. A horse trotted past her tent. In a moment she smelled the tantalizing aroma of fresh coffee. Jessie stared past the thin sheet of canvas into the growing light, reaching out and trying to find him, trying to see him wherever he was.

Don't, Ki, she cried out in the silence of her mind, *don't come . . . don't let them take you too . . . !*

★

Chapter 21

Ki rode out of Miles City at first light, heading north across the open prairie. The broad green expanse stretched as far as the eye could see. A slight breeze rose with the coming of day, rippling the stirrup-high grass.

The first riders appeared some five miles out. There were two to the left, another pair to the right. They rode along with him, matching their pace to his, always keeping a good two hundred yards on either side. Ki wasn't surprised. They'd told him to come alone and they intended to make certain that he did.

She's up there, waiting. They've told her that I'm coming and how it's going to be. They'll work it so I can get close to her, close enough to see her eyes, the expression on her face. They'll have a man beside her; they'll fix it so I know what they can do, how they can hurt her or kill her in an instant.

He urged the mount on, searching the sea of grass. He figured he'd ridden fifteen, close to twenty miles. The riders were still with him. The land rose up in a gentle slope just ahead. Before he reached the crest, the riders slowed to a halt, taking up flanking positions. Ki's stomach tightened in a knot. He closed his eyes and took deep, calming breaths. It was coming, it would happen any moment.

A rider suddenly appeared atop the slope. He looked down at Ki and waved his rifle to the left. The instructions were clear enough. Ki was to veer off left, keep to the narrow valley. He understood. There was little high ground, only uncounted miles of tall grass. The shallow slope was less than ten feet high, but they intended to keep it for themselves. From there a single rider could see all he wanted to see for miles around.

Past the rise two riders stood waiting. One raised his rifle

171

and aimed it directly at Ki's chest. Ki reined his mount in quickly and sat perfectly still in the saddle. The man without a weapon rode toward him. Ki recognized him at once. It was Henry, the man who'd found him at Easter's the night before.

Henry stopped a few feet away. He looked at Ki and shook his head. "See you didn't bring the girl," he said flatly. "You're a damn fool, mister."

"I've been told before," said Ki.

"Get off and stand clear of your horse. Fold your hands on top of your head."

Ki obeyed. Henry slid out of the saddle and ran his hands carefully over every inch of Ki's body. Ki looked past his shoulder, past the rider with the gun. There were other men on horses, thirty yards away through the grass. A dozen men, maybe more.

"All right," said Henry, "if you got any weapons I can't find 'em." He straightened and stood away. "Start walking, right over there."

Ki made his way through the waist-high grass. One of the riders moved aside to let him pass. He was acutely aware of what they were doing. It was an open show of strength, a way to let him see he was helpless among them—an unarmed man on foot, walking through a rank of armed riders.

They stood in a small clearing, past the shallow bed of a dry creek. Ki had prepared himself for the moment, readied himself for the instant he saw her again. He was determined to show them nothing, to hide his feelings behind a mask of confidence and strength. If they could play the game, so could he.

At the sight of her, the mask nearly crumbled and fell away. It was all he could do to contain the rage that swept through his veins. He knew at once they'd hurt her—it didn't show but he knew. He could read it in her eyes. In the single beat of his heart he saw her between two gunmen, her hands bound tightly behind her back, saw Heller a few feet away, struggling to stay on his feet. Damn, they'd worked him over badly, left his face a ruin! And Copperhead, where was he? The half-breed was nowhere in sight. Instead there were two middle-aged men, one short and balding, the other taller and slimmer. Now who the hell were *they?*

Ki ignored them both. Quickening his steps, he left Henry behind and walked boldly across the clearing.

"Jessie, how are you?" he smiled. "These people treating you all right?" Jessie beamed, smiling back through her fears.

"Goddamn it, get back here!" Henry cursed. He grabbed Ki's arm and jerked him roughly away. "We'll *tell* you where you're supposed to be!"

The short man in thick glasses looked curiously at Ki. "It's all right, Henry. Leave him alone." A small furrow creased his brow. "You were supposed to bring Angela with you," he said coolly. "Where is she? Why isn't she here?"

Ki shrugged. "I told your man I'd come and talk. That's all. Who *are* you, mister? I never saw you before."

The owlish eyes blinked. "I am Ernst Heydrich," he said curtly, "and I will ask the questions, not you."

My God—Ernst Heydrich himself! Ki tried to hold back his surprise. "All right. And who's that supposed to be?" he asked, nodding at the taller man. "I never saw him either."

His tactics didn't rattle Heydrich at all. "I will ask you again. Where is Angela? Please, don't play foolish games with me." He glanced at Jessie and back again, his meaning perfectly clear.

"There isn't any game," Ki said evenly, "unless it's one you're playing. I don't have the girl and that's that. I did have her. And if you're thinking about trying to get more out of me, go right ahead. All you'll get is where I saw her last."

Heydrich's eyes narrowed. He started to speak, but Ki pressed on. "I'm not a damned fool," he said. "I knew what you'd try to pull. I got her away safe—with someone I can trust. Only I didn't let him tell me where they were going." He looked Heydrich straight in the eye. "Which means I can't tell you, now can I?"

"You are lying," Heydrich said calmly. "It's a bluff, and a foolish one at that."

"Is it? You real sure, are you, mister?"

Heydrich almost smiled. "If what you say is true, I have no further use for you, now do I? Or Miss Starbuck, either."

"Friend, you're not thinking," Ki said evenly, "I rode in here, didn't I? Now why the hell would I do that—so you could put a bullet in her head and mine?"

173

"Mr. Ki," Heydrich said curtly, "you are wasting my time!"

"Well, I'll try to make it quick then," Ki told him. For an instant he let his gaze touch the tall, silent man to Heydrich's right. The man watched Ki intently, but his features betrayed nothing at all. "Here's the way it is," Ki said boldly, "*my* terms, mister—not yours. I don't have to tell you about Angela. You likely know her better than anyone else. She pulls a lot of fool tricks, but she can think straight enough when she has to." Ki showed Heydrich a crooked grin. "She's got that list of yours, mister. Only it's not just *one* list any more. There are copies in Kansas City, St. Louis, Cheyenne, Denver—and a couple of other places in between. That girlfriend of yours sure did get around."

"That's a lie!" Heydrich blurted. "A damn lie and you know it!" Ki saw the first crack appear in the man's armor. His fists went tight at his sides, and tiny beads of moisture peppered his brow.

"Angela wouldn't tell me a thing about the list," Ki went on. "The girl's a lot smarter than you figured. You were afraid the names would fall in our hands—but Angela had a better idea. She knew the only way she could possibly stay alive was to make sure *no one* got a hand on that list. Not your people, and not us. She doesn't give a damn whether the cartel's agents are exposed. She wants to stay alive, period." Ki paused for an instant. "You see how it works? You keep your agents in place. Nothing happens—as long as Angela Halley stays healthy. And once a year the folks who are keeping those sealed envelopes get a birthday greeting from Angela. If those greetings keep coming, nothing happens at all."

"And what do you get out of this? There is something else, yes?" For the first time, Heydrich's tall companion spoke. His English was perfectly precise, but his Prussian nationality was clear.

Ki showed him an easy smile. "I get to stay alive. Jessie and I both, and Mr. Heller there. That's Angela's thanks for getting her free of you. If we don't make it back, she'll let the list go. There's a U.S. Deputy Marshal who *knows* you people and what you are. If he gets his hands on that list, he'll damn sure do something about it."

"No, my friend." Heydrich gave him a weary smile. "It is

174

all a fabrication. There is not a word of truth in it."

"You're willing to bet the pot on that, are you? You speaking for the cartel now?" Again Ki met the taller man's eyes. Heydrich caught the action and flushed with anger.

"I am willing to bet on my knowledge of that foolish girl," he said flatly. "You are right—I know Angela well, and I know it would never cross her mind to leave copies of that list with anyone." Heydrich gave a quick, disparaging laugh. "She is incapable of such a ruse. She had the mind of a selfish child!"

"You know what I think?" Ki said quietly. "What I think is you're letting your pride get in the way of your good sense. That little girl made a fool out of you: She got you in hot water with your people and you don't much like it. You're not going to *let* yourself believe she's smart enough to beat you."

Ernst Heydrich went rigid. His lips spread in a taut white line and his eyes blazed with hatred at Ki. "Take him," he shouted over his shoulder. "Take him and make him talk. He'll tell us where she is."

"No, Ernst." The tall Prussian laid a restraining hand on Heydrich's arm. "I think we shall talk to the man; I think we shall hear him out."

Heydrich stared, disbelief turning to cold anger. *"You* think? You're not making the decisions here, I am!"

"No, you are not," the man said calmly. "Not anymore." His eyes found Heydrich and held him. "The man is right. Your anger at this girl has clouded your reason. You let her get away with the names. This is a thing that should never have happened. You put everything we've accomplished at risk. We gave you a chance to get her back—"

"Damn you," Heydrich flared, "it's all a lie, don't you see that! It—it's not true, not any of it!"

"You may be right, yes," the man agreed, "but we cannot know this, can we? If it is not a lie, what then? How do we know the girl won't—"

"No!" Heydrich blurted, "by God you're not putting all this on me!" He took a step back, his hand darting to the folds of his jacket. The Prussian saw the gleam of metal, cried out, and flailed at Heydrich with his fists. Heydrich swept his arms aside, came in fast, and slashed the pistol hard across the Prussian's cheek. The man bellowed in pain, brought his hands

175

to his face, and staggered back. Heydrich swung the weapon about in a blind rage, squeezing the trigger as fast as he could. Ki dropped to the ground, saw the deadly bursts of fire reach out for Jessie, and knew he'd never reach her in time. Suddenly Aaron Heller lowered his head and threw himself at Heydrich like a bull.

"Aaron—*no!*" Jessie cried.

The pistol exploded as Aaron took Heydrich to the ground. Ki was already moving, his stiffened fingers lashing out in a blur. The gunman next to Jessie folded as Ki snapped bone in his solar plexus. He turned on his heels, kicked another man in the belly and lifted Jessie into his arms. Bullets whined past his shoulder as he ran across the clearing and leaped for the cover of high grass. Men shouted behind him. Gunfire clipped green blades above his head. He heard the horses' hooves strike rock in the dry creek and knew the riders would be on him in an instant.

"Ki, don't!" Jessie shouted, "you can't make it with me!"

Ki didn't answer. He kept his body low, dodging through the grass and holding Jessie close against his chest. He heard them coming behind him, turned, and saw two riders closing fast. One fired wildly with his Colt; the other danced his mount in a quick circle, a rifle at his shoulder. Ki couldn't stop— turning and fighting was useless, especially with Jessie bound in his arms.

A triumphant shout arose from his right; he saw the other riders coming, four, five abreast, cutting in from the south. Lead plowed a furrow across his shoulder. Ki staggered and fell. Jessie cried out as she tumbled from his arms through the grass. Ki came up in a crouch. He searched about frantically for a weapon—a rock, a stick, anything.

"Ki, look out!"

He turned on his heels at Jessie's desperate cry. The barrel of the Winchester struck him in the back and sent him sprawling. Ki staggered to his feet, pain numbing his shoulder. The rider hit him again, using the barrel as a club. Ki tasted blood and went to his knees. The rider laughed. Ki shook his head to clear his eyes. They were all around him, half a dozen riders crowding him close. He stood shakily over Jessie, trying to fight them off. They were playing with him now, kicking out with their boots, using their mounts to knock him to the ground. Ki saw the man called Henry loom above, his face a grinning mask. Ki clawed out for his leg. Henry kicked him savagely in the face. The butt of a rifle caught him squarely between the shoulders. Ki went down. He couldn't find Jessie; she was lost in a tangle of deadly hooves. Henry laughed aloud; he thumbed back the hammer of his shotgun and swung the weapon directly at Ki's head. Ki stared at the dark barrel, waiting for it to happen. In some far corner of his mind he knew there was thunder and wondered how that could be. The day was clear; there wasn't a cloud in the sky...

Henry's chest exploded.

Bone, blood, and tissue sprayed the riders around him. The thunder rolled again—a gunman flew out of the saddle as if a giant hammer of air had kicked him loose. A rider shouted in fear; another drove his horse in the mount beside him, spilling his companion to the ground. Ki found Jessie, covered her against the flailing hooves. The riders above bolted, fleeing in every direction. Ki wiped blood from his eyes. A rider lay dead a few feet away. Ki crawled to him, found a knife at his belt, and quickly cut Jessie's bonds.

"My God," she said, "Ki—your face!" She tried to wipe the blood away.

"I'm all right," he said shortly, brushing her hand aside. "There's no time. Here—take this." He turned the dead rider over, pulled a pistol from his belt, and handed it to Jessie. A Winchester lay nearby. He rammed the butt into the ground and pulled himself to his feet, using the weapon to hold him up.

"Can you—can you make it all right?" Jessie asked.

"Yeah, I think." Ki waved her down and raised his head cautiously out of the grass. Riders were scattered across the prairie, firing blindly at targets they couldn't see. As Ki watched, another man fell from the saddle. Again and again the heavy, unmistakable cough of a Sharps .45 or a Big Fifty rolled over the sea of grass.

"What is it—what's happening, Ki?"

"Keep low," he warned her. He pressed her shoulder down

and urged her ahead. "Come on, I'll tell you in a minute. I want to put some distance between us and those riders. It isn't over yet."

"Ki, did you see Aaron? Is he—"

"I don't know," he told her. "He went down, Jessie. It didn't look good." A riderless horse trotted by, eyes white with fear. For an instant Ki was tempted to stop it. It wasn't a good idea—anyone on a horse now was a target. They were better off in the grass.

"This way," he told her, "I want to work back east around the riders. We've got friends out there, and I'd feel a lot better close to them."

"You don't look like you're going to make it another foot," Jessie said.

"Hell, I'm getting used to it," Ki said darkly. "I wouldn't know how to act if something didn't hurt. Hey, hold it—" He waved her down and peered through the grass. "It's the other end of that dry creek. I'm going over. You come after."

Jessie nodded. The booming sound of the Sharps rifles was closer. Heydrich's men answered with scattered fire. Ki paused as a rider cut through the grass to his left, then bolted into the open and ran for cover. He turned then, pumping the Winchester over his head to signal Jessie forward. She nodded, bent low, and ran for him over the shallow gully. Halfway across she suddenly stopped, turned, and looked back, a curious look on her face.

"Come *on*," Ki muttered under his breath, "what the hell are you doing? Let's *go!*"

He saw her body go rigid, saw her hand come up with the revolver and squeeze the trigger twice. The dark form came out of the grass, hurled her savagely aside, and kept coming. *Copperhead!* Ki's blood surged with anger. He levered a shell in the rifle and aimed it point blank at the charging figure: The rifle clicked empty. Ki grasped the barrel and swung the weapon from the waist. The stock hit the half-breed in the chest and splintered, the blow tearing the weapon from Ki's hands. Copperhead bent double and staggered back, his ruined face a mask of pain. Ki's right hand lashed out like a snake. He caught the man in the face three times before he could get his bearings. Copperhead grunted, shook his head, and stared in disbelief.

Ki didn't give him a second to recover. He drove his fist like a wedge into Copperhead's jaw, pounding him with one savage blow after another. He had to end it fast and he knew it. He was drained, empty—his body wouldn't accept more punishment. If he gave the half-breed a chance, even an instant—

Copperhead bellowed, raised his big arm like a club to block Ki's blow, and drove his other fist in Ki's chest. The blow lifted him off his feet. Ki rolled away in the grass, gasping to fill his lungs. Copperhead came at him, determined to catch him on the ground. Ki came up fast, slammed his body hard against the half-breed's belly, jerked up straight, and sent him sprawling.

Copperhead scrambled to his feet and came in low. Ki let him come, leaped in the air, and hit him in the mouth with both feet. Copperhead shrieked like a cat, the blow tearing fresh wounds in his face. He spit blood, swayed on his feet, and blinked at Ki with glazed eyes. He'd never faced Ki's peculiar brand of fighting, and he didn't like it at all. He tucked his head low against his shoulders, waving his big hands from side to side.

Ki backed off. He'd landed punishing fists but his strength was failing fast. Copperhead sensed it and grinned. Ki weaved in and out, landing quick blows and leaping free. For his size the half-breed was incredibly fast. Ki landed a cutting jab to the man's mouth, another to his nose. Copperhead took the punishing hands, brought a ham-sized fist up from the waist, and hit Ki full in the face.

The blow shook everything inside him. He could feel the ground coming up to meet him, the darkness closing in. He hit hard and rolled desperately away. Copperhead laughed and kicked him in the ribs. Ki cried out, throwing his arms before his face. The half-breed's boots lashed out again and again. Ki retched and tried to bring himself erect. Copperhead kicked him in the head. Ki folded, tumbling on his back. He tried to move but nothing worked. The half-breed towered above him. Ki blinked, trying to bring him into focus. Copperhead planted a heavy boot on Ki's chest, pinning him like a bug. Ki struggled to tear himself free. The half-breed stepped back, raised his foot for a blow that would drive Ki's ribs into his heart.

Ki brought everything he had to the motion, willing his legs

179

to come alive. As Copperhead's boot came down to crush him, Ki brought his knees up flat against his chest, snapped his legs high like pistons, and drove his bare feet into the half-breed's groin.

Copperhead went rigid. A high, unearthly wail escaped his throat. He jerked his arms in crazy circles, fell on his back, and hit the ground hard. He gripped his vitals and curled in a ball, rolling in agony through the grass.

Ki tried to stand. His body wouldn't work. He came to his knees, collapsed, and tried again. Wiping a hand across his face to clear his eyes, he saw Copperhead pulling himself to his feet. Ki stared in disbelief. The half-breed held one hand between his legs. Blood flowed through his fingers and his face was twisted in pain. Dragging one leg, he came through the grass toward Ki.

"Damn you, stay down!" Ki's voice was a hoarse, ragged cry.

Copperhead kept coming. Now Ki saw he'd found the broken rifle. He clutched the steel barrel in his fist like a club. Ki brought himself up on one knee, then the other. He braced his hand on the ground and forced himself halfway erect. Nausea threatened to pull him under. Copperhead took a lurching step forward, swung the steel weapon, and missed.

"I've had about . . . all of you I can take . . ." Ki muttered between his teeth. Swaying on his feet, he gripped his hands together between his legs and brought them up with all the strength he could muster. The clasped fists hit Copperhead just below the chin and kept going. The half-breed's neck snapped back. The life went out of his eyes and he fell limply to the ground.

Ki staggered back. The world swam dizzingly before his eyes.

Jessie . . . got to find Jessie . . . It was hard to keep the thought in his head. He turned, trying to find his way to the dry creek. Everything blurred and went dark. He thought he saw men with heavy rifles running toward him. His legs gave way and the ground came up swiftly to meet him. He didn't give a damn who the men were or what they wanted.

★

Chapter 22

He opened his eyes and saw her sitting beside him. When she saw he was awake she leaned down and kissed him lightly on the cheek. He smelled the scent of her skin and felt her soft hair brush against his face.

"You feeling any better?" she asked gently. "You want anything—a drink of water or something?"

"Water'd be good," he told her. He tried to lift his head, fell back, and gritted his teeth against the pain.

"Hey, you don't *have* to do that," Jessie scolded. She pressed him back down, lifted his head, and helped him drink.

Ki settled back on the pillow with a sigh. "You're right," he said grimly, "I'm not ready to do much moving." He glanced about the room and recognized the familiar surroundings of Silas Easter's quarters above his wagonyard. "How long have I been out?" he asked. "I don't remember real well."

"You've been *in* and out for three days," Jessie told him. "More out than in, I guess."

Ki shook his head. "I'm afraid I don't recall a whole lot. I—" He stopped then and frowned curiously at Jessie's face. "Hey, are you hurt? You all right?"

"I've got a little bruise is all," she assured him. "That half-breed hit me kinda hard. He was real anxious to get to you."

Ki frowned, the thought suddenly filling his head. "Copperhead..." Tasting the name brought back the savage features. "Is he ... dead? Did I—"

"He's dead," said Jessie. "Copperhead and eight of the riders working for Heydrich. We found Heydrich dead, too, only no one's sure who put a bullet in his head. I can make a good guess. The other Prussian and some of their gunmen got away. Over east toward the Dakotas." Jessie let out a weary sigh.

"The army's trying to find him. They won't, though. You can be certain a man like that left himself a hole to crawl out. 'Course the law and the army both are calling Heydrich's bunch outlaws and raiders. They figure Montgomery's men were massacred for money and horses."

Ki cursed under his breath. "I saw that camp. All Copperhead's gunmen did was kill. They didn't steal a thing."

"I know," said Jessie, "but a raiding party's easier to swallow than some far-fetched story about a foreign cartel. Nothing's changed, Ki." She laid a hand on his arm. "I just came from down the street. Aaron's going to make it. He took Heydrich's bullet in the chest and almost bled to death before we could get him back to Miles City. Doc Cuppscott says he never saw a man come closer to dying."

"I'm glad he'll be all right," Ki told her. "He's a good man. I still don't know what you two went through up north, but I'm glad you had some help. Damn it, Jessie—I never should have left you to go chasing after that girl. If I'd have—" Ki stopped. He stared straight at Jessie. A look of shock and surprise suddenly spread across his features. "Good God, I forgot! I left her out there—on the Missouri. Angela, she's holed up in a hollow up there on the river!"

"Hey, easy, friend." Jessie laid her hand on his brow. "She *was* up there, Ki. She's not now. She sorta got tired of waiting—four or five hours after you left her. An army patrol scouting up from the Judith Mountains found her walking."

"Walking?" Ki shook his head in disbelief. "That figures," he groaned. "Is she okay? She's all right, isn't she?"

"Oh, yes, she's all right," Jessie said dryly. She looked right at Ki. "Until I talked to her, I had no idea you were bluffing—that you made the whole thing up. All that stuff about leaving the list in half a dozen cities..."

Ki gave her a long and sober look. "Maybe I didn't make it up, Jessie. Maybe that's what happened. I know she didn't have it on her. What did she say to you?"

Jessie made a face. "That she didn't know what I was talking about. You know what I think? Really? I don't think she hid it or left it with anyone, Ki. I think she lifted some of Heydrich's papers for spite and came away with that list. Maybe she knew what she had and maybe she didn't. I'll bet you a sack of double-eagles she threw the whole mess away before she even got out of Chicago."

Ki remembered the wild, free-spirited girl, as erratic and unpredictable as the wind. Sweet as honey one minute, and mean as a she-cat the next. "Where Angela's concerned, I'd believe almost anything, Jessie."

"Oh—before I forget, Silas Easter wants to come in and see you when you feel like it."

Ki grinned. "He came through that business all right then. We lose any of the men with him?"

"Not a one," Jessie said fiercely. "It was a smart move, Ki, sending Silas and those hunters out the night before."

"It was more Easter's plan than mine," Ki told her. "We couldn't figure anything else to do. There was no way of knowing where they'd set up the meet, and we didn't dare try anything in daylight. Easter and his boys made two or three camps a few miles apart. The idea was to send scouts out from each group with a good pair of binoculars, track me, and Copperhead's riders, then lead the whole bunch in."

"It worked," Jessie grinned. "The hunters set up a hundred yards off in the grass and picked off the riders. It didn't take long to send them scattering."

She leaned down to kiss him again, then stepped back from the bed. "You rest," she said gently, "I'll be back later with something good for your supper."

"Jessie..." Ki dug his elbows into the bed and forced himself up on one arm. "What we did, this whole thing with Angela and Ernst Heydrich... It wasn't all for nothing. We didn't get the list, but we beat them."

"Yes, we beat them, Ki." Jessie faced him from across the room. "The cartel can't take the chance. They don't *know* where that list is, and they don't dare risk exposing their deeply placed agents. They'll have to remove every person on that list. All those years of work and planning are down the drain. We won the round. They didn't."

"What about Angela?" Ki asked. "We've still got to protect her, Jessie. Get her away somewhere. Whether she has the list or not."

"Ki..."

"If she's not doing anything, I'd—well, if she'd like to

come up and visit, it'd be all right with me."

Jessie looked at the ceiling and blew out a breath. "I've been trying to figure how to tell you this," she said dryly. "It's—well, it's kinda embarrassing, I guess."

"What?" Ki's eyes widened in alarm. "What is it, Jessie? She—something's happened to Angela!"

"Something's happened, all right," Jessie said evenly. She set her hands on her hips and raised a brow. "You remember I said an army patrol picked her up walking south? Well, there was this young lieutenant named Oliver, real nice-looking boy. This morning the lieutenant was missing from his quarters and, uh—Angela's gone, too. Along with a couple of army mounts."

Ki stared at Jessie's expression, then burst out laughing. "Hell, Jessie, I don't know why everyone worries about Angela. No matter how often she falls, that girl's going to land on her back every time!"